Praise for

CHARLES FRAZIER

"Frazier is a superb prose stylist who elevates the historical fiction genre." —*USA Today*

"Frazier lyrically resurrects the blasted but hauntingly beautiful Southern landscape. . . . Beautifully rendered." —*New York Times Book Review*

"There are things so masterful words can't do them justice. Frazier's writing falls into that category." —*Asheville Citizen-Times*

"Frazier's historical research generally sits lightly on the story, almost always embedded gracefully in dialogue, a small telling incident, or a sharp memory of kindness or brutality. His prose is both of the characters' time and perfectly evocative." —*Washington Post*

"Frazier's superb novel is both a large-hearted homage and a sensitive reckoning. . . . A banquet of first-rate storytelling." —*Wall Street Journal*

"A writer of evocative prose, Frazier possesses the rare capacity to impel the reader to stop, reread, and savor a passage." —*Richmond Times-Dispatch*

The
TRACKERS

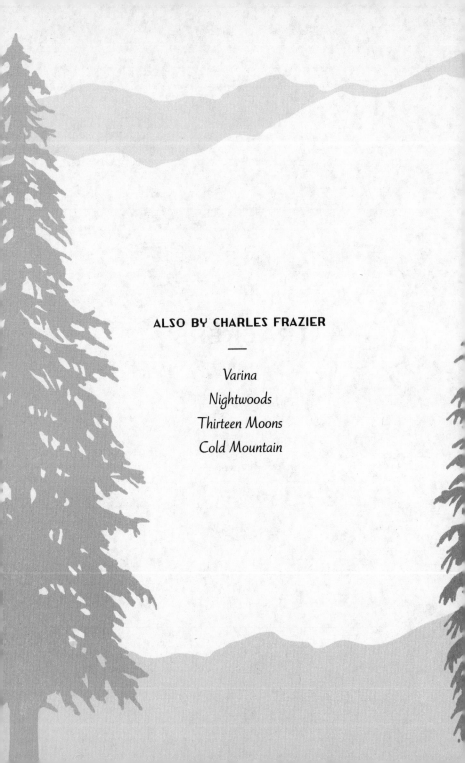

ALSO BY CHARLES FRAZIER

—

Varina
Nightwoods
Thirteen Moons
Cold Mountain

The
TRACKERS

A NOVEL

—

CHARLES FRAZIER

ecco

An Imprint of HarperCollins*Publishers*

THE TRACKERS. Copyright © 2023 by 3 Crows Corporation. All rights reserved. Printed in the United States of America. No part of this book may be used or reproduced in any manner whatsoever without written permission except in the case of brief quotations embodied in critical articles and reviews. For information, address HarperCollins Publishers, 195 Broadway, New York, NY 10007.

HarperCollins books may be purchased for educational, business, or sales promotional use. For information, please email the Special Markets Department at SPsales@harpercollins.com.

Ecco® and HarperCollins® are trademarks of HarperCollins Publishers.

A hardcover edition of this book was published in 2023 by Ecco, an imprint of HarperCollins Publishers.

FIRST ECCO PAPERBACK EDITION PUBLISHED 2024

Designed by Jennifer Chung

Interior art: Douglas fir and spruce trees © Max_Lockwood/shutterstock

Library of Congress Cataloging-in-Publication Data has been applied for.

ISBN 978-0-06-294809-0 (pbk.)

24 25 26 27 28 LBC 5 4 3 2 1

For David and Elizabeth

As soon as you embark, you'll be free . . .
But don't go astray.

—**Sophocles,** *The Trackers*

————

. . . hunger and cold and death ride the green
light of every train the child tramp flips. Soon
he knows them as old acquaintances.

—**Thomas Minehan,**
Boy and Girl Tramps of America, **1934**

A MUDDY BLACK-AND-WHITE NEWSPAPER PHOTO-
graph. I'm standing on a scaffold made from two tall stepladders with boards running between them. I've barely begun the mural, haven't even started putting color on the wall of the brand-new post office. In the photo, the wall looks almost blank, though if you know what you're looking for, you can faintly see the penciled grid I've been laying out, where I'll soon sketch the underlying form of my plan—curving lines moving across the space, swelling and rising and breaking like waves, the flow of energy moving left to right like a line of text. Up on the scaffold, my head nearly touches the ceiling. My tousle-top hair needs a trim. I'm wearing baggy khaki pants and a workingman's T-shirt and an old pair of Converse All Stars. In the photograph, the paint stains barely show. I'm holding a brush in my hand, not because I've been using it but because the photographer asked me to hold it where the camera would see it. Long and Eve stand a few feet apart on the new black-and-white tile floor, their chins lifted, looking up at me. Eve is wearing a fancy show business cowgirl outfit. She looks a little silly, and at that moment somewhat ordinary. Long wears a dark business suit with subtle Western yokes on the chest. The photo highlights the gray at his temples and emphasizes the difference in their ages. They're tired, having driven hours from Cheyenne after a few late nights of political business, lobbying and glad-handing. The flash-bulb pops and records the moment we first met, and it was news. The caption on the front page of the Dawes Journal *read,* After Cheyenne trip, prominent rancher John Long and wife greet WPA painter.

I

—

TEN THOUSAND FOOT BLUE

MID-AFTERNOON, MAY, UNDER AN EMPTY HIGH-altitude sky, cool but the sun blazing like it yearned to cinder you, I took a right turn off pavement and passed under a massive *H*-shaped ponderosa-log entryway. A nearly discreet sign swinging on two chains from the crossmember read *Long Shot*. Down the dirt drive, two black arcs of telephone and electric lines drooped pole to pole for half a mile of tallgrass and sage.

At the end of the road, the ranch house sat long and dark brown. It wasn't old—not much is out there except the land itself—but this was aggressively new. Its angular flattish rooflines looked like Frank Lloyd Wright had been hired to draw up an enormous log-and-stone cabin one morning and had tossed it off in time for lunch. The center of the house stood tall and angled, and the two wings stretched low and flat. My first thought was that it hunkered against the world, as if attacking bands might still roam the plains. As architecture, it made me wonder who it was afraid of or, conversely, who its anger was aimed at.

To the left of the house, the paved highway ran far enough away that vehicles passed miniaturized, barely visible and totally silent. To the right, open country stretched west across sage hills to distant blue-black pine mountains in front of ghostly snow peaks flat as drawing paper against the sky, the Wind River Range. Centered in my windshield, heavy double doors, tall and wide enough for a locomotive, or at least a Packard, to pass through, stood closed. Above the shoulders of the house, a herd of red cattle grazed a near hillside. They drifted all in the same direction, paired with their shadows, moving slow as a tide change. Sky stretched blank and blue to the horizon in every direction.

I stepped up on the porch and knocked three times. The knocker was a stylized bronze horseshoe big as the mouth to a five-gallon bucket. I waited and knocked again.

No response.

To the right of the house, a pole-fenced round pen with sandy footing sat next to a massive hip-roof horse barn. In the center of the circle, an elder slim cowboy in a frayed straw hat lunged a young quarter horse on a long line, the horse shorter both front to back and up and down than the thoroughbreds some of my father's clients rode to kill foxes with packs of dogs. Handle and lash, the cowboy's lunge whip was twice as long as he was tall. He swirled his right hand loose-wristed, making a figure eight with the whip, apparently just for the slow, rhythmic whooshing sound of it, the music. The tip never touched the horse. It trotted in circles, head and tail up and ears back.

I walked over to the corral and waited to be noticed. The cowboy didn't even look my way. He seemed to be muttering low to the horse. Sometimes he let the whip end fall to the ground and barely tapped the horse with the long handle across its chest or upper legs. A reminder, like tapping someone on the shoulder. The horse would stop, change directions, change gait with tiny movements of the cowboy's right hand or his muttered words. One time he let the horse slow to a stop, and then he slacked the line and let it fall to the ground. He lowered his head and looked at his boot tips and backed away a few slow steps like he had no expectations of the horse, required nothing from it, had in fact forgotten all about it. After only a few seconds, the horse stepped toward him, curious but wary, and then the cowboy pulled the line until it was off the ground but still loose. He made a slight mouth noise, and the horse trotted in a circle along the fence line. The succession of events was a communication, a language, and when the horse started circling with only a quick sound, it felt somehow like coming to the end of a stanza.

—Mr. Long? I said.

The cowboy kept his eyes on the horse, his beat-up, big-knuckled hands fully occupied with the lunge line and the whip. He tipped his head back and aimed his chin toward the front of the house. When the shade of his hat brim lifted, sunlight caught his face halfway and lit up white whiskers. First glance, he appeared to lack a mouth, since from nose down nothing revealed itself but bristles. He wore Levi's worn pale at the rear end and a faded blue plaid Western shirt with the sleeves cut entirely off. Under the saddle-tanned skin, his forearms and upper arms and shoulders looked like an anatomy study. Muscle and tendon and veins squirmed and clenched in ropes and knots. His gray face looked grafted onto a younger body.

I stood there awhile by the fence wondering what to do until the cowboy, without breaking his concentration on the horse, finally said, G'on in.

And then to the horse he said, I've about got you to know the word *whoa*. So let's us quit and head to the barn.

I CLIMBED THE STEPS BACK onto the porch, knocked again, and then opened the heavy doors and stuck my head in and said, Hello? Hey? Anybody home?

Apparently nope.

So I stepped into the entryway. As my eyes adjusted, the room swelled dark and wide, and taller than expected, shaped by massive timbers and log walls and Douglas fir plank ceilings. Daylight filtered down from narrow clerestory windows like slits in a fort wall for firing. A circular projection of amber light from a big mica-shaded lamp on a round oak table defined the center of the space. Shelves of books absorbed sound and light, but all around, rising high toward the ceiling, I could see paintings, layers of them rising high toward the ceiling. On pedestals and shelves, bronzes of horses in various rodeo contortions.

On a shelf higher than arm's reach, a rifle with a long telescopic sight occupied a horizontal shelf that looked made for it, a space to display an art object. The rifle's muzzle end was supported on a skinny metal bipod, and the belled rubber eyepiece of the scope flared like a coronet. Several little knurled knobs and wheels interrupted the long body of the scope and made me want to climb on a stepladder and twiddle with them to feel their precision. The forestock reached almost to the muzzle, and the whole thing, wood and metal and glass, shone like it had been polished yesterday.

At the end of the room, brighter hallways led off to left and right and straight ahead, but I hesitated to keep moving forward. I circled, looking at the art, mostly Western. I'd have needed a flashlight to see the signatures but guessed Russell for a lot of the bucking horses and Plains Indians hunting buffalo. A few Remingtons clustered together, including a very nice stark snow scene, almost black and white, of horsemen climbing through boulders up a rough mountain trail, very nearly abstract if you stood back and squinted. The sorts of paintings I studied photos of while I developed my mural proposal for Hutchinson to pitch to his committee.

Off to the side, I found a small and very handsome mountain landscape, surely a Moran. And then, surprisingly, at least at that first moment, two French paintings. One I guessed was probably a Matisse—a woman lounging on a chaise in a red room with a door opening to a blue sea. The other was, almost certainly, a tiny Renoir—a haze of landscape, bits of shiny water, a meadow with flowers, a female figure in the distance barely distinguishable from the vegetation. The painting itself couldn't have been even five by seven. But it was framed deep, wide, and dark—almost more frame than image—to enhance its luminosity and its tiny preciousness. You looked into it, and it magically enlarged and expanded away from you.

I ventured farther into the house, calling out greetings now and then to avoid being taken for a burglar. Eventually, at the back of the house, I found a woman in a very large and bright modern kitchen. She chopped vegetables and tossed them into a huge pot of dark stock for stew.

The woman set down her knife and wiped her hands and said, You'd be the painter boy.

—I'm Val.

—Julia, she said. If you're looking for Mr. Long, he's gone. Be back in a few days, maybe. Or sometime after that. He goes to Cheyenne and you never know when you'll see him again. Eve, she's gone with him. You go out back to that first little cabin, blue door. That's yours. The big one with the brown door is for the hands. Don't ever go in there. It stinks something awful. And the one with the red door is Faro's. You don't want to go in there either, for different reasons.

—Blue door, I said.

—Round about six, come back in here and have a plate at the kitchen table or take it back to the cabin. In the morning, breakfast at six if you want meat and eggs and hash browns. The old man who cooks for the cowboys—he used to cook in chuck wagons on cattle drives—does breakfast and will bring it over if you're up. After seven, nothing but coffee and toast and jelly and a glass of milk. Serve yourself.

I thanked Julia for her help and got my bag out of the car and walked around the house toward the blue-door cabin. Between the house and the barn, four cowboys stood in a gathering off to the side of another young cowboy who was clearly drunk. He was stocky and red-faced and wore his hat pushed back to his hairline so that the afternoon sun struck his face full on. It shone oily and golden. He wore a pistol in a low holster on his thigh like an old-time gunfighter in the movies. None of the other ranch hands carried guns.

One of them said, Come on, Wiltson, let's go inside and settle you down before you make a fool of yourself.

Wiltson waved his fingers over the pistol butt like it was a magic wand. He claimed he was in no mood to be told what to do by anybody whatsoever.

The ranch hands conferred among themselves, and then one of them headed to the barn. In a minute, the old cowboy I'd mistaken for Long came out and walked toward the drunk cowboy. He still had on the sleeveless shirt, though the sun angled and the day had turned cool. He was not armed.

Wiltson said, Faro, you may be head man around here behind Long, but this ain't the moment to dick around with me. Not a good time a'tall. Call it a bad mood, but you better step away and keep stepping.

Faro kept walking up. When he got close, Wiltson settled his hand near his right hip above the pistol butt. He locked his eyes on Faro and quivered the open hand like a threat to draw.

The skin of Faro's face clinched tight against the bones. He swiped his left palm downward to smooth his face hair. He ran his tongue around in a circle inside his closed lips and rubbed his right thumb and forefinger together like he needed a toothpick.

He said, One chance, son. Shut up and go to bed and sleep it off.

Wiltson laughed and said, Old men supposed to be real wise and shit. But out here they don't seem to make nothing but crazy fucking dumbass old men.

He got halfway into laughing at his own wit when Faro shuffled three steps very fast and grabbed Wiltson's left wrist and yanked it sharp straight downward, and when the boy pitched forward from the waist, Faro met the face with a knee. Wiltson's nose burst with blood, and he bawled like a branded calf and staggered half a step. His knees buckled, and as he began to fall, Faro reached for Wiltson's pistol and pulled it from the holster and whipped the barrel of it against the back of his head as he fell. It happened almost too fast to follow.

Wiltson's hat landed a few feet away, right side up, and Wiltson came to earth facedown with arms and legs splayed. He didn't move except for struggling to breathe around the blood from his broken face. Faro stuck the pistol under his belt and walked back toward the barn.

One of the hands said, What are we supposed to do with him?

Another one said, He didn't mean nothing.

Over his shoulder, Faro said, Neither did I. Wipe his face and put him to bed. Quit acting like somebody died. It might look bad right now, but this is not beyond the ability of the human body to heal. Tomorrow morning, if he's sobered up and can walk and still wants a job, tell him to come see me by noon at the latest. Otherwise, hit the road with all the other railroad bums and hobos.

THE GUEST CABIN WAS LOG outside and inside, one large brown room with a gigantic bed at one end and a smooth riverstone fireplace at the other. Two fat stuffed leather chairs angled in front of the fireplace. A cozy two-chair breakfast table sat by the window, and that, together with the great bed, were as sad as checking in to the bridal suite when you're traveling alone. If you were looking for something to criticize, the bathroom was maybe a little dim and narrow. You had to watch banging your elbows on the wall while brushing your teeth. Otherwise, the cabin was luxurious. Without Long's offer to Hutch, I'd have been spending a slice of my earnings on a dingy room over a store in town, a filthy shared bathroom down the hall.

I bedded down early, right after dinner, anxious to get an early start on my mural. But I couldn't sleep due to anticipation and altitude. I looked through some of my folders of information and found that the county was over six thousand feet high.

I went out and sat on the little porch. Laughter came from the bunkhouse until an hour after dark, and then silence. The big house showed light in only a couple of windows. Half an hour later, Faro walked by from the red-door cabin toward the barn. As he passed, he glanced at me and said, Can't always count on those turd cowboys to do night check right. Too bad you had to witness that little transaction. These days, some of the young ones especially, you have to remind them they're not the boss.

I HAD NEVER TRAVELED FARTHER west than Louisville, so the rail portion of my journey to Wyoming felt epic and magnificent. All the different trains and stations, the elements of landscape but not full landscapes, only linear swipes of color flying past through the windows, flowing in muted horizontal bands. Beige, blue, gray, green, white. And the smell of coal smoke and the acidic odor of cinders. Names of insignificant towns along the rail lines became briefly important waymarkers. Same with redcap porters, their names passed along among fellow travelers. Oh, look for Johnny on the Kansas City to Denver run and mention my name, he'll take care of you.

Those long stretches west of St. Louis, the train became a temporary mill town, rattling and throwing smoke into the air and waste from toilets onto the ground between the rails. People moved in and moved out, and the population reconfigured town by town. Late night, the moon-bleached prairie landscapes outside the scratched windows flowed and fled in the moonlight, no more substantial than the landscapes of dreams. I hardly slept, afraid I'd miss something. Long after midnight, the car jolted to a stop at a tiny town, a station with three metal-shaded bulbs lighting the platform. Only one passenger—a tired-looking woman—stepped down from the train. A brown pasteboard suitcase patterned to look like alligator tugged against her right hand. She looked neither left nor right, and nobody ran to greet her. She walked toward the station door but stopped to remove her hat, one that would have been in fashion five years ago. She dropped it in a wastebasket as the train jolted forward. By the time the few lights of the town gave way to darkness, I faded back half asleep wondering who she was, why so alone? By choice or not? Images drifted in and out of dream through the night, town by town. Three in the morning, a sleepy towheaded boy maybe seven years old stepped from the platform onto the train. He carried a half-empty tray of chewing gum and candy bars. A few streetlights glowed in the town beyond the station, and then black sky swelled up all around. I bought everything left in the tray so the boy could walk on home in the dark, but then I worried that this bleak station might be better than home.

A cough of steam, wheels rolled, town ended, and the only lights were in the sky. Hazy Milky Way, Jupiter bright and hard. I figured I could spend the next ten years painting that train ride.

Traveling the country, town by town, I felt a heavy drift of grief and sometimes a breakthrough of optimism from the long Depression. So many lives and ways of life were going or gone and would never return. So much confusion, so much loss of security and faith and wealth, livelihoods wiped away along with fundamental trust in the idea of America and its institutions. Those institutions had been what failed people, the loss of trust in them inevitable. Some days those past few years, I felt a sliver of hope that the country could scrabble its way out of the hole we'd found ourselves in, hope that if we actually tried to make life better for folks who'd been ignored or trampled on for so long, we might even come out better than we'd been before. Other days it felt like too massive an undertaking, that nothing could ever free us of the hard times we'd been living for years. The Depression had gone on so long it had become divided into epochs. The horrible shocking months after the crash, the dreary years afterward, the hopeful months, and then the dreadful backsliding of the economy toward hopelessness, like surges of a medieval plague sweeping over you again and again. The last morning of my journey, like punctuation for my sense of having witnessed a slow march toward apocalypse, I walked into the dining car, and on every newspaper facing me, the front page blasted huge images of the *Hindenburg*, its gigantic shape reduced to nothing but collapsing geometric framework by a storm of turbulent fire against ink-black sky.

FROM DENVER I DROVE UP to Wyoming in a '28 Model A woodie wagon I bought from a lot out on East Colfax. It had been a good vehicle for somebody back before the crash, but by the time I got it, all the good had been driven out. The canvas roof over the back end leaked and needed swabbing with melted wax. Varnish peeled off the graying wood side panels in flakes the size of thumbnails. Three of the tires dry-rotted in checkers that seemed to enlarge and multiply by the day. But on the plus side, I'd paid less than a hundred for it, and some previous owner had installed a radio. It hung awkwardly from the dashboard like a shoebox, but it got good reception. In a pinch, I could sleep in the back end. And plenty of space left over for hauling painting materials for the job I was busting to get started on.

It was a New Deal art project, a post office mural. Art for the people. Mostly those government murals for post offices and libraries all over the country were actually painted by better-known artists in their studios on pieces of canvas measured to fit the wall in question. For a small-town PO, the painting usually needed to fit the awkward space on the same wall as the door to the postmaster's office. When big-time city artists finished working on their commissions and their paint had dried, they rolled the canvases and sent them somewhere out into all that inconvenient land between the coasts, where somebody glued them in place. To find subjects for their murals, the artists looked at photographs of the local landscape and read up a little on local history and whatever details the Federal Writers' Project people were putting together for the state guide series.

I got lucky getting the Dawes commission. The known artist chosen for the job—who planned to paint on canvas in an apartment in Brooklyn and mail it off to be pasted on the wall—had died. And even then, I wouldn't normally have had a chance if the PO had been in anything like a real city, or even in a town near a real city. I mainly got the job because Hutch—my benefactor and old art professor back in the early days of the Depression when it felt like a phenomenon soon to pass—now occupied a job of some significance at the Treasury Department's Section of Painting and Sculpture in Roosevelt's Washington. Hutch was the right kind of idealist for the times. He believed public art could be like a pebble thrown into a still pond, a small influence but spreading in all directions. He also saw Dawes as an opportunity to try an idea he'd been thinking about for some time, but hadn't had the chance to play with, that murals ought to be painted on-site in the old style. When Hutch told me I had the commission, he said he had convinced himself that this was a young person's job. Fewer roots and ties. And maybe we need fresh naivete. God knows we have plenty of the other, with all these elder artists lined up for a shot at a government paycheck but not willing to leave home for it.

The goal Hutch expressed was that in these forgotten towns, people would see their tax dollars working to build a handsome PO on Main Street. On top of that, they get to watch a real artist create public art painted specifically for them, depicting something important about their community, its history, or its main economy— wheat or cows, cutting timber, mining ore. Maybe a celebration of their picturesque landscapes or specific historic events. Some element that had formed the place, including maybe some Indians fading in the distance. So the mural's main argument, however it was shaped, was that this particular place held importance and was not forgotten after all. Let people of the town see every brushstroke from start to finish. He wanted them to feel ownership of the art for decades to come. Every time they stopped by to check for mail or post a letter or buy stamps, he wanted them to leave with an image of an artist up on a scaffold being a genius, or at least a good craftsman. Way in the future, if we were lucky enough to have one, old folks might say to grandchildren, I seen that picture painted when I was your age.

Hutch had stressed that in planning the mural, details of subject matter were of extreme importance, and had sent folders of pertinent information about Dawes—history, economy, flora and fauna. I read the pages and looked at the photos and made a list of possibilities. Cattle, grass, pioneers and their sculptural covered wagons, cowboys, Indians, sage plains and distant snow mountains, antelope, bison, elk, possibly a stray grizzly. I read that Dawes was the county seat of Dawes County, named after a Mr. Dawes who had been a rich railroad man, but I never even considered finding a way to add him to the painting like I might have if he'd been a famous gunfighter or fur trader or explorer.

I tried hard to take a smart-aleck tone toward everything, but really I took the work itself as seriously as Baptist missionaries sharing the gospel. I had a job in a jobless time doing what I loved and what I had some talent and a lot of education to do. And the work I was planning could possibly mean something to an audience, however small, into a future perhaps beyond my span, however long or short, bright or dim. And also, I wanted to do right by Hutch, who had given me a shot when most of my old art classmates were struggling to find paying work of any kind. I was getting slightly over a hundred dollars a month and also an allowance for room and board. But as a bonus, a rich art-lover college friend of Hutch's, with a vast ranch outside town and many back-East connections, had offered to contribute living quarters and meals on his ranch. And Hutch had made sure I still got to keep all the allowance. The rancher's name was Long and his big ranch was Long Shot, which either suggested a sense of irony or none whatsoever.

When I finished my mural and cashed the last Treasury Department check, I would have little expectation of making a living painting for some time. Back home in the Tidewater, I had nothing left but my nearly worthless inheritance, an acre of sand

and dune grass on the Chesapeake Bay. Parents both dead, brother an enemy after he successfully strip-mined all the value out of our father's estate and his law practice following his death a couple of years after Black Thursday when he took a terminal sailboat ride out toward the mouth of the bay.

Then, more recently, the woman I was supposed to marry, my fiancée, eloped with someone else out of the blue, last minute. Specifically, three days before we were penciled in to be wed at the Episcopalian church. Everyone—meaning her family and their friends and her friends and my friends—assumed I was broken for life. Poor Valentine, the groom left waiting at the altar. How dramatic and humiliating.

Very quickly, though, I discovered that I didn't much care who she married as long as it wasn't me. I felt no heartbreak, no shame, no yearning, no sense of loss. I felt relief, like I had won something, though I couldn't specify the prize beyond the fact that her expectations of me didn't matter one scratch anymore. And also, since I was widely seen as the victim of her impulses, a certain amount of sympathy began flowing my way. Mostly, though, I felt like I could breathe properly again without constriction, complete lungfuls of air in and out for the first time in a year. But respiration, however much it seemed like a soothing miracle, didn't really give me any more direction in life than before she cut me loose.

The mural commission, though, gave me at least temporary direction. Go west. Paint for a few months.

DAWES WAS A LINEAR MAIN-STREET kind of town, not a crossroads. It stretched less than half a mile east to west across the high plains. Seven blocks, five stoplights. The businesses mostly came doubled—gas stations, banks, drugstores, hardwares, barbershops and beauty shops, dime stores and diners and groceries. But five bars and five churches spaced along the front street. And of course only one post office. Past the businesses, houses stretched a few blocks in either direction, and beyond the city limits, the only paved road was the east-west highway. If you wanted to go north or south, you had to go somewhere else.

I arrived at the PO a half hour after it opened for business and introduced myself to the postmaster, a skinny man about midway to retirement with the crisp name of Don Ray. He wore a gray well-maintained pinstripe suit from the previous decade, and he took his position very seriously and expected everyone else to do the same. After all, he saw himself as the ranking representative of the federal government in Dawes County. Which, when I gave it some thought, he actually was.

The building was brand new, in service only a month and still smelling of paint and varnish, new wood and masonry. Same floor plan as most of the recent POs in towns this size. Walk in the front door, and the counter stood straight across a rectangle of space representing the lobby. Off to one side—in this case the right—mailboxes with brass doors and combination locks and tiny glass windows to peek in and see if you had mail before you wasted time remembering your numbers and twiddling the little knobs. At the end of the boxes stood The Wall, as Don Ray called it. In the middle of the wall was the heavy oak door to his office, his name and title freshly painted in blocky gold letters. On either side of the door, dark wood wainscot and framed corkboards featuring overlapping notices of commemorative national park stamps and mug shots of FBI most wanted criminals crowded each other for space. That range of plaster above the door and descending to the corkboards was my field of opportunity. It rose before me blank and white in what amounted visually to three parts—the two tall spaces to left and right, and in the center the shallower space above the door frame.

Don Ray and I stood back from the wall studying it. I told him my plan was not to see the space as three smaller panels, as some muralists did, but as one large space. Let the image, its forms and its narrative, rise on the left and crest high in the center, above the door, and fall on the right. A wave. One of the fundamental shapes of motion and energy.

Don Ray said, Like at an ocean?

—Or the rolling plains.

—I've never seen an ocean.

—You should go. Atlantic or Pacific, either one. The Pacific's a little closer from here.

—Unlikely, he said. By the time I made it there, I'd need to head back. I've not got unlimited time to roam around like some.

Don Ray paused and looked at the wall and said, Those corkboards bugger up your space for painting.

—Sort of. But it comes with the territory.

—Doesn't look right, all those mugs of the *hostis publicus* taking attention from your picture.

I might have unintentionally raised an eyebrow or looked surprised.

Don Ray laughed and said, What? You think this is the most ignorant ass end of the whole world?

I skipped forward and told him I'd be putting up simple scaffolding, ladders and boards, and would first be attaching the wood panels, already shipped by rail and waiting to be loaded on a delivery truck. I'd need to find a carpenter or two to help me install the panels. Next I would put on gesso, the ground of the painting, the surface you paint on. Gesso is messy, like swabbing a layer of white plaster over the surface of the panels, but I told Don Ray not to worry, I'd put down drop cloths to protect the new floors. And I told him even after all that, there's still more tedious, meticulous work left before actually getting to paint.

—As boring as watching someone else working algebra problems, except not so boring if you're the one doing it, Don Ray said.

—Exactly, I said. But really, it won't be too long before I'll begin painting with tempera.

I assured him I'd clean up at the end of every day, but I warned that the eggs were messy and might create a smell now and then because you saved money buying old eggs. And, by the way, I'd need a lot of eggs, so who should I talk to about deliveries?

—Eggs? Don Ray said. No cooking in the building.

—No, of course not. Raw eggs are for the paint. You separate the whites from the yolks and discard the whites and pat the yolks dry with a cloth and then mix the yolks with dry pigment to make the paint. Tempera can last thousands of years. Egyptians painted with it.

—Messy, Don Ray said. Eggs and dirty cloths and slopping water around. This building's brand new, and I'm responsible for it.

—I'll do the messiest parts outside.

—I don't want some mudhole of dumped egg whites right outside the building.

—I promise I'll keep things clean, and I'll flush all the leftover whites down the toilet.

Don Ray said, If the toilet needs clearing, I'm handing you the plunger.

He studied the blank wall a while longer and then said, What I can't figure is how I'm going to get in and out of my office once you get your scaffold up. Am I supposed to go outside and climb through the window?

—Which way does your door swing?

—In.

—No problem. Open the door and duck a few inches.

—Well, I guess that might work, Don Ray said. So, good luck to you son. We close up the counter and roll down the tambour at five, and everybody goes home. Course the front door stays unlocked so people can check their boxes all night long. You know, in case you get inspired at two in the morning and need to get in.

ABOUT SIX, I WANDERED OVER to the big house and found Julia in the kitchen.

She smiled and said, Dinner'll be ready in about half an hour. You want to eat here at the table or take it back to your cabin?

—Happy to eat right here, I said. If you don't mind.

—Long as you don't mind me eating with you. Nothing fancy tonight. I'm doing a couple of tenderloins with a pan sauce. Mr. Long likes me to call them filets, but to me, that's something you call fish.

I watched her work. A blazing hot pan, a very short noisy time for the two steaks. Then, with the steaks in the pan off the heat, she did something very fast with butter and wine. Another pan held something that looked like carefully browned home fries. Julia said, Sorry, nothing green tonight. The last load of vegetables that came in wasn't fit to eat.

My first bite, I said, This is something special. You've been working here awhile?

—Little while now, Julia said. I started out cooking for pay in a diner over in Lander when I was about twenty, give or take. Just the usual—beef stew, meatloaf, roast chicken, fried chicken,

chicken-fried steak. Once or twice a week the menu included steak browned on the flat-top grill with french fries. People kind of liked the way I did it, but I didn't think much about it. Fairly thin steak, potatoes cut skinny and rinsed and then deep-fried in beef tallow. Plop of butter on the steak. No big secret. Most people like beef fat and butter. Well, one day Mr. Long came in and ordered it. When he finished, he said it was the best steak frites he'd had since his last time in Paris. He hired me on the spot for too good a wage to turn down, and I've been trying to learn how to cook French ever since.

I nodded, wondering what level of wealthy you'd have to be to enjoy a meal and hire the cook right then and there to come live on your ranch and cook for you every day.

—You like working for Mr. Long?

Julia said, I do. He doesn't mind me setting my own schedule. I don't start until about ten in the morning, and I don't work after about nine at night, even when Mr. Long and Eve stay late at the table. A lot of days my work starts with cleaning up the mess in the dining room, but I'm not a housekeeper. There's a couple of them who come out and clean two or three times a week.

She pulled a book off a shelf near the stove and handed it to me. *French Cooking for American Kitchens.* She said, When I first got here, I didn't know any of the French foods he asked about, so he gave me that cookbook. Don't look at the picture on the first page. Skinny women with their little titties out riding a cow and holding up pigs and poultry and big fish.

A torn corner of paper marked a page and when I turned to it, a recipe for beef stew with wine and onions and mushrooms. A sentence was underlined in pencil—*However, for the best results, make use of every trick.*

I held up the open book and said, Good advice?

—You bet, Julia said. And not just in cooking.

DON RAY HAD FOUND CARPENTERS to haul the panels off the delivery truck and fix them to the wall. Even during that boring stuff, people stood and watched for a few minutes as they came and went. They asked questions like, What's it going to be? Are you a real artist? And of course, as one stout, square-headed little man in dungarees and a yellow straw hat said, You know what we call the WPA?

—What? I said, trying to sound bright and interested and not at all like I knew exactly what he'd say next. Hutch had told me to expect a few townspeople to take their opposition to New Deal art programs out on me. He had also beat it into my head to be patient and gracious since these folks—whether they or I liked it or not— were part of my patronage, their tax money enabling my art.

As expected, the man said what people all over the country said, tongues pressed into cheeks, We Piddle About.

I wasn't ever going to find it funny. And besides, my job wasn't even through the Works Progress Administration. But I forced a fake Ha-ha at the punchline and asked, Did you make that joke up right on the spot by yourself?

—Heard it said.

—Well, you remember that and keep saying it, because it's a good one.

THAT AFTERNOON, BACK AT THE ranch, Wiltson met me as I passed the barn like he'd been watching for me. He walked up and said, I need to say something.

The swelling had gone down some on his face, but deep purple bruises still marked his cheekbones and one side of his head at the temple and ear. When he talked, I was surprised that he hadn't lost teeth in his encounter with Faro.

Wiltson said, I don't remember it, but the boys tell me you saw that shit with Faro. I want to say I wished I hadn't done what I did to get him that fired up.

—He was really rough on you.

—Aw hell, he went easy. Didn't even break my nose. Pull a gun on somebody like him, you're lucky to walk away.

—You didn't actually pull your pistol, just acted like you might be about to.

Wiltson said, Same difference. I was asking for it. But we've kissed and made up. Or at least I've kissed his ass and we've made up. I said I was drunk and idiotic, and he said, Who hasn't been? So we're square. No grudges.

—Well, that's good news.

—That Faro's a mystery, ain't he?

—He's very gentle with the horses, I said. He reasons with them, like he can communicate with them in a strange way.

—Everything he does is strange. Watch him. Like every day isn't enough work to suit him, he's poured cement in a pair of buckets with loops of heavy rope sticking up for handles, and he swings them around and lifts them and throws them and runs stooped over hauling one or both of them for a hundred feet or more. He looks at you sometimes like he doesn't know who you are or even what kind of animal you are, surely not the same kind he's a member of. He's got an old big cannonball welded to three feet of steel rod like you'd use to reinforce a concrete wall. Swings it around in strange patterns for as high as ten minutes at a time.

—Like circles and figure eights?

—Yes.

—I'd guess if you were swinging a cannonball on a rod, those would be the first shapes you'd come up with. Not many choices given the limitations of physics and the human body. You wouldn't be making pentagons in the air.

Wiltson said, He might start that any day. Sometimes I think Faro is some kind of warlock or a wizard.

—Nah, I said. He's from the last century. People were all strange back then.

THIRD DAY OF WORK, DON Ray invited me to supper.

I said, Sure, when?

He said, Tonight, of course. We eat at six, and Lucy gets rattled if people come late.

I said, I won't have time to drive out to Long Shot and change clothes.

—Doesn't matter. You'll look like an artist.

I wasn't sure what looking like an artist meant, but after work I changed into a clean blue chambray shirt from the back of the woodie. My baggy work pants would have to do, but they had only a few old paint smudges on the thighs.

I showed up at the Ray house on the dot, expecting Lucy to be high-strung, with hair springing out of a tight do, acting agitated with tiny beads of sweat blooming on her upper lip, maybe not knowing where to hold her hands because she's dusted with flour halfway to the elbows. But Lucy Ray didn't seem all that easily rattled. She was a very pale brunette about halfway between my age and Don Ray's. She set her cocktail glass on the coffee table and rose from the sofa to greet me with a brief touch of her fingertips to my forearm. She wore a lavender summer dress patterned with tiny yellow flowers.

—What a treat, Lucy said. I've never met a real artist before. Unless you count that woman from Rawlins who'll paint the portrait of your horse or bull if they're famous enough and you pay her enough.

—Really? I said. Famous horses, I get. Like Man o' War. But cattle?

—Bulls, specifically, Lucy said. Some are known throughout the West. Famous for throwing rodeo riders into wheelchairs and for throwing good progeny. You know, strong seed.

Don Ray looked at me and smiled and then said, Lucy, maybe we could talk about Val's painting. I'm sure he'll be starting to make headway any day now.

I said, I'll admit so far it's looked more like carpentry than painting. And thank you for finding the carpenters for me. Soon I'll start laying out the mural using some of the ancient techniques to enlarge my careful small drawing to fit your big wall. Once that's done, I'll begin painting, layer by layer. The first stages are tedious, but it's the way murals have been done for centuries.

Don said, Every job has its own little lore. Don't get me started on rare stamp collectors or on the kind of accounting books I have to keep. Stonemasons can talk your ears off telling you the deep wisdom they've learned from handling rocks all day. Constructing the post office building, one of them said to me that the main thing he'd learned about turning a pile of stones into a wall is—his exact words—*the stone you're looking for is always right beneath your hand*. Now what's that supposed to mean?

Lucy said, Don, it means the answer to any problem is always close, not far away.

—Yeah, Don said. Tell that to the engineers and construction crews for the new Golden Gate Bridge.

Lucy turned to me and said, You were saying something about going from small paintings to filling a wall. It sounds like magnifying or expanding your original picture?

—That's exactly right. Sometimes I think it's like blowing up a balloon. It feels that way in my head. It's not an abstract process. Very concrete and particular, more craft than art. This first part can be like doing geometry proofs at the same time you're nailing shingles on a roof. And I haven't even gotten to laying out the grid, the cartoon, scheduling the *giornata*. Believe me, I can't wait for the day I start putting color on the walls. But with tempera you have to paint thin layers to get deep colors. You can't glob it on thick. And each layer needs to dry, at least a little.

—Good, Lucy said. We'll have you with us for a while.

We went to the dining room, and Lucy Ray very effortlessly materialized a beautiful hunk of medium-rare roast beef and sharp-flavored greens and soft yeast rolls. She could leave the table for what seemed a few seconds and come back with another basket of hot rolls and a fresh pitcher of martinis. I waved the drinks off after two because I had to work the next day, but the Rays pressed forward, refill after refill, and hardly seemed fazed.

We were having warm apple tarts with whipped cream and coffee when she asked for my impressions of the Longs. I told her I hadn't met either of them, and that it was still unclear when they'd be back from Cheyenne.

Lucy said, It's no secret he'd like to move down there, at least temporarily.

I said, My understanding is that he's not from around here.

—No, Lucy said. But he's been around awhile. He got that land before the crash. Afterward, when livestock prices bottomed out and the government was killing hundreds of thousands of cows and pigs and bulldozing them into the ground, it was hard times for ranchers all over. But Long's probably rolling in money now. They say four years ago he made a million on some government deal. Grazing rights or water rights down on the south part of the ranch along the Bison River. Maybe a hydroelectric dam. You know, big men getting their big cut off the top. But they haven't even started on anything. Now and then people say they see surveyors down there working, but then nothing happens.

—Jobs like that don't happen overnight, Don said. And Long's done a lot of work to get electricity to the ranches outside town.

—Yes, Lucy said. A couple of summers ago, he convinced some other ranchers to sign up for an electric co-op. Of course, he made sure lines were run to his ranch first. But anyway, these days his interest is mostly in Cheyenne.

Don said, Strange state where you decide to plop your capital city nearly rock-throwing distance from the next state's much bigger capital.

Lucy said, You ever know a short man who got really aggressive around tall men?

When nobody answered she said, Every time somebody asks him, Long claims he has no political ambitions. Nevertheless, he seems to go to Cheyenne a lot. I think that government land deal got him interested in politics.

Don said, Mostly they stay at the hotel near the capitol where the lawmakers stay, but if there's some special occasion where he's donated a pile of money, they stay at the governor's mansion.

Lucy said, We subscribe to the Cheyenne paper, and it seems Mrs. Long is a big hit down there, like a bottle of 7Up that Long shakes and spews all over the politicians.

I asked what kind of office Long might be interested in, and she said, Speculation is, anything short of governor would be out of the question for Long. Like state legislature would be almost humiliating. Really, US senator is what they say he's eyeing most closely.

The Rays talked about a popular politician, Senator Philson, a cattleman with roots going back to the Indian Wars, who'd have to be hauled out of the chamber on a gurney with a sheet over his face for the seat to open up. But given the senator's age and bad health, short of supernatural intervention, his passing shouldn't take more than about half a term. With a well-timed death, Long could ease into the job as an interim appointment by his friend the current governor. Long would enter the US Senate in mourning, his heart heavy laden with respect for his fallen predecessor who had served so honorably and so long, and whose seat Long would be humbled to fill until the next scheduled election, by which time he would have run a careful and well-funded campaign. But in case old Philson suddenly started looking rosy and like there might one day be a photo of him all wrinkled and caved in upon himself and angry, with the headline *Senator Celebrates 105th Birthday*, then the junior senate seat might offer possibilities. It was currently held by a slick and vulnerable fifty-year-old oilman with ethical liabilities both personal and business. Downside was, Long's fight to take that seat would be ugly and costly, especially so since they were both of the same party.

Of course I didn't know how many martinis Lucy and Don had thrown back before I arrived, and neither of the Rays seemed very drunk, but they were unexpectedly candid in talking about Long and what they represented as the town's general attitude toward him. Though I guess if you go to any town, small or large, the richest or most well-known person agitates opinion and uninformed guessing of motives.

—Long's lived here a good while, Lucy said. But he's not from here. And he'll never ever be from here.

—Obviously, Don Ray said.

—You know the name of his ranch, Long Shot?

—Yes.

—He tells people it's because that's what his buddies called him back in the war. Because he held some record for the farthest kill.

There was a pause and then Don said, I assume Mrs. Long is with him in Cheyenne?

I said, All I know is she's not at the ranch.

—They're an interesting pair, Lucy said. Long floated along until he was in his forties as a bachelor. Just him and that scary old cowboy that they say has about a hundred notches on his gun. All kinds of stories about him. The hands come and go, but the old cowboy's permanent.

Don said, Long could have had a wife back East when he was a young man.

—Could, Lucy said. But I'm not talking speculation. He'd been a bachelor as far back as anyone here knows. And then he goes on one of his long trips and comes back from Denver or Santa Fe with a shiny young wife nearly half his age. Some speculate he brought her in so he'll have an heir, like Henry VIII. So Eve better watch her head if she can't make a boy child. But she's probably plenty tough. They say she was on the road with the railroad bums for a while before she started singing with dance bands. I'm not judging. A lot of people have been out there a long time looking for work and doing the best they can. I'm just saying she's maybe seen a lot, and then she landed Long. Jackpot.

Don Ray looked at me and very slightly shook his head. To change the subject he said, Lucy, your arithmetic might not quite work. I don't think there's as big a difference in age as you're making it out.

—I guess you've studied on it some, Lucy said.

Hoping not to be pulled into any more of the local gossip, I said, I'm looking forward to meeting them both.

NEXT MORNING WAS CHILLY, AND as I walked out to the woodie for my drive to work, Faro walked toward me like he was too preoccupied to even say good morning. But as we were about to pass, he stopped and said, In the future, people won't give two shits about rivers. That's how bad it's gonna get. People won't even write songs about them anymore. That's how you'll know the world has gone to hell. Maybe you'll be unlucky enough to see that world. Me, I'll have floated on downstream.

I said, I'll have to think about that.

Faro said, No, you don't.

That afternoon Faro sat alone on the top board of the fence to the empty round pen. He looked off to the west. He didn't seem to notice me as I passed on the way to my cabin. But then he said, Hey, Val.

I turned and said, Hey, Faro.

He motioned me over and pointed to the Winds and said, Before he left for Cheyenne, Long had been saying that when you got here, if you didn't turn out to be some delicate soft little artist, we ought to trailer the horses over to the mountains. Maybe take a two- or three-day ride. Him and Eve and you. I'd be the guide. Couple of cowboys to take care of horses and set up tents. He's been studying maps, called it a welcoming excursion.

Faro said it like he was embarrassed by the cute moniker.

A two-hour ride was the longest I'd ever done, and I was sore after only that. I couldn't imagine days of riding and then sleeping on the ground.

I said, I'm going to be pretty busy working, but what are your thoughts about it?

Faro said, I'm no guide. I've never paid much attention to maps. Back when I did a lot of my traveling, plenty of places hadn't been mapped yet. Get to a point, and then nothing but white space. I've been lost a hundred times and found my own way out. There's not but one true trail through the world, and all the truth you can say of it is it's there. Everything else is a guess, your own made-up bullshit. There's really no such thing as a guide. Just the trail.

I said, I might agree.

—Think on it, Faro said. And as for the ride, we'll see if Long brings it up again. Sometimes he gets going on an idea and then lets it float away.

A COUPLE OF DAYS AFTER MY DINNER WITH THE Rays, on into the afternoon, I finally met Long and Eve. I stood seven feet up on my wobbly scaffolding working on the grid. They came in together to post a few letters, check mail, and check me on their way back to the ranch.

They looked like what they were, local ranch aristocracy, the kind turned out in crisp Scully shirts and polished Justin boots that had never touched the inside of a corral. I knew nothing about those brands before I came there. My father, a lawyer, had tended toward Hickey Freeman suits, Harris Tweed overcoats, Allen Edmonds footwear.

Still, both ignorantly and judgmentally, I whispered to myself out of the side of my mouth, Cowboy formalwear—John Wayne and his young cowgirl friend need to buy a book of stamps. But maybe my tone fell short on generosity. After all, I'd been living in their guest cabin for almost a week. I couldn't help noticing the stack of magazines Long drew from their oversized mailbox with its scrolled brass door, *The New Republic* on top. Mighty progressive reading, which I maybe hadn't expected from a wealthy Wyoming cattle rancher.

From the moment she had entered the room, Eve acted as if she were onstage, every movement meant to convey some nuance about the character she was playing. The way she walked and pushed her hair back from her forehead with the inside of her wrist, how she drew a cigarette out of the pack and tamped it with a few percussive taps and then waved it around between two fingers without ever actually lighting and smoking it. She seemed used to having people watch her, and she wanted to put on a good show, give the audience their money's worth even though her audience had paid nothing.

Don Ray came out of his office to greet them and let them know a photographer was on his way from the newspaper office down the street.

Eve said, How thoughtful, Mr. Ray. She waved her cold cigarette in a gesture of thanks.

Don Ray said, Well, Val, you finally get to meet your patron.

Long looked tired from their week in Cheyenne, his face matte gray. Where his brown hair was clipped short over his ears a little stubble shone white.

I climbed down and shook hands and thanked them for their generosity in supporting the project. Long waved the gratitude away and made small talk about public art and government buildings. He talked about Europe. Go there and realize the importance of public art immediately.

He said, These PO projects broadcast art across the continent in a scope like nothing before. A hundred years on, at least some of what these New Deal programs are producing right now will still exist and be like an electrical charge, giving a tingle or maybe even a jolt of positive energy to anyone open to receiving it.

Eve said, Like a big battery.

Long sounded a lot like Hutch with his optimistic vision of

how art in every small town, right there in your face filling up a whole wall every time you bought a stamp, could elevate the country, maybe by only an inch, but every upward movement, however small, accumulates.

I said, That's the hope Hutch pushes out into the world. How was your drive from Cheyenne?

Long said, A lot of time has passed since I saw Hutch, but we send little messages by postcard several times a year. I'm glad to be helping out on this project. But to answer your question, we left Cheyenne after lunch and made it back in five hours with the accelerator pinned to the floor every time the road was straight for more than a hundred yards.

Eve said, More like after late breakfast. I mean, we ate eggs and bacon, and for me that's breakfast. But who's counting.

She looked at her unlit cigarette as if a bright green parrot had suddenly lighted on her two extended fingers.

Long said, Apples and oranges. My point is, every time I'm in Cheyenne, I'm overwhelmed with embarrassment that our state capital is so near Denver. Like we intentionally crowded it as close as we could without violating their sovereign territory. If I were ever governor, I'd start recruiting like-minded office holders to draft a plan to move the capital. My first choice would be Lander. Hell, even Casper would be better than Cheyenne. But Casper would open its own can of worms, if you know what I mean. Or maybe I'd have some fun and piss almost everybody off and propose moving it to Jackson. Start almost from scratch and build a capital to suit ourselves.

—Maybe it already does suit, Eve said.

I watched Long's reaction, and he seemed kind of charmed by her comment. Also, I had no idea why Casper might be a political can of worms and didn't really care, so I said, Where's Jackson?

—About as far from Denver as state lines allow, Eve said, a little singsong and sarcastic as if reciting something she'd heard a hundred times. Very beautiful mountains. The Tetons. Surely you've seen pictures. You should take a couple of days off and drive over sometime while you're here. And John's kidding about moving the capital.

Don Ray said, Well, I'd for sure vote to move it.

I was still somewhat vague on the details of Wyoming geography, so I smiled and said, The Tetons. Bierstadt?

Long said, I have a couple I'll show you. They're upstairs.

He paused and said, Dinner tonight?

—Sure, I said. But aren't you both tired from the trip?

—The drive's as restful as a good night's sleep after you've spent several days talking to politicians.

—Fucking amen to that, Eve said.

Long smiled and tapped her forearm.

—Oops, sorry, she said.

—We eat late. Come over about seven thirty or eight and we'll have a drink to get started.

In Virginia most people ate about five thirty. Six thirty would be what most people considered late for supper. Eight would have been crowding bedtime.

The newspaper photographer arrived, and the three of us lined up side by side. He looked at us through the camera and then backed away and looked at the room. He said to me, Hey, how about climbing back up on the scaffold and let me see how that looks. And hold a brush like you're doing something.

After the flash popped, Eve and Long headed out.

At the door, Eve turned and looked up at me and said, Have Julia and Faro been taking good care of you?

—Absolutely, I said.

From my perch, I looked through the high window as they climbed into their big Brewster town car with the strange, heart-shaped grille, scooped and narrowing to a spear point at the bottom.

I EXPECTED DINNER THAT FIRST night to be short, polite, perfunctory. But like so many to follow, it stretched late into the night and ended with wine bottles scattered about the table and Eve, at some point, drifting off while Long and I kept talking.

Early on, Eve said, What's Val short for?

—Valentine Montgomery Welch III.

—Oh my, there's three of you?

—Were, I said. I and II are gone. Hard to imagine inflicting that name on three generations, isn't it? My school friends called me Valmont, but now everybody just calls me Val.

Long dove right in, probing around looking for my theory of painting. I hardly had any theory. I felt bad about that because Long made it seem like a requirement.

I said, Back in college, Hutch wasn't much interested in theory. All that mattered was the thing itself, whether you were talking about the subject or the final product of art. I'm more interested in how physical and material the world is. Basically, I mean vision. What we see. So talking about art theory to me is like having a theory of walking or of the color blue.

—Hmm, so that's your theory, Long said. We'll have plenty of time to go over that. Maybe we'll formulate the theory of blue.

Eve said, So these years of bad times, you've ridden out a big chunk of them in school? I bet now and then you had to eat franks and beans in the dorm room. But I'm not judging.

Long leaned and tapped Eve's arm.

She said, What, am I wrong?

—Not really, I said.

Given what Lucy Ray had said about Eve having lived hobo for a while, I reined in my impulse to be defensive and mention my father's death.

She moved on and talked about being a little embarrassed wearing a version of her stage costume that afternoon. She said, That silly outfit, I hate wearing it except behind a microphone with the lights blaring and the band driving forward like a freight train and a crowd of people drunk and dancing. I haven't done that in a while, but in Cheyenne those outfits go over really well with horny middle-aged politicians.

She and Long talked over each other about how she played Cheyenne a number of times back when she sang in cowboy swing bands, including a big and memorable show at Frontier Days. Which I'd never heard of but was apparently one of the oldest, most major of all rodeos across the West.

—That was many years ago, Long said.

—Yes, almost three, Eve said.

Pretend arguing, they explained that still, even now, various government officials remembered her warmly. Uncomfortably so sometimes. But Long knew how to work those memories, and Eve was willing to go along now and then.

I wanted to know more about the bands Eve had been in, about the music I had heard on the radio driving from Denver to Dawes. The sound was different from what got played back on the East Coast, yet you could tell it pulled from some of the same influences—jazz, swing, hillbilly fiddle music, country. But all wound into its own thing by the whine of twin fiddles and steel guitar. But before I could get a word in, Long and Eve had pressed on with their talk.

Eve said, When I start to balk at the attention in Cheyenne,

John asks me how I'd feel about being first lady of the state, or a US senator's wife.

Long said, You're exaggerating. I'm not running for anything.

Eve said she guessed she could play either of those parts for a couple of hours at a time if she had to. It wouldn't shape how she felt about herself, though. She'd spent enough time onstage with smoky cylinders of yellow light aimed at her to know that the person standing in the crosshairs is not the person you are. In Cheyenne, at governor's mansion dinners, she always felt like she was bluffing her way through, trying not to make grammar mistakes such as stepping a foot wrong into those *I*-and-*me*, *her*-and-*she* minefields.

She said, When it comes to the difference between *that* and *which*, I gave up long ago and decided, fuck it, life's too short.

—Hardly anyone at those dinners is speaking perfectly either, Long said.

—You are, Eve said.

After a pause she said, John, honey, you think you have good taste and I don't, and mostly you're right. But you like me blond better than my natural color.

She looked at me and said, I'm really halfway between auburn and mouse.

Long said, I love every version of you. But you know how it is in Cheyenne.

I sat and listened as they talked back and forth about how well the shiny show business version of Eve worked to moderate the more refined image Long couldn't help but project. If he ever became a candidate, she'd smooth away the New England part he couldn't wholly shake. They styled themselves that night as partners, their strengths and weaknesses perfectly complementing each other.

—John can't pass for a local here, but I can, Eve said.

—Marginally, Long said.

I was a little surprised that they talked so openly in front of someone they'd just met and wondered if they were a little desperate for company and playing to their audience of one, like Fred and Ginger sparring in the early minutes of a movie before they fall in love.

Long said, You make me look young and full of energy.

—*Full of spunk* would be how they'd put it in Cheyenne, Eve said.

—Let's leave it at energy.

Eve looked less tired than she had at the PO, less makeup, more natural, more relaxed. She wore a delicate peach-colored sweater and a deep blue skirt with buttons in a tidy line down the front, no Western embellishments to be found. Candlelight at the table softened her brassy hair, and she looked beautiful and golden. A small scar below her left eye, almost like the dent a fingernail might make on the page of a book, was fascinating. I had to keep reminding myself not to stare at it.

LATER—WE WERE PROBABLY EATING PIE by then—I said, When I first walked into the lobby, the paintings were overwhelming. And not just the Matisse and the Renoir.

Long laughed and said, Lobby wasn't what I was aiming for in designing this house, but maybe it's the target I hit. Sometimes you have to accept slips between cups and lips.

I might have blushed a shade, but before I could apologize for my word choice, Eve said, I've been looking for the right word to call that room. From now on, *lobby* is it.

Long said, Well, I'd propose *gallery*, but looks like I've been outvoted.

He went on to say, I bought the Renoir and the Matisse in Paris right after the World War. After the Grand Armistice—the eleventh hour of the eleventh day of the eleventh month of 1918—I decided I didn't want to get on a boat and go home right away. My father arranged for me to be discharged in Europe, urged me to stay in Paris awhile and sent me a monthly stipend via American Express for a year, after which I was supposed to come home and get to work. But I stayed in Paris as long as the money kept coming, which was closer to three years. I had a grand time and bought a few paintings with little thought of value or bargains. I bought what I liked and could afford and didn't care about other people's opinions. The exchange rate for dollars in the aftermath of the long war made my stipend pretty luxurious, and I bought paintings for a few hundred dollars here and a thousand there. I still love most of those paintings and look at them almost daily. Among them, the Renoir and the Matisse you noticed. More upstairs.

I said, That rifle with the long scope looks like it's in a place of honor. That must have a story too.

Long said, It's a Springfield M1903. I used it in the war, but a .30-06 isn't very special. The scope, though, is fairly particular. I was a sniper. You know, climb up a tree or crouch in a trench and shoot somebody you can hardly see with your bare eyes.

He went on to talk about how his father saw the war as a terrible mistake but also as an opportunity to make a lot of money. He wanted Long to stay at home and help him, but his arguments failed. Long volunteered. He wanted to experience war like Hemingway and Cummings and Dos Passos and so many other smart young volunteers did, except that in training before leaving

America, he showed an unusual ability at target shooting. So instead of driving an ambulance, he spent his time blowing holes in Germans. He claimed kills from nearly a mile away and seemed to remember that year of sniping with great affection. He preferred to put down officers for moral reasons, but any head rising over the lip of a trench for long enough to aim and fire was fair game.

—We weren't saber fighting with a complex code of honor, Long said. Both sides were poisoning masses of soldiers with clouds of mustard gas and chlorine gas. You don't want to see what that's like, and don't expect me to describe it in front of Eve.

—I'm too delicate to hear that crap, Eve said. She shifted in her chair and propped an elbow on the table to rest her cheek in her hand, like settling in for a conversation she knew might take a while.

Long said, Those battlefields had their own rules and standards. They didn't look like anywhere else on earth except maybe a volcano caldera. Everything blasted and the earth churned up. I wasn't there looking for rank.

—For what, then? I said.

—For kills. Snipers—the good ones anyway—didn't need to keep score. Others did it for them. Getting into the war late as we did, none of us Americans were ever going to come close to Pegahmagabow's record. He was from Canada, an Indian, and for some reason he believed he couldn't be killed, so he took all kinds of chances. I worked more remotely, cloaked and hidden, up a tree half a mile away. But people said Pegahmagabow liked working up close. He would go into no-man's-land late in the night and wander like a ghost in German trenches and take little personal items from sleeping soldiers. Their eyeglasses, a book, a pistol. Or he'd just rearrange their lapels or take their caps off to show he could do it. He volunteered for the riskiest missions. The officers let him be sort of a free agent. He went out sniping alone on long hunting trips, and observers with binoculars would see German officers jerk back dead before they hit the ground and then hear a faint crack, a shot coming from blown-up ground and blasted trees where no troops were positioned.

—And what was his number?

—Short of four hundred, officially. Just confirmed kills, so add at least ten to twenty percent, since some would have died later. And, again, don't get humanitarian. The other side were doing the same thing, and they had the advantage of German glass in their scopes.

I'd drunk enough of Long's expensive wine to say, If kills was how y'all kept score, what was your number?

After a silence, Long said, I'll ask a more serious question. Do some people, based on nothing but their behavior, need to go, cease to exist, right this second? Is it better on the larger scale for some few to be canceled out, whether it's to endless oblivion, the land of the dead, or to the next incarnation? Easy case in point, early evening of April 14, 1865. If you could pull the trigger on John Wilkes Booth, would you? It would likely change the history of our country, but no repercussions, no one would ever know? Take him off the board?

—Truth?

—Of course.

—I'm not sure. We don't know how any minute of history will play out. I don't want to be the one making those kinds of decisions.

—That's an easy answer, and if I didn't like you, I'd call it a cheap answer. We never know anything past right this second. But what if you were there and you couldn't dodge? You have an instant to choose. Would you feel guilty for the rest of your life because you did it? Or because you didn't do it? Another human being, you pull a trigger and he's dead on his feet. Hardly felt a thing. Messy for a second, but all the violent, evil shit in his mind goes blowing out of his head like the bulb burning out on a movie projector. And factor this in, it's not just that Booth gets turned off, it's also that Lincoln stays lit and his force in the country continues. So turning off one light is like turning on another. And maybe the world's better for it. Not just for you but for some larger sense of existence on earth. Turn off mad Sherman when he was beginning his plans to kill off all the buffalo in order to kill off the Plains Indians. What result? Maybe everything—the earth, humanity, the sky and trees, the damn weather, and a pine tree and the squirrel up in the tree eating a pine nut—all better off because this one person got turned off. To put it in current terms, does the good of the one outweigh the good of the many? I need you to answer that question, but not tonight. We're both half drunk and tired. Tell me in a day or two. Or next month.

I already knew that in a day or two I'd still think that Long's question was faulty, an oversimplification at the very least. The good of the many being decided by one so often becomes a slippery slope. But I'd need a more complete argument than that.

I said, This is just a thought experiment.

—So is everything, Val. Deciding to drive into Dawes to paint a mural or to buy a box of fence nails, just a thought experiment.

At the same moment, Long and I both looked over to see that Eve had fallen asleep with her head resting on her crossed forearms and her tousled blond hair, darker at the roots, covering her face, all but a curvature of smooth cheek and a taper of lips.

—It appears we ought to call it a night, Long said.

EVEN ON A BRIGHT BLUE afternoon, sepia barn light fell from the high rafters and rose from the bedding in the stalls. I followed Eve down the long center aisle, pausing now and then for her to introduce me to famous horses.

—This is Painted Black. He won big cutting-horse prizes everywhere from Fort Worth to the National Western Stock Show in Denver and Frontier Days in Cheyenne. But that was all before I got here, and he's retired now. So we have that in common. These days, he earns his living making babies. He's a cranky old boy, so don't put loose fingers near his stall. Might lose a joint or two.

She walked over to the half door, and Painted Black stuck out his nose and she kissed it.

—Ferocious, I said.

—Not with me.

As we walked on down the aisle, she introduced Just Jack, Bucephalus, Mercury, and an older bay named Mopsy. Eve said, He'll safely pack around the rawest beginner. So you'll probably be riding him someday soon.

Farther along she said, If you've never been to a cutting competition, you can't hardly imagine what these horses can do working cattle. Once they lock in on the one they're cutting from the herd, it's like a combination of ballet dancing and sword fighting. The rider sits in the saddle and looks like all he's trying to do is stay out of the way. An innocent bystander. Sorry, Officer, I didn't see a thing. But like most skills, it's a lot more complicated than it appears. I'm still just learning how to watch and understand what I'm seeing.

At the end of the reception line, near the big barn doors, she stopped and said, This is Pálida.

A pale gray mare nudged against the stall door, making a

sound like a deep chuckle. Eve took an apple and a carrot out of her jacket pockets. She handed me the carrot and said, Do I need to tell you how to hold it?

I said, I didn't grow up in Manhattan.

Pálida took the carrot in three careful chomps and then turned to Eve and took more time with the apple. She butted her long face against Eve's shoulders and chest.

Eve smiled at the mare and pressed back against her. A game between them, it seemed. Dim light, quiet sounds of horses chewing hay and stomping flies all around us, I noticed dust smudged across Eve's cheek where she'd leaned against the mare's neck moments before. She and Pálida were both luminous—bright-eyed and delighted with each other. I couldn't look away.

Just then, Faro walked through the barn door from the round pen, leading a young horse, talking to it in a low voice. Maybe he was startled to see me there inside the barn, or maybe it took a couple of seconds for his eyes to adjust to the dim light after the blaring sun, but Faro locked his eyes on me with an expression so cold it struck me as reptilian. It came with a quick movement of head only—eyes fixed, a short jerk and slight tilt to the side—like a lizard having its attention caught by the movement of a bug, something edible. Nothing in his body reacted or moved or tensed. Only the shift of eye line a couple of degrees indicated interest. The look seemed inhuman until I realized that just because I might never have felt or thought whatever passed through Faro's mind and body in that flicker of time did not mean it wasn't human. Listen to the rumors and speculation in the pool hall and the bar and beside the cattle pens, and you'd think he'd killed dozens of men fairly casually back in the distant past. Maybe the chilly expression that moved across his face in a second was a relic of the old West. An artifact, like finding an arrowhead. An instant image I could save and try to paint someday.

Faro eased back and studied Eve and Pálida. Then he said to me, There's something about horses. They know every true feeling that passes through you, and you can't hide it from them. They don't ever fall for your lies. You can fool a dog, but you can't fool a horse.

He led the young horse away and Eve said, When he says that stuff, I pay attention.

We walked out into the sun, and Eve said, Have you ever watched him ride?

—No. Just watched him train young horses in the round pen.

—He sits more relaxed in the saddle and more fluid with the horse than any twenty-five-year-old cowboy on Long Shot, except that at a canter his head bobs more on its stem. One time I said, Faro, I hope when I'm your age I can ride half as good as you. And he said, I'll tell you what I tell all the cowboys when they say that shit. You can't ride half as good as me right now, so best of luck with your condescending ambitions.

She laughed, so I did too. Her admiration for Faro was surprising. I'd mostly seen him as strange and self-contained and quick to violence, but Eve's tone of reverence toward him interested me. We walked to the blue-door cabin, and I thanked her for the tour of the barn. She headed into the house and I sat on the porch awhile. I hadn't seen her seem so genuine before. No performing there in the barn. Just a girl and her horse.

DAY BY DAY, MY WORK on the mural progressed. I finished laying out the grid and penciled the design on the blank wall, an expansion of my miniature gridded sketch, based on the small color painting I'd submitted to the Section for approval.

To prepare me, Hutch had emphasized a teaching element as

integral to the job, explaining how to make a traditional mural and encouraging people to observe the work—see the process, smell the paint and watch me mix it, feel a connection to this image that aimed to express a fundamental truth about the place they occupied. In short, help people see that it was painstaking work with plenty of planning and preparation, not just inspiration and a genius flinging paint around in a frenzy, that there was craft too.

As Hutch had hoped, a lot of people stopping by for postal business or simply out of curiosity did ask questions. In those early days, mostly they asked, When are you going to get started? I explained the process over and over, the many steps necessary to make a mural in roughly the ancient way, which was how my boss liked them done, and that some days those steps felt like ten thousand plodding tiny increments.

Mostly, people wanted to know what the picture was going to be, meaning the subject. I never came up with a perfect answer. Sometimes I'd say, The energy of America. And leave it at that. Or I'd say, The natural and human history of this place. Landscape and all the people and animals that ever lived here. Their struggle to make a home. Indians and buffalo, the fur traders, pioneers and covered wagons, the arrival of ranchers and cowboys and the railroad and bankers and farmers. The passage of time will move left to right. And then I'd say, Up toward the ceiling, up in the right corner, the most recent part of the mural, will be a little bit of the night sky and the constellations stretching back beyond cavemen, back forever. Mighty Orion and Big Bear, the Seven Sisters. Or I'd say what I said to Don Ray the day I met him, The mural is going to express waves of history always swelling and cresting and breaking and rising again, and all the images will be slightly tilted forward, leaning into the future.

I was twenty-seven, so take that into consideration.

One man said, Well hell, boy, You could have boiled it down to cattle and railroads and been done with it.

Sometimes, if I was talking to someone who seemed really interested in the process, I contrasted what I was doing to Lucy's interpretation of the stonemason's wisdom, the pile of rocks and the incomplete wall like a puzzle where each immediate piece is always the solution to the problem at that moment. So you solve the larger problem rock by rock, piece by piece in every immediate moment. I said that if I relied on that kind of intuition, I'd have lost the battle before the start. Planning, not spontaneity, was at the heart of a mural. On the other hand, some people, for lack of anything else to say, but wanting to seem interested, asked questions like, Is that pencil a number two? Or, Does that paint ever wash out of your clothes?

Aside from the public-education aspects, Hutch had also emphasized other responsibilities of my job. Right before I left heading west, he had given me what he probably saw as a pep talk. He said, This isn't art school. We're well past whether I give you an A or a B anymore. I'm sticking my neck out giving you this chance. Screw it up and you'll lose this commission, and any possible further work for Treasury will be, at best, assisting real painters who understand what we're trying to accomplish. Go out there, do good work, and be careful. Never forget, the people of Dawes are your real patrons. Stick with the idea you've submitted and that has been approved and don't mess around being witty and clever in the corners. We've had problems with that. So nobody walking down the street carrying a copy of the *Daily Worker* or the *New Masses*. Or some bum in the background with Herbert Hoover's face. The Rockefellers tore down a mural by your idol Rivera for exactly this kind of cheeky shit. Don't start wanting to be this year's new young smart-ass. I know you'll be tempted, like so many young painters and writers and musicians, but somebody will see it and complain. You can't afford it and neither can we. The Section needs all the support we can get. This is not the Roaring Twenties—that world is gone and may never be back again. Essentially, don't screw up. Remember, hitting bottom right now is a lot farther down than it used to be.

And Hutch was right to remind me of the different, harder world we were living in after the giddy, limitless feeling of the previous decade. After the crash broke like a tidal wave, the country had been tossed along in a series of crests and troughs. We'd been near a hopeful crest for a few months the year before, but all the indicators showed us again sliding down the face of a massive wave toward another trough, like surf-riders in Hawaii. The horrible conditions in the dust bowl—over much of the country, but worse in Kansas, Oklahoma, southeast Colorado, Texas, eastern New Mexico—had followed the same patterns, those rolling repetitions. Things had been better for more than a year, but drought conditions had stopped improving and downward movement seemed inevitable. Soon we'd be seeing front-page apocalyptic photographs again—biblical dust storms, black blizzards towering into the sky and scouring the landscape. Heat waves threatening to burn out the center of the country. Seventy-five percent of the nation in drought. Not even two years ago, high temperatures had reached one-twenty, and not only in Texas. And overseas, the fascists and imperialists who'd snatched up political power were whetting their appetites for war. A couple of newspapers came to the ranch every morning and a stack of magazines every week, and some days the converging portents felt like the end of the world was approaching, like the next logical progression would be a plague erupting or an asteroid plunging straight for us.

LONG AND FARO HAD BEEN together for a while, a decade and more. They talked to each other in a clipped shorthand that involved the names they'd given sections of land within the ranch boundaries, the names of horses, of tools needed for a job, of illnesses cattle and horses are prone to. They strung together fragments of grammar using vocabulary like *thrush, headstall, singletree.*

A couple of weeks into the work, I walked by Long and Faro and caught the tail end of a conversation. Faro said, In that big section of fence, some of it always needs mending. You could tend to every foot of it, repairing and replacing, and by the time you come back around to your starting point, you'd think, I need to get back to that. And then you could keep right on going for another circle. You know, time and weather and forces of decay.

Faro walked away, and Long said, At first you think he's wise, but then you see that mostly he's working off a bigger calendar in his head.

—Longer? I said.

—No, I think he's looking at more pages at one time, Long said.

I asked, How big is this ranch anyway?

—Big how? Long said.

—Acres, I guess.

—Oh, by that measure I wouldn't know.

He waved his forefinger a few times north to south and said, We go about twenty miles this way.

He paused and waved east and west and said, A little less that way, approximately. But it's not a perfect rectangle. The property line follows Elk Creek for a lot of the north boundary, but that creek meanders. And of course down south, the land along Bison River that I sold doesn't count anymore. So figure plus or minus about ten percent. I think there's about six or seven hundred acres to a square mile. Look it up next time you're at the library.

He walked off toward the house, and I climbed the steps and sat on the porch of the blue-door cabin to read, like I did most afternoons. There were a few recently delivered issues of *New Republic* that I'd wanted to get to, including one with dispatches from Hemingway covering the war in Spain. I flipped the thick pages, reading about hopeful newly formed unions of steel and aluminum and auto workers, but also about the horrific bombing of Guernica and Franco's fabricated propaganda about it, using tactics borrowed from his pals Hitler and Mussolini. Soon I had to stop reading, lift my eyes from the page, and focus on landscape instead.

It had been a week of cool blue skies, dry thin air magnifying the mountains, so different from home in Norfolk. There hadn't been a solid rainy day since I'd arrived, though on rare occasions turbulent swirling piles of steel gray and charcoal clouds built and a thunderstorm would rage for half an hour and then be gone, leaving the blank blue sky again.

Before long, not quite sunset, Faro came by my porch carrying four clinking beer bottles by their necks. He asked to come up, as if the guest cabin operated by nautical rules—permission to come aboard. I gestured toward the other chair and said, I thought you had fences to mend.

He said, Tomorrow, and came up the three steps and popped the caps with the round end of a church key and reached me out a Coors. We sat and sipped in silence. Finally he said, How's your picture coming?

—Slow. But if you're in town in a week or so, swing by and take a look.

—I'm guessing people have been telling you stories about me.

He looked straight at me, clear gray eyes not giving away anything, mouth clamped shut leaving no expression there, only a wall of white whiskers.

I said, People come in for postal business and to see what I'm doing, how I'm spending their tax dollars. They like to tell me what they think is interesting about Dawes and what ought to be in the mural. Your name comes up.

Faro said, What? A historic figure?

—A survivor of the Wild West. A remnant of the past. One of the last of the . . .

Faro broke in and said, I'm not the last of anything. Plenty of people older'n me still roam around above ground. Aim yourself toward one of those elders. I knew a fellow over in Nebraska, an old Sioux warrior named He Dog. Died not long ago. About a hundred. Rode with Crazy Horse. Fought at Little Bighorn. You ought to have painted him. He had a face looked like the side of a canyon.

I said, Well, if all the stories they tell about you were true, you'd have to be about ninety yourself.

—Some days I feel it. Some days I feel twenty.

—They say you did all kinds of things. That you were a gun-fighter.

—Good God. Being in a couple of gunfights doesn't make anybody a gunfighter.

—They say you were down in New Mexico during the Lincoln County War and that you and Billy the Kid were friends. That you helped him and Pat Garrett set up the con where he wasn't killed but went to Mexico.

Faro looked off and thought. Real flat he said, OK, you got me on that one.

I was startled and showed it. I said, What? You knew Billy?

Faro said, So we've established you'll believe anything?

I said, Ha-ha. They also say you were the young infantryman

who killed Crazy Horse with a bayonet. Said you were about six-teen.

With no pause to calculate, Faro said, Yes, I admit there was a time when I was sixteen, so the story must be true. I ought to write a book—*I Stabbed Crazy Horse.* Make me a fortune. Then for a se-quel I'll write about how I helped Billy the Kid fake his death and escape to Mexico. I was a busy boy.

He opened the second pair of sweating brown bottles and said, Some of those gunfighters down in New Mexico in that mess peo-ple call the Lincoln County War were straight-out killers. If they weren't getting paid for it, you'd call them crazy. You wouldn't want to exchange three words with them. Their eyes weren't right. But Billy Bonney was different, partly because he had a sense of humor. They call him the Kid, but a lot of us were a couple of years younger than he was. Nobody expected to make it much past twenty. We were drunk most of the time and not ever for a minute in a mood to be shoved around by old people, meaning anybody past thirty. We'd light up violent at the least feeling of offense. There wasn't much law there. The law was whoever had the most guns, same as it always was throughout history. Difference was, a lot of the time we kids had the most guns, which is a heady feeling when you're seventeen and two-thirds drunk. I wish I could say I helped him get to real Mexico.

He looked off toward the darkening mountains all wistful.

I decided not to risk being gullible twice in a row. I said, Any-way, the subjects of this mural were decided and approved a cou-ple of months ago. But when I'm done with the mural, I'd like to paint you.

—What color? Gray or brown?

We sat and finished our beers, and Faro got up to leave. But he stopped at the foot of the steps and said, Firstly I'm not sitting and letting you paint my picture under any circumstances other than I'm dead and you prop me up with a forked stick to keep my head from flopping to the side, the way so many famous outlaws got their pictures made. Shoot a man dead and wait a day or two in summer heat and then take his picture and he presents an expression worse than daybreak of a Sunday morning in Deadwood a year before statehood. Stunned drunk. Crazy Horse got in and out of life without getting photographed, and that seems like some kind of victory. Granted, it was a short life, but still. Secondly—and you need to listen up—I don't go to the post office much. But if I walk in a year or two from now and study your picture and find a gunfighter that looks like me, or even an everyday cowboy looking like me, then we've got a big problem. And these days, the last way I want to spend a couple of months is tracking you to New Jersey or whatever shithole you live in to settle up. I don't like going east, but I've done it before and I'll do it again if I'm forced to.

I said, You've been east?

—What? You think all I know is sagebrush and pronghorn? Desert buttes and little pueblo villages down toward Mexico? I've been all over. Seen both Atlantic and Pacific. I've known San Francisco in many different versions, including before 1906, when the earthquake and fire made crazy people think God wanted to wipe it away. Been to New Orleans and down around the top half of Florida once. It's a big continent, but seems like there was more time back then. You wanted to take six months to go to New Orleans, well, that seemed reasonable. I've been a lot of things, not just a private in a frontier army or a cowboy. Name a city. First one that falls out of your mouth.

—Washington, DC.

—Been there. Smelled rank in the summer, but the buildings were handsome and had space between them.

—New York.

—There too. Don't remember much. There was a bar that served oysters, and I liked them so much I ate a couple of dozen over the course of the night and then was sick the next morning. But the night was worth it. And don't picture me wandering around in dungarees and beat-up packer boots, at least not after the first time I went to a big city. Easier to be anonymous if you wear their clothes.

THAT NIGHT I COULDN'T SLEEP. I didn't look at the clock. Never do. I don't want the alarm to ring in the morning and I come crawling out of bed knowing I was awake for a specific number of hours and then feel foggy and sleep-short all day. I'd rather wake up thinking maybe I hovered in and out a little bit overnight and then move on with the work. However long I lay awake hovering during the middle of this particular night, at some point, through the three-inch space in the one raised window, I heard sounds outside. A single horse at a canter in the soft footing of the round pen. Quiet voices.

Without turning on a light, I eased out onto the porch. Under a full moon, a crisp geometry in the cloudless sky, I could see Pálida circling in the round pen, a ghostly shape like pale moonlit water or a spirit stream of ectoplasm flowing wavelike in the material world. The voices, I realized, were Eve and Faro.

I moved a little closer, to the porch rail, and saw that Eve was having a riding lesson. Faro sat on a fence rail, murmuring suggestions. I could only be sure of half the words, and I couldn't tell the difference between when Faro talked to Pálida and when he talked to Eve. I'd never heard him use that voice with humans. When Eve spoke back, it sounded like listening in on a confession, a tone of great calmness and respect.

Pálida came to a slow stop, a stutter of muffled hoofbeats like a jazz drummer at the end of an improvisation on a well-known ballad, trailing off to silence having run out of ideas. Faro kept saying words like *better* and *good*. Then I heard him say, You're learning to listen to Pálida.

Their voices had the tone of a tryst, a secret meeting. I realized it would be awkward and bad in several ways to be caught listening in on this three-way private conversation among Faro, Pálida, and Eve. I backed through the door and closed it carefully, wondering not so much what they were saying to each other, but why they were there in the middle of the night. Back in bed, I did look at the clock. 2:35. And of course I hardly slept until the alarm rang at six thirty.

∿

THE WAY I'D BEEN TAUGHT WAS, START WITH SKY.
So there I was, scaffold boards as high up the ladders as they
would go, everything ready for color, for breaking some eggs. After
two weeks, my schedule—my calendar, my *giornata*—finally read,
Ten-thousand-foot blue.

If whites get mixed with yolks, you've got a problem. So you
take great care to keep yolks whole, move them hand to hand letting the slimy whites drain, then dry them off with cloths. Then
pierce the yellow yolk and let the liquid run into a bowl or cup.
Finally you mix dry pigments with runny yolk and make color.
It took a while to get that hard, high-altitude blue right, but by
lunchtime I thought I had it. So I started at the top left corner of
the wall. Below, chalky gesso and penciled mountains and plains
and ghosts of animals and human figures.

I was up there, reaching high into the sky, all the way to the
angle between wall and ceiling. The girl was small and thin and
solemn, maybe five. Wore a blue-and-cream plaid shirt and a pair
of new indigo Levi's with the pale inside of the fabric rolled up
four inches above her ankles so they might last a couple of years of

growth. She looked up at the mural from right at the base of the ladders, and then she started backing away in six-foot increments. She backed and stopped and looked and tilted her head left and right and backed again until she reached the far wall. She stood there a minute and then ran forward and climbed quick as a squirrel up onto the scaffold. When she got there and found herself standing on the boards with me—the wall suddenly only inches away and huge and the floor farther down than she had expected— she seemed unsure why she'd made the climb.

I said, My name's Val. What's yours?

She said, Anna.

She studied pencil lines at the top of a mountain, the pinnacle, and traced the angle with her finger without touching.

—I'm glad you came up to visit, I said. Want to help paint some sky?

I circled my finger on the area of wall where I'd started and touched a brush into the tempera and made a smooth, sweeping motion and handed it to her. She didn't swab it on. She touched the surface lightly, pecking with the tips of the bristles to see what mark the brush would make. Then she looked at me.

I made small sweeps with two fingers and said, Very light and easy.

She painted a space the size of a saucer. When she was done, I climbed down first and was going to hover arm's length away as she followed me down the ladder, but her father stepped up and said, Let her do it. Got to learn how to take a fall in life.

Which struck me, a childless man with the first number in his age still two, as a better position on child-rearing if you meant it metaphorically and if the floor wasn't rock-hard hexagonal tile laid over a slab of concrete.

Anna came down more slowly than she went up, and when she

had both feet on the ground, her father said, This painter fellow was watching you climb down and got to worrying.

Anna turned to me and said, You didn't have to look.

I walked Anna back about thirty feet from the mural and said, Part of that sky is yours. Can you remember where it is?

The girl pointed left, exactly to the spot.

—Where that mountain is going to be, she said. You go to the top, and then keep straight up almost to the ceiling.

—Exactly. Look at it every time you come in here, OK? So you won't ever forget, no matter how long from now. Promise?

She reached her hand out, and we shook on the deal.

Of course I wrote Hutch a long description of that moment, expecting effusive praise for my realization of his vision that a mural, this particular public mural, would create ripples spreading forward in the pond of time. What I got back was a color linen postcard of the Washington Monument with a terse message scrawled big—
See What I Said?

DAYS AND DAYS PASSED WITH the same pattern—beautiful late May weather, warm days and chilly nights, snow still halfway down the highest mountain peaks, days spent painting and talking to people. Then, more often than not, dinner with Long and Eve.

One night the Depression rose up dark as Nosferatu from his coffin. Long talked about how in the early days, the first couple of years after the crash, everybody thought it would be over soon, but then it kept hanging on and on.

He said, It's been tough on everybody. No one has gone unscathed.

—Really? Eve said. Everybody including you?

—Of course. That first couple of years, cattle prices hit bottom.

And then in '33, when Roosevelt outlawed owning gold, well that was hard to take. A good idea in general for the country, but I decided to hold on to mine. I know, that's like a hillbilly burying money in the backyard in a lard can. But walking into a bank and swapping a box of gold for a stack of paper was a hard sell. A no go. So it's still hidden, and I don't know what to do with it. I've thought about hiring a trustworthy person to take it to Mexico where it's legal and bank it for me. Faro will do it. He proposed crossing a wilderness stretch of border in Texas with three horses. One to ride, one to pack the gold, and a spare. Rotate them so they get to rest. Go down, deposit the gold in the bank, sell the horses, buy a first-class train ticket to El Paso. But he wants a fifty percent commission, no negotiation. He won't even discuss it with me. I'm thinking ten percent would be totally fair and generous. Hell, twenty percent if that's what it takes, and that would be philanthropic. But Faro says fifty or forget it.

Eve said, John, you know why you're so mad about some gold you can't do anything with right now? It's purely that you aren't getting interest on it. And so in terms of being scathed, what you have is a bad year for beef prices and lost interest on a spare box of gold. So on a scale of one to ten, with one being least scathed, what's your number.

Long said, I'd say a five.

Eve laughed and said, Wrong, totally wrong. If Faro was here, he'd say straight out he's a zero, and he's probably right. Nothing bothers him much. And you're close to the same. So let's give you a two. Really, a one, but call it a philanthropic two.

She looked at me and said, Your turn, Val.

—If Long's a two and Faro's zero, then I'm maybe the five.

—Way too easy, Eve said.

—Then I'll elaborate. My father was a ten, but he was easily scathed, so maybe the scale doesn't completely apply. He was a law-yer in Norfolk, not a rich New York or Washington lawyer, but a comfortable Norfolk lawyer. He spent the latter twenties buy-ing up land along the bay he thought could become valuable if his tea-leaf reading of county documents involving extensions of wa-ter and sewer lines foretold what he hoped it did—an explosion of growth in one particular direction rather than another so that a big chunk of worthless land could suddenly become a fortune in bayside building lots because a few pipes got laid. He realized that in a world one step beyond wells and outhouses, how you get your water and how you say so long forever to your waste is an issue of great financial importance. So back in the boom times, he'd bought a number of parcels adding up to nearly a thousand scrub acres of sand and dune grass and pine trees, all financed to the throat.

You could argue that the original sin that took him down was that speculation based on hope and an educated guess. By the time he sailed away, investors in stocks had already shot the tops of their heads out or taken an endless dive from a high window onto pave-ment. Real estate losses came later, of course, but I still count my father among the jumpers. He took the little dinghy that my cous-ins and I used when we were kids and sailed out into the Chesa-peake past Point Pleasant, and when he got halfway between Cape Charles and Cape Henry, he roped one ankle to a concrete block and took his own softer dive. A little clean splash. So after a pro-cess too boring to talk about, my distribution, the final remnant of his failure, was a single acre of waterfront sand that my father had specified was to go to me. The only reason my brother or the bank hadn't taken it along with everything else is because it isn't worth the bother. I think if I ever have kids I'll write my will to follow Oedipus's example and tell them to divide their inheritance by the sword.

Leaving me nothing would have felt more satisfying than that acre. I spent way too much time trying to decipher the message he intended to send from beyond the grave. Maybe it was no more complex than a bitter laugh or slap in the face or raised middle finger.

On the trip out here, I brought the deed to my acre with me. I don't know why I need to keep it close at hand. That acre is useless except to build a two-room beach shack, which I already did. Some of my friends call it the Tiltin' Hilton. When I go out there for a few days, I have to bring in five-gallon cans of water and use an outhouse no different from what most of rural America uses. When I get back, I'll probably spend my days setting traps for blue crab, surf-fishing for greasy-tasting spot and hoping to catch a flounder now and then. Sit on top of a dune in a folding chair with an easel and paint sappy watercolor sunrises and sunsets and sell them in Virginia Beach gift shops.

Eve thought a moment before saying, OK, I'm going to have to subtract two points since you've got a vacation house, but because of your dad, I'll add one back and judge you a four.

—Generous, I said.

Just then Julia bustled into the dining room and said, Last call and then I'm going to bed, folks.

She took our dirty dinner plates and silverware but left all the wineglasses and bottles, both empty and full.

Eve said, Thanks, Julia. See you tomorrow.

Once Julia had disappeared back into the kitchen, Long said, Val, your family situation sounds a lot like mine. I inherited this ranch by losing something, at least by my crooked family's measure. To beat my father and brother and sister, I had to make them think they'd won. They kept score by dollars as valued by people like themselves, and by their terms, they did win. But for them winning wasn't nearly enough. They had to see me as losing. I couldn't ever let on that the thing they wanted least was what I wanted most. This ranch. They'd have seen that as weakness. Like how they saw apologizing when you were wrong as a weakness. Strength was bullying the person in the right into apologizing to you.

He said, Getting disconnected from that bunch of cannibals was the best thing I ever did. Those first few months after the crash, my family wanted to keep thinking I had been an idiot to settle my inheritance for this land, but now some of them have little left but paper, and I still have this piece of the planet. Plus what I got from selling that Bison River piece, which I made sure they heard about.

I said, Yeah, we're exactly alike except I got one sorry acre and you have too many thousands to bother counting.

Long laughed and shrugged and sipped his wine.

Eve said, My turn, boys. Nobody I knew back home in Tennessee shot out the top their heads or jumped off a tall building or hung themselves in the garage. Nobody had an inheritance to lose or owned stocks or even really knew how the stock market worked. What we did was keep on going. But every day it seemed like we lived in a smaller box. And then at some point you could see it in all the grown-ups' faces, they knew it wasn't a box. We had all been dumped in the top of a big funnel and were getting pulled real slow down toward that hole at the bottom, and nobody knew where it emptied. My older brother took off when he turned seventeen. A year later, I took off too. Our parents had made it real clear—if you can't find a job here and you're taking food from the little kids, you need to go and look for work somewhere else. Some people, married people, are so broke they've had to go hand over a new baby to an orphanage because they didn't have money to feed it. That's not just a story or a rumor, I've seen it. So I guess my parents sacrificed us older kids to protect the little kids. One of the many possible consequences of having babies, especially for folks who aren't ready or can't afford them.

Those of us who'd been tossed out on our own kept on going however we could, even though the world kept falling to pieces every day. Pick up yesterday's paper thrown on the street and look at the front page, and it punished you, especially the bleak photographs of dirt farmers and fired factory workers and their families staring blank into the distance. Shamed people standing in breadlines. They're looking into their future and seeing nothing out there but dread. Read the stories with lots of numbers, and those punished you too and stole whatever belief you still had in the declarations that formed the country. A number like this: three hundred thousand to a million kids, some as young as ten, living out on the road on their own. That's burned in my mind because when I read it I was one of those teenagers riding freights, crisscrossing the country, following the seasons picking fruit for pennies a day, looking for food and shelter. Many girls among them, prey to all manner of danger. But a boy wasn't safe either. Predators everywhere on the roads and on the rails. The kids call them wolves, and there are all kinds of wolves, some with badges.

Some counties meet the trains at the rail yard and throw everybody in jail for a night or two, and they get a mattress and food and a shower and then get escorted by a deputy—with the warning not to come back too soon—to the rail yard to catch another freight. Other counties, they'd meet the freights with shotguns and billy clubs. Step a foot off the boxcar and you get beat down and thrown back on the car no matter how much they hurt you, whether you're nineteen or twelve. In the good jails, you get stewed prunes with your oatmeal. But just one night in jail, even a good one, and the smell hangs on for days. One summer I kept my hair cut short like a man's, mostly for the smell. Then there's the shelters. Some of them, preachers come yell at you for hours about how you're soaked in sin. My opinion? The main thing preachers want is to rule the world. Always has been, from the pope on down.

Point is, out on the road, the world comes after you the same way the banks have done with our parents since '29—steal everything they can with a fountain pen. Which is why a lot of the tramp kids made heroes out of outlaws, especially the Barrow gang because Bonnie and Clyde were a doomed love story better than *Romeo and Juliet*, which those of us who had gotten at least halfway through high school knew about. But those outlaw heroes robbed with a Thompson gun, not a fountain pen, and mostly they robbed banks. If anybody had it coming, it was banks.

I lived that life more than two years. Hard as it became, the first six months was glorious, the blazing freedom of it. Winning two dollars shooting craps with dice stained amber from a thousand dirty hands. Sitting in the door of a boxcar watching scenery pass by. Seeing and feeling in your body how damn big this country is, how different its parts are, what a big curve of the globe it stretches across. Start in Savannah and wander a jagged path to San Francisco and it makes you dizzy when in your whole life you hadn't been more than thirty miles from a town of a few thousand people and only one particular set of plants and animals and weather and ways for people to make a living. Nothing seemed real. Going from Memphis to Denver was like having a vision. The land lay flat and the sky wasn't even the same, and then suddenly jagged mountains had snow even in June. And then from Denver to San Francisco, an entirely different vision unfolded.

She paused and Long refilled our glasses. Eve sat with her hands in her lap, staring blankly at the candles burning low. She looked like she had more to say, and neither Long nor I spoke.

Finally Eve said, Let me give you one day of the Depression

for me and then y'all figure what my number is. This was my second year out on the road, at this camp in Tennessee or Kentucky. Sometimes you'd find a good, safe hobo camp and stay awhile. Some of the best ones became semipermanent. Folks built shelters from rusty scrap tin and planks and old canvas thrown over ropes stretched between trees. You could count on them still being there your next time coming through. Little yellow campfires lighting the night, people cooking and sharing food they had scrounged during the day, making hobo stew. The best places were safe havens surrounded by trees and bushes, a quick walk to a rail yard where the bulls with the billy clubs mostly looked the other way.

The bad thing about those established camps, you got fifty feet into the woods and the smell would burn your nose, and you really needed to watch your step. This one big hobo camp I'm talking about, almost a village, sat on a flat ledge alongside a peaceful, slow river, but that river killed some people, maybe a lot of people. Happened one night when big storms upriver pushed heavy brown water downstream throughout the night. Before dawn water washed up and over the ledge, and all those shelters people had built broke apart as easy as they'd been slung up.

Everybody was asleep and a good many were drunk, and the water rose so fast. Some people, it was water flooding into their sleeping pallets that woke them up. Fires washed out and the moon was covered with clouds. People tried to scramble up the steep bank above the shelf. We grabbed onto tree limbs and brush, and in the pitch dark about all we knew was what gravity told us. Up was hard, and down was easy. Daylight came and we huddled desperate in the thin light where we'd found purchase. The river swept by heavy and brown and full of stuff, pieces of houses and dead animals. We looked for people we knew, but everybody was transient and the flood had scrambled them from their little groups. In that gray dawn nobody looked recognizable, their clothes soaked or stripped away, their faces muddy and their mouths open and dragging in air. Could have been fifty people camped along the river that night, could have been a hundred. I'd managed to climb the bank with a little satchel over my shoulder, so I had a couple of pieces of clothing and my shoes. Everybody ran around looking for their friends, calling their names. It became clear that a good many people were missing. Hard to reckon the number of people sucked away by the river and drowned. Three or fifty? Of course washed away didn't mean certain death. Maybe in a hundred yards you'd fetch up on a rock or grab an overhanging tree branch and save yourself. Anything was possible. You could also die and the heavy water spit you out in the middle of wilderness or pull you down and down to the river bottom for the catfish to eat. Either way your life came to nothing at all, not even numbered. Like it never happened.

Eve got steely toward the end. She said, As far as the regular world was concerned, what happened that night was invisible. No newspaper stories, nothing. The newspapers write about real people who get killed, important people, but that wasn't us. The people on that riverbank who were wiped away that night were nothing.

Long and I both sat quietly.

—Now you men factor all that in and tell me what my number should be, Eve said.

Long reached over and touched Eve's hand and said, A nightmare. I'm sorry.

—Yeah, she said.

Long said, That's where you lost your childhood husband, isn't it? The one you said was sweet?

Eve nodded and said, A lot of people lost somebody that night. A lot of searching downstream for days, but at some point you don't have a choice. You go on. Life's like a movie, one direction. Forward.

NIGHT AFTER NIGHT FOR NEARLY a week, I dreamed Eve's stories. A series of snapshots, film clips. A newsreel featuring teenage Eve in a mass of young people moving like a rain cloud all around the country, hungry and dirty and scared. And then the rain cloud became a flood sweeping away rickety tents and shacks. I'd wake with a jolt, the image of Eve clawing at a riverbank—eyes wide and blazing in the dark—lingering in my mind.

ᨠᨠ

A COUPLE OF WEEKS AFTER HIS FIRST VISIT, FARO
reappeared at the cabin porch with sunset beers. Evidently talking
about his old dead friend He Dog had stirred up memories.

He said, Last time I saw him this side of the veil between
worlds he was about ninety-five. I saw him out at Pine Ridge, not
so far from Fort Robinson, where Crazy Horse was killed, which
you tried to pin on me. I figure his place, when I get to the other
side, might be different from mine. I'm not talking heaven and hell.
But I can't count on seeing him over there.

Faro began describing He Dog like a witness to a crime helping make a police sketch. I had a pad in my lap, pencil and gum
eraser at hand, beer on the porch rail. I worked as he talked, and he
didn't object or suggest he might need to kill me.

Eventually, Faro scooted his chair over to watch me work and
to comment.

He said, No, his eyes were farther apart, lips thinner, more
wrinkles all over his face. No, not that way. Deeper wrinkles, not
all going the same way. Make him look less angry around his mouth
and eyes. Don't make him look angry at all except a little around
the eyes from way back in the past. Make him look bigger like his

head was the side of a mountain. Make his nose look like worn leather, and make his eyes look like he's squinting to see something you can't ever see no matter how long you look.

Faro kept revising my sketch until he finally gave his seal of approval, saying, Well shit, that's probably about as close as you're ever going to get.

The portrait was smeared, rubbed partially out, erased and re-drawn until it mostly gave the impression that He Dog was either fading away or emerging out of fog. Still, the face did look al-most massive as a mountain. Folds of skin across the forehead and around the mouth looked topographic.

I thought maybe someday, off in the future, I might make a painting based on this sketch, or at least my memory of it. I'd paint the face mostly the deep color and sheen of an old well-oiled saddle. The eyes looking with nonattachment toward a horizon be-yond your furthest comprehension. Behind He Dog, a faint wave-like suggestion of a plains landscape, almost monochromatic. Half the canvas would be sky in all its gradations of color.

Faro looked at the sketch and said, I wouldn't mind having that. What would you take for it?

—Not a thing.

I pulled the sketch out of the pad and handed it to him.

He looked at me straight on, evaluating. Then he said, Val, I don't know how you plan to make a living on art by giving it away. But I thank you.

He stepped off the porch, holding the paper at the corner be-tween thumb and forefinger.

ONE AFTERNOON I CAME HOME from work around four to find that Long had set Eve and me up for a riding date. He met me at the car.

—Hurry, he said. The horses are already tacked. Eve could use the exercise. Good for her mood. Dinner at eight.

I rode Mopsy, of course, the easiest horse in the barn.

After we mounted up Eve said, Just don't ask him to go faster than a slow, easy lope. It annoys him.

We followed a ragged two-track farm road westward. Grass hills etched in curves against the sky, and then the Winds rising gray-blue with snow tops in the distance. A herd of brown cattle grazed on a hillside.

I said, My first couple of weeks here, I thought Long must not have a lot of cattle since I hardly saw any. Then I realized that he had more land than I could imagine.

—There's a whole other barn and bunkhouse way south, Eve said. Takes almost an hour in a pickup to drive there on the farm roads. Lots of cattle grazing free range between here and there.

We rode farther, and I waited for Eve to speak again. When she didn't, I finally said, Your singing career, I'm interested. Do you ever miss it?

—I do. Sometimes I miss it a lot.

—The performing aspect?

—Sure, partly. Get to the end of the show, we'd play something raging, fiddlers sawing so hard strings broke, and then we'd stop dead and the band leader would say, Good night, friends, see you next time around, and we'd start walking off. But the audience, the sweaty dancers, didn't want to stop. They'd clap and stomp the floor and shout for more until we did two more songs. For a while, life seemed like it went from one ovation to another. But it's more than the applause and the lights cutting through the air in smoky dance halls. I miss singing hoarse on early-morning radio shows knowing wheat farmers and cowboys were listening while they ate their breakfast in the dark. I even miss the long bus rides. I guess

I miss the life. It was the only time I've ever felt like, This is what I do. A couple of years. Since then, I don't know what I do except heat up John's politicians and businessmen, and that's no challenge at all.

We rode on a minute, and then I said, You're learning to ride. That must be a challenge.

—It helps. Sometimes when I ride Pálida it feels like going to church.

—Been meaning to ask why you and Faro do lessons in the middle of the night.

—You've seen that?

—One night when I couldn't sleep. It seemed mysterious.

—Started out, I just wanted to surprise John. One day out of nowhere, get on a horse and amaze him with my skills. But some nights in that dark ring, it feels like being in a cathedral, like a ceremony. At least how I imagine it, since I've never been in a cathedral. Faro can be kind of mystic, you know. Sometimes around the ranch he's scary, but never at night in the round pen. I can relax on Pálida, and he talks like everything's all right and always has been and always will be.

—A ceremony?

—As close as I've ever been to one.

—Weddings and funerals?

—Funerals, I've been to a few when I was a kid, quiet and quick. No weeping and wailing. But out on the road, when people die they just go away. Like a pal who probably died chopped up under boxcar wheels one night in western Nebraska. No funeral for him unless you count the buzzards carrying him away piece by piece, lifting him to Glory. And as for weddings, the only ones I've ever attended have been mine, and those have been fairly casual so far.

THAT NIGHT AT THE TABLE, a lull in the conversation, I said, Eve, I can't figure out the big jump from traveling hobo all over the country, ocean to ocean, to traveling around the West singing in a cowboy band. Got to be a story there in that stretch.

Eve said, I guess maybe. It didn't feel like a story. It felt like it was fall and I'd been all over the east half of the country since spring and was tired from nonstop fruit tramp work and from constant motion. I don't remember where I was going, but there was this town in Oklahoma, and I'd saved a little money from the picking season. I was walking through this neighborhood a couple of blocks off Main Street looking for a cheap boardinghouse, and a woman my age was hanging a line with diapers. She said hello as I walked by and then after I passed she called out for me to come back. Said she had some clothes, almost new, that would exactly fit me.

She said, They're too young for me now. At least my husband says they are. He says no matter how new they are, I'll never be new enough for them again since our son came along. He tried to make that a joke, but . . .

The woman went in and brought the clothes out, a good-sized tidy bundle, a brown paper rectangle tied with jute twine, a gift she'd been saving for somebody. She said, He wants me to give them to the ladies at the church, but I want somebody they'll look good on to wear them.

I thanked her for her bundle and decided this town must be pretty nice. I found a room, women only and a bathroom shared with one other person. In a few days I got clean and rested. With the very nice sweaters and blouses and wool skirts the new mother had given me, nobody would have taken me for a railroad bum. Within a week I had a job in a three-chair barbershop, sweeping up bales of hair and cleaning the sinks and wiping down the counter where all the shiny scissors and razors lived spread out on white hand towels. A couple of times a week, I washed and bleached those towels and the cotton capes that snugged at the customers' necks and draped over their clothes from the neck down. I scrubbed ten years of cigarette smoke off the inside of the big front window. The barber who hired me said, Don't worry much about the toilet. Nobody expects a barbershop toilet to be too clean.

I was making ten cents an hour plus a free haircut whenever I wanted one. I tried it once, said, Just trim an inch, and it turned out to be no better than when I'd grab it up at the back of my neck in my left fist and scissor it across with my right.

That job went on through the winter and spring. They paid once a week, and I lived carefully. I bought a couple of pieces of brand-new clothes all my own. Of twenty-one meals a week, I cooked eighteen on a hot plate. I went to the movies one night a week and a double feature on the weekend. Mostly the people in them were living like 1929 never happened. Everybody in fancy apartments big enough to play basketball in the living room and wearing tuxedos and shiny, slinky dresses and talking sort of like they're from England. And after that lovely dream, next morning I'm back in the barbershop, and still glad to have the job. But one morning I go to work and there are three strangers in the chairs waiting for haircuts, and only one barber there that day. While they waited, the strangers talked about traveling around playing music. They'd done a long string of shows through Texas and Louisiana, and after Oklahoma they were heading through Kansas and across to Colorado. And then they said one of their girl singers, the better of two, had run off unexpectedly. Met a man and got married in three days. Hard to find replacements when you're on the road in the middle of a tour playing five or six shows a week not counting the live early-morning radio sets along the way.

I listened awhile, and by the time the first one was laid back in a barber chair with the paper band tight around his neck and his face lathered up and the barber stropping the razor, I said, If y'all need a girl singer, I can sing.

The one in the chair lifted his head and looked me over and said, Hmm.

One of the ones in the waiting chairs said, You're good-looking enough to make a girl singer, and you'd probably fit the costume. Let's hear you.

So I sang the first thing that came to mind, a minute of Anything Goes. And then, only because I'd seen *Flying Down to Rio* recently, I tried some of Music Makes Me, singing it as close to the cocky way Ginger Rogers did as I could manage.

When I was done, the one in the chair with the lathered face worked his hands out from under the cape and applauded. The barber said, If y'all are going to steal my employee, I expect free tickets next time you come to town.

A day later, I was on the bus with the band, rolling down the road toward the next show. The last girl's stage outfits fit exactly except I needed to lower the hem of the skirts a couple of inches. It took a week to get the smell of her armpits out of the cowgirl clothes, but even having to do laundry didn't damage the shine of riding on the bus, walking onto the stage into the spotlights. We played at least five nights a week, so to stand in the light that much created a feeling like I was growing, every moment like a tomato seedling in the sun.

And the other part of growing was riding all night in the dark on two-lane blacktop and chip seal to get to the next town and do it all again. Sometimes we rolled out right after the show and rode for hours and checked into a hotel at three or four in the morning. If we had an early-morning radio program scheduled, only a handful of us had to show up. That always included a singer, though, and I was always ready to volunteer. I remember a morning when four or five of us doing a before-dawn radio show got dressed up for it, being silly and ironic. The guys couldn't find their ties, so they fashioned them out of toilet paper. I plastered on powder and lipstick, and we giggled all the way through our performance, and I guess we sounded like what we were—still half drunk from the night before. I mean, those days did feel a little like magic.

Long said, First time I saw Eve she was singing.

—I've been wondering how you two met, I said.

Long said, It was in Casper. I was in town for business, a meeting—cattlemen or, more likely, oil and gas—and some of them talked me into going with them to the show. Of course all the guys in the room fell in love with her. I was standing way back from the stage to keep out of, you know, the crowd. But when she started singing, I eased forward along the left flank until I could see clearly. So, though every man there fell in love, I fell in love enough to give the bandleader a twenty to meet her. That was all. Shake hands and say her voice was wonderful.

Eve said, That was Ronnie. So he catches me on the way out to the bus and says, There's a guy wants to meet you real bad. And I said, Stop the presses. And Ronnie said, I know, happens every night and I don't bother to tell you. But this guy might be different. The manager of the hall says he's loaded. And, surprise, he's not even real old.

Eve smiled at Long when she said it, and Long said, What he said to me was simple, that you always told him it would take something big, somebody special, for you to get serious. The exact way he put it was that you weren't looking for a man, and it would take Prince Charming and King Arthur rolled into one to get your attention.

—I don't remember saying that last part, but, anyway, Ronnie convinced me to talk to you. He said, Trust me, Eve, this guy might be that big thing. And what does it hurt to say hello?

Long said, Obviously, the story goes on from there.

Eve said, Yeah, but we tell it different when we're in Cheyenne, don't we?

ALONG ABOUT DESSERT LONG SHIFTED our conversation to art. Most nights he tried to engage Eve on the subject and clearly wanted me to help. She wasn't exactly resistant, but she tended to drift off when Long talked about technique.

He mentioned Renoir, and I'd had enough wine to be impolite and say, Renoir is not my kind of art. Prissy art. My models are Rivera and Benton. Not vaporous bits of landscape or weather or some woman swinging in a swing wearing a gauzy dress. Rivera's paintings, and Benton's, are about something solid. The struggle and strength of the underclass, the power and bulk of their muscles on the wall representing the power of their spirit, of their souls, to endure and survive.

Long said, So you need art to be *about* something? An image expressing a thesis? Equivalent to writing an opinion piece for the newspaper?

—Not exactly.

Eve perked up and said, What I always wonder about the little Renoir and the Matisse in the lobby is, who were the women? What was their relationship with the men painting them?

Long suggested those were not valid questions, but Eve required a better answer than that.

—There's a story in all those pictures, she said. The cowboy pictures are easy, not worth wondering about. Men and horses, an Indian now and then. But that red picture with the woman in the room, the Matisse? Outside the big window, looks like sunshine, a palm tree, a white sand beach and blue water, all bright and sunny. But she's inside wearing a floppy old robe, looking dazed or depressed. Maybe drunk or hungover. She could be facing out at the view or looking at the vase of flowers, but instead she's blank, looking at nothing. Black eyes. So tired she has to prop her head on her hand. I like beaches. When I've been at one, I like to look at the water, but she's broken up, not looking at anything. She's not even lying down on that lounge chair. She's sitting half up. Might as well be saying, What do I have to do to get out of this shit? So my question is, did the painter do something to put that woman in that mood, that situation? Probably. Or did she do something to him she regrets and doesn't know how to fix? And doesn't know if she wants to fix? The main thing is, why did some man want to paint that particular messed-up minute and freeze it forever?

I waited for Long to answer, but he sat still. I did too.

Eve said, And that precious tiny Renoir, the young woman, let's call her a girl to keep it simple, standing in the flower garden. That one's simpler in a way, but harder in another. Every inch of it is so pleasing to the eye. Too easy to see nothing but the pretty and move on. She's in some kind of situation, but I haven't figured it out yet. Could be the painter keeps putting her on display and she's tired of having to be the center of attention every minute by being good-looking. Do things she doesn't want to do, like stand there in the weeds getting bug-bit and being painted. Maybe she's a great actress or maybe she's not, but nobody cares, especially the guy painting the picture. She's a pretty girl in a field of flowers. That's all anybody needs to know, and that's all she needs to be, so shut up. That's what I see when I look at that one. Pretty stacked on top of pretty. I keep thinking there must be more to it, so I keep looking at it and keep trying to figure it out. Except maybe there's nothing else to figure out.

Long tried to dismiss her interpretation of the two paintings, but it seemed personal to her, like she needed him to hear it. And to me it felt like she might be on to something.

Long, though, fell back on an easy argument. He said, I would argue that the painting is more about structure, color, and form.

—If that's all you've got, then paint a few black squares and yellow triangles and call it a day, Eve said.

Long said, All right, I'll fold on that line of reasoning. But consider that *pretty* may have been Renoir's goal, possibly the core of his aesthetic. Did you read that article about the current exhibition at the Metropolitan Museum of Art? It was in this month's *Vogue*? It mentions that prices on Renoir's major paintings are amazingly high right now.

—John, we get stacks of magazines every month. I can't read every article. Some of them, I just flip through looking at the pictures.

Long said, Of course my Renoir is not at all a major work. It's a little something he painted on a napkin to give away. He did quite a few of those. Gifts for friends and girlfriends.

Eve said, Enough about paintings.

She stood and appraised the table and then said, We've made such a mess tonight. Why don't we surprise Julia and clean up? Do the dishes and everything.

Long said, What, as a sort of joke?

—No, Eve said. A courtesy.

Long shook his head and wandered off upstairs.

Eve and I carried plates and serving dishes and stemware and empty bottles. At the sink, I washed and Eve dried.

—Don't know if I'll ever get used to having a live-in cook and housekeepers that come three times a week, she said. Some nights, when it's only the two of us and we're up past Julia's bedtime, I sneak back down once John's asleep and wash dishes. He laughs when I make the bed. Seems like the least I can do. He says I'm trying to steal their jobs, but it still doesn't feel right, being waited on all the time.

PROBLEM WITH THOSE LATE-NIGHT DINNERS was, next day, Eve and Long could sleep until late morning and drink coffee until noon, but I needed to get up about dawn and get ready to paint. Driving into town with the rising sun soft and yellow and the sky blue with bands of clouds impossibly purple and peach and apricot above the rolling hills to the east, all I could think was that skies are so hard to paint because if you paint them real, they look fake. Sometimes a radio station from Lander or even all the way to Casper would have a live broadcast of the kind that Eve had talked about. In between farm reports and news—workers strikes in the Midwest, economy clinching tighter again, horrifying developments in Spain and Germany and Italy and Japan, quick snatches of Roosevelt declaring the country's deep desire not to be dragged into any new faraway wars but seeming more pessimistic by the day—there'd be a burst of wild music like Eve had talked about. A few members of a cowboy band, dazed from playing at a dance in Nebraska or Montana or Colorado until midnight and then driving two or three hundred miles to a small-town station with an early-morning program, sawing at their fiddles and banging at their guitars and singing all bleary, but it's making music, and they love that life better than any other.

EVERY DAY FOR A WEEK, sunlight had looked and felt thin and sharp. Tiny needles. It hurt. It didn't just strike the surface of your skin, it penetrated. The higher the elevation, the more I felt like I was being rendered transparent by X-rays or gamma rays or whatever. How to reproduce that kind of light on canvas?

That Sunday I drove west for hours into the Winds, looking at the landscape, trying to see it topographically, all the fine lines of elevation, the shapes of watersheds. How to paint that on canvas? I made quick black-and-white watercolors, wondering if it was possible to catch the scent of pine and fir, of needle beds a thousand years old, in nothing but gradients of black and white.

All that day of overwhelming vertical landscape, though, my mind kept circling back to Long and Eve, a feeling of something unsettled, something wrong, something hidden. I tried to separate my attraction to Eve from that feeling. Tried not to be yet another guy love-struck by the girl in the spotlight. Even Long hadn't been able to help becoming one of those guys. And he also couldn't help being the winner.

A MONTH OR SO INTO THE WORK, THE MURAL, square by square, had begun to come together. A sweep of time passing, cresting in the center with a trio of trackers—two Crow guides and John Colter. In planning I had wanted those three figures to give the mural its title and for that image to embody the hinge of time in this place, that moment not far past first contact between the Plains Indians and whites, the point where everything changed except landscape and weather. The buffalo in the background going from a vast herd on the left, a shadow on the land extending as far as you could see, and then dwindling as you moved right, to a few beaten-down stragglers, standing near a herd of brown and white cattle. I wanted all the figures to have mass, as much like Rivera and Benton as I could manage. I wanted all the living creatures to look comparable to the mountains and the vast plains and the big, empty, sprawling sky.

Standing with my back against the mailboxes, I felt like, finally, *The Trackers* was starting to look like a real mural. I was thinking of layering in more tones of blue to deepen the sky along the top edge of the mural when Eve and Long came in to empty their mailbox.

They seemed genuinely surprised with how much I'd done in the past week. Long particularly focused on the underlying forms and said I hadn't let the ideas get in the way of the painting, whatever that meant. Eve praised the richness of the colors, and before I could say it, Long told her how with tempera rich color comes from layer after layer of paint.

Long said, By the way, we have dinner guests tonight, three businessmen from Casper, members of a natural gas producers organization. I really want you and Eve to be there, and I'll apologize in advance for the inevitable boring conversation.

Eve said, That's an understatement.

—An artist and a singer in a cowboy band, Long said. You'll confuse the hell out them, that's for sure, which is a good thing.

Eve looked at me and said, So we're supposed to be the entertainment. And serve as an example of why John is not entirely like other politicians and businessmen.

—You and Eve can duck out right after dessert, Long said.

Eve said, Trust me, Val, we want to gobble and run. Follow my lead. Cattlemen are bad enough, but don't get me going about how deadly boring the natural gas passers are.

Long sort of laughed and said, Natural gas *producers*.

—And that's different how?

—Difference between production and distribution? It's the name of an organization or a federation or whatever. They want to keep the state and federal government from regulating their operations and profits in any way whatsoever, and they think I have some influence. They want what everybody wants, utter freedom, a total lack of restriction or responsibility. So tonight I've got to convince them I'm enough of a capitalist to temper my New Dealer tendencies.

THE DINNER LIVED UP TO Eve's prediction.

Before Long's guests arrived, Eve came downstairs wearing dark tan slacks cinched tight at the high waist, then wide in the legs with sharp creases down the front. White collared shirt with the sleeves rolled up to her elbows. Not her typical dinner attire.

Long said, Eve, you look as mannish as Katharine Hepburn. You look like you borrowed a pair of Val's trousers.

Eve and I looked at each other. Long wasn't too far off the mark, though the legs of my gray wool trousers turned up at the bottom in deep cuffs.

—Seems to be the style these days, I said.

Eve spread her arms wide and said, You wanted us to confuse the gas passers. Here we are.

I laughed, hoping Long would follow suit. He ignored me and looked at Eve without humor, then glanced at his watch and said, No time to do anything about it now.

The gas men—three almost identical beefy fifty-year-olds with hard, jutting bellies—did seem a little confused by how to make dinner conversation with an artist and a singer. I had expected to get a glimpse of the sparkly, shiny Cheyenne Eve, but she hardly spoke. Even the simplest questions, such as how she was liking Wyoming ranch life, got very terse answers—Like it fine. A time or two, I saw Long give her slight puzzled looks.

One of the men felt the need to unload the We Piddle About gag on me. As usual, I pretended a slight laugh, but Eve muttered an annoyed Great God.

I'd had two sips of coffee and two bites of Julia's excellent cobbler when Eve gave me a nod and we dashed. Very quickly I said, Nice to have met you. By then Eve was already out of the room. She walked fast through the house and out the back door. I followed her to the porch of the blue-door cabin, and she flopped down in a chair.

She said, Fuck, what am I doing? I don't belong here. This is supposed to be my home. I'm not going to be put on show here. That loudest one managed to brush his hand across my ass as we were taking our seats. Well, cupped would be more accurate. It was all I could do not to knock the living shit out of him. A punch, not a slap. Might have done it if I hadn't taken damn Nembutal to get through that dinner. I'm not a show horse or a fucking broodmare. I hate those bastards and the ones in Cheyenne, and I hate John too when he has his nose stuck up their asses. I thought he was better. I *know* he is better. I don't like what they do to him. And he wants that to be our lives. Cheyenne or Washington.

Eve swept her hand in front of her face and then past her shoulders and breasts and stomach and hips before flipping it off to the side like backhanding, dismissing, shooing away a persistent fly.

—I didn't ask for this, she said. It's no different from finding a gold nugget or dying in a car wreck. Chance, not an accomplishment. People get confused.

She paused and said, What do you have to drink in there?

—Nothing but water.

—Go in the kitchen and bring back something.

I found half a bottle of Irish whiskey and two glasses and brought them to the porch.

She poured three inches in each glass, and after a long pause she said, I can picture a life where, you get to the end, you've never even had a home. You've lived on the bus and in hotel rooms, traveling show to show, making music and standing in the smoky light until you died, whatever age that was. New towns, new places, nothing but the music is the same.

—Worse ways to go, I said.

I thought about my father, betrayed by the world he believed in so deeply.

Eve said, Faro talks about people who hurt horses. He says those people die of cancer. Natural justice. A rich man puts down a perfectly good horse for his own convenience because money has gone tight. That man is setting himself up to die. Faro says he's seen it over and over all his life. He knew a man back after the crash who hired somebody to come in and kill a barn full of very fine horses. Went stall to stall shooting those beautiful animals— and by the way, what kind of shit human would take on that job? That man, the one that owned the horses, got a tumor the size of a lemon inside his brain. Another time, a guy Faro knew found out he could include his horses in his ranch insurance and then figured out a way to electrocute them so that it might look like an accident. That was not long after the crash. That guy died a year ago from every kind of cancer there is, rotting head to toe. Very bad way to go. Faro says he could name a dozen more examples going back to the big depression in the 1870s. He doesn't have an explanation for it, and neither do I. I don't much believe justice exists except as a theory, but it makes me feel something—not happy, but maybe calm—when I hear that those kind of men, killing good horses, died in a hard way.

She waited and then said, Right this minute, I feel less like I have a home than I did five years ago in some hobo camp.

I tried to say a few stupid soothing things, none of which seemed to help.

Finally she said again, Not a show horse, not a broodmare.

She stood and came over and kissed me on the forehead like you'd do an old grandparent and said, Thank you, Val, for listening. If you bring this up in the morning, I'll swear I don't remember a thing. Then she kissed me not at all like a grandparent.

I wanted to take her hand, ask her to tell me what was really going on. What was wrong. Instead I said, You sure you're OK?

By then she was halfway down the steps. At the bottom she half turned and, without stopping, said, Fucking bulletproof, Val.

I sat on the porch late, watched the lights in the big house go dark room by room until the only yellow window was the big bedroom of Long and Eve's upstairs. They hadn't thought to close the heavy curtains, only the sheers. Sitting in the dark looking at the window like a peeper, I could see nothing really. Only shapes moving around and then the light shutting off.

TWO DAYS LATER, LONG MET me at the car as I was getting out. He wasn't urgent or alarmed, but the first thing he said was, Have you seen Eve? Was she in town?

—I didn't see her. Why?

—Her car's gone. She didn't say anything about going out. It's been since this morning.

—Except for about half an hour when I went down to the drugstore lunch counter, I was working. So if she wasn't checking the mail, I wouldn't have seen her.

Long walked back toward the front door, and I walked around toward the cabin. Faro stopped me at the porch.

—Have you seen Eve?

I said, Long asked me too. Are you worried?

Faro said, Not worried. But she usually says something if she's going to be gone awhile.

Along about sunset, Eve drove up. Top down on the convertible, red paint and windshield dusty. Lenses on her sunglasses dusty.

Apparently we'd all been listening for her. If the wind wasn't blowing, you could hear a car coming up the gravel drive at least a quarter mile away. John and Faro and I, not bunched up or coordinated but awkwardly spread around the front of the ranch house, met her.

She swiveled out of the car and stood in the driveway leaning her head side to side, lifting her shoulders, stretching her arms. She said, Went for a long, long drive. Back roads all the way into the Winds. Togwotee Pass. I ate at a diner on the way back, so don't plan supper for me. I'm going to wash off the road dust and go to bed.

A WEEK LATER, SHE WAS gone again. Took off in the morning and didn't come back. The convertible turned up at the edge of downtown. No goodbye, no kiss-my-ass note.

Long wanted me to call the Dawes bus station. He said, They might recognize my voice. Which struck me as an odd concern at the moment.

He said, Don't use her name. Just a description. Don't want gossip.

I said, She might be using another name, like maybe her maiden name.

—Miles is what she used when we got married. It was her show name and might have been her maiden name. She never used the other married name while I've known her. Her first husband's name was Jake something, but I think she may have told me two or three different surnames. Ar-something, O-something. Two syllables I think. Arnold? Owen?

Then he repeated, No names. Describe her kind of generally.

So I made the call, asking if anyone matching my vague

description of her had taken one of the four daily buses from Dawes to the outer world, meaning to Cheyenne and south to Denver or straight east toward Casper and on to Nebraska. If you wanted to zigzag your way westward, it was a damn long trip to anywhere, unless you considered Salt Lake City somewhere.

No, they hadn't seen anybody like that.

Long decided I should call every bus station within a hundred miles and also the railway station in Rawlins. No one I talked to had any recollection of a woman matching my description and no record of a ticket under the name Miles, but there wouldn't be if you paid cash just to go to Cheyenne.

Long sat quietly in his desk chair.

Eventually I said, That dinner with the gas guys, she was very upset afterward.

—She's hardly talked to me since then. But, really, that was already going on before. I've tried to ask what was bothering her, but she didn't want to talk.

BY THE THIRD DAY, LONG was fairly agitated. When I said it was time to report her as missing, he flared up and called the suggestion ridiculous. This was personal. She was mad about something, or sad about something. Something now or out of the past. Absolutely not a matter for the goddamn sheriff's department.

He said, She took the little Renoir with her. She knows what it might be worth. A little precious thing you could fold in a tea towel and stow in a handbag. With prices what they are right now for Renoirs, and sold to the right buyer, she might get out of it enough to buy a two-bedroom bungalow in San Francisco or Los Angeles. Who knows how much house it would buy in someplace like Omaha.

SOON, WITH NO EVIDENCE WHATSOEVER, Long became convinced
Eve had run off to join a cowboy band and live her old life. So two
days later, I drove into a town in western Nebraska called Black
Hawk or Red Wing. A color and something about a bird. Dawn
barely swelled at the eastern horizon as I left the grasslands and
entered the huddle of brick buildings. I stopped at a diner and ordered a cup of coffee and a Denver omelet.

The waitress said, What's that?

—An omelet with cheese and ham and mushrooms and onions
and green peppers.

—So a ham-and-cheese omelet?

—Sure.

—I wouldn't even try guessing how far you'd need to drive to
the nearest mushroom.

When the food came, the coffee was so grainy and bitter that I
asked for a glass of chocolate milk as a mixer.

I drove all the downtown streets in ten minutes and found a
ten-year-old bus parked around the corner from the third best of
the four hotels in town. They'd painted over the greyhound below
the windows and replaced it with the name of the band. *Billy and
His Buckaroos.*

In the lobby, nobody. I rang the bell at the desk and waited, and
then rang it again. A woman with bleached hair came from a back
room. She fluffed her hair on the side where it lay flat from a pillow.

—I'm looking for someone with the band.

—They won't be up and moving until nearly lunchtime.

—It would be a girl singer I'm trying to find.

—All you boys are looking for that. A good-looking girl singing in a band.

—No, it's a particular person. A friend. Her name's Eve, and
she has blond hair, about twenty-five.

—Real pretty?

—I think she is. And talented and very sharp and bright.

—So, kind of prickly?

—That's not what I meant.

The woman said, You're describing a lot of girl singers. But let me tell you, most of them aren't all that beautiful once they scrape the makeup off. Including the one sleeping upstairs. Besides, she has to be pushing forty.

So in Black Wing, I learned that Eve hadn't become a Buckaroo, and in other towns down the line, I confirmed that she hadn't joined Willy Green and His Greenies or the Plainsmen.

BACK AT THE RANCH, I learned that Faro, who'd been tracking south into Colorado, hadn't found anything either. He said, I found seven bands all down the Front Range from Fort Collins to Pueblo, three of them in Denver. A couple of those fellows remembered Eve from before, but nobody had seen her or heard anything about her being out looking for work.

Long said, Well, I found something. He handed me an innocuous linen-texture picture postcard labeled *Elliott Bay Looking Toward Bainbridge Island*. Postmark Seattle. On the back, the message was a couple of penciled lines, a cramped hand, most likely a man's. *Sorry. Of course I remember back in the days. Maybe I can help. Remember that place near the water? We stayed a week or two? Somebody there will know where to find me.* Unsigned. The postmark was less than a month old.

Long said, This would have come a couple of weeks ago, about when she started getting more distant by the day. What does she need help with in Seattle? What's the connection to back in the days? Her hobo husband, Jake? I think she might have said he was born in Seattle or they met in Seattle. There's some connection with Seattle.

I said, Didn't he die in that flood she talked about?

—Well, I've been thinking, she's never used the word *died* when she talks about him and that flood, always uses *lost*.

He paused and then said, Whatever she feels, whatever is bothering her, she isn't able to hide for long. She couldn't stop feeling things about who she was back then, the life she lived. More than once she said, It brands you.

THE NIGHT BEFORE I STARTED my trip to Seattle, Long slid a stack of bills across the dining table. He called it a retainer plus expenses. It was more money than I would be paid to paint the mural, more than double in fact.

He said, This is a job, not a favor. And don't fret about the mural. How much do you have left to finish it, as a percentage?

I said, Twenty at most.

—Close enough. I talked to Hutch and told him ten. And I said glowing things about the work you're doing, but I told him a situation has come up, and I need your help for a couple of weeks. He said no problem.

I said, Why not send Faro?

—I will if I need to, but a little finesse is what's called for right now.

—I could drive my woodie all the way or, maybe better, take the bus to Denver and then go by train to Seattle.

Long wouldn't hear of it.

—That wagon is likely to break down a dozen times between here and there. Take Eve's little roadster. It's almost new. Driving it, you could be halfway to Seattle by the time you'd get to Denver by bus. And she's obviously not using it. I've made a reservation at the Olympic in Seattle, a good hotel, convenient location, not some flophouse on Skid Row. So get on out there, and see what you can find. She seems to be looking for something or somebody. I don't think she could have much money with her, beyond what she could get for the Renoir. Which she may not even try to sell. She probably took it to send me a message. She could have driven away in the car and sold it easily, but she didn't. It's likely she'll soon need money, so check traveling bands and bars where she could be making a few dollars singing torch songs. If Seattle's a complete dead end, come on back, but if you find a trail, follow it. Let me know how it's going. If something important happens, send a telegram. Telephone if it's an emergency.

After explaining my mission in Seattle, Long walked into his office and came out with a flat box and set it on the table in front of me. He said he'd been planning a gift to celebrate completion of the mural, but figured I could use it now in chilly, rainy Seattle. Inside, neatly folded, a muted red-and-green plaid wool shirt and a waxed waterproof jacket.

Long said, Pendleton Woolen Mills and J. Barbour.

He liked to say the names of his things. The names of the men who had painted his pictures, of course, but also the breeds of his cattle and horses, the model names and numbers of his trucks and cars and tractors, the makers of his clothes. A couple of weeks earlier—before I knew the name—I'd commented on a Barbour Long wore, particularly the muted color, dark brown in one light and deep green or charcoal in others. The shirt in the box seemed carefully chosen to look handsome with the jacket. I was genuinely touched by the gesture and thanked Long profusely.

Back in the cabin, I tried the clothes on and enjoyed the smell of the wax, like a musty canvas pup tent, and the slight scratch at my neck and wrists from the wool. I liked knowing I could smell and feel those garments for decades if I took care of them and kept myself from becoming too thick to fit them. And if that happened, it would be all my responsibility for failing to live up to clothes of that longevity. I looked at myself in the mirror and wondered if Long had given the gift early to pull me closer to him. I looked like a son sneaking into his father's closet and dressing in his expensive hunting attire.

II

—

CHARCOAL
AND UMBER

ALL DURING THAT DRIVE TO SEATTLE IN EVE'S good-looking red car—angling south to Rock Springs, west to Salt Lake City, then northwest through Idaho, Oregon, and on into Washington—I started early enough in the mornings to drive at least a couple of hours before dawn with the top down and the heater blasting in chilly mountain air. The roads were empty. For a while before sunrise, the radio still picked up stations from far across the country, all the way to Chicago. Very early one morning, sky full of stars, an image flashed in my mind unbidden like a memory. Eve in the passenger seat, slouched over, sleeping with her head in my lap, face and hair lit faintly by the dash lights.

After daylight I would watch for the next diner and stop and eat a big leisurely breakfast and drink coffee until I started vibrating. At least three hours before dark, I'd stop at a motor court with a scatter of little cottages and sit on the porch and read or sketch awhile. At that pace, a thousand miles took three long days. Some of those empty, straight roads, I could open the V8 up and drive for miles and miles at eighty with the tires humming loud on chip seal. Other times I'd drive long, slow stretches on unpaved roads that varied from heavy gravel to sandy silt. Local radio stations spent a great deal of time on current prices of wheat and cattle and potatoes and apples, depending on where I was. But some of that territory was so blank I had to study maps the night before and consider the wide spacing of little towns to plan where I could eat and fill the tank and find a place to sleep.

I passed through a lot of brown empty land and grassy cattle land and high mountains and then occasional green valleys of farm communities where you could almost be fooled into thinking the Depression never happened—not like bleak cities with breadlines and dust bowl blasted to a moonscape. For long stretches, you could believe we were still the imagined country whose overall movement was steadily and surely upward, like those moments in Fred and Ginger movies when everyone wears tuxedos and ball gowns, and the dancing is only lightly regulated by the laws of gravity.

I drove past Salt Lake City at dawn on the second day, and the tabernacle and temple in yellow low-angle light looked like a movie set, a reminder that America is oddly not monopolistic about who can dream up a religion and attract a congregation and start passing the collection plate every Sunday, but very much so when it comes to allowing corporations to treat us all like we live in their fiefdoms at their pleasure. Case in point, the Supreme Court year after year dealing blow after blow to any attempt at regulating industry to protect workers and the economy. They'd claimed such regulations could only be made by the states for a while, but when New York made a law about minimum wages for women, they changed their minds and declared that even the states lacked the authority to fix wages. Among those nine crusty, bitter old justices, the majority interpretation appeared to be that the Constitution demanded sacred capitalism exist wholly unfettered, no matter the crisis and the human toll. After all, the ultimate expression of capitalism is not Democracy. It's a dictatorship not of individual men but of corporations with interchangeable leaders. I wasn't sure if the Depression was straining the structural limits of our Constitution or simply revealing that its fundamental ideas were faulty. Those revolutionaries of old had left so much space in their documents, so much fog and vagueness. Like scribing a draft and getting a laugh imagining people in the future trying to figure out what in hell they meant.

Coming across Washington, I passed out of old dark uncut forests into hills logged down to bare dirt, forests converted to stump ranches with cattle grazing in low brush growing where the huge trees had stood.

FIRST THING IN SEATTLE AFTER checking in to the unnecessarily grand Olympic Hotel—a water view from a large west-facing room—I walked to the main PO and asked for general delivery mail under Eve's name. The postal clerk at the counter had seen everything and wasn't fooled by my lie that Eve was my wife and lay coughing and feverish in a hotel room up on Madison and needed her mail, and to complicate matters, my wallet had been stolen yesterday. The clerk looked to the side and shook his head like I was one more idiot in a long line spoiling his otherwise flawless life, which maybe I was. He recited by rote that I needed, bare minimum, some identification with the same last name as the recipient.

—You can't just walk in and take somebody's mail, he said.

He refused even to tell me if any mail existed under the name Eve Long or Eve Miles, though once I had stretched the lie spiderweb thin, I realized that Eve was smarter than to use either name for forwarding mail.

Long had warned me not to take anything for granted. He said he'd started wondering if the name Eve had told him when they met was her real name. Everything could be semi-false, he said.

Stage names. I don't say that to fault her, he said. Being unsure is one of the entertaining features of being married to her.

That afternoon was beautiful and clear with oxygen-thick sea-level air. I went to a long list of downtown hotels showing Eve's pictures to desk clerks, and the same at Union Station and King Street Station, and at every bus station and cabstand in town. That night, I wandered down by the water for dinner and then drove all the way up around the university, stopping at larger clubs with dance bands, scanning faces onstage and then standing off to the side and looking at the audience in the dim secondary light. I focused my mind on blond hair, an oval face, red lipstick, and dark brown eyes. I stayed out late and drank too much. I visited the roughest dives, but also plenty of places I couldn't have afforded without Long's envelope of bills. Next day, I strolled through the library hoping to find Eve sitting at a table reading a history of France or something by Jane Austen. I imagined her looking up, happy to see me so unexpectedly.

My wandering made clear that Seattle was still a new place. I mentioned that to the desk clerk at the hotel, and he said, It's not even been a hundred years since white people first got here and built shacks at Alki Point and lived on fish and clams. And now there's everything from mansions to slums. Ain't progress something?

I appreciated his tone, so I said, Yep, it sure is.

THE BIGGEST OF SEATTLE'S SLUMS, its Hooverville, had risen out of the mudflats alongside Elliott Bay early on in the Depression, a logical downward transition from the flophouses near Pioneer Square. Like Hoovervilles all across the country, the neighborhood was ironically named after the much-despised former president who in public estimation had plunged the country into depression.

That first day in Hooverville was high broken clouds, bright filtered light, almost windless. You could see across the metallic bay to the dark line of Bainbridge Island. I walked from Pioneer Square into the camp, and my first reaction was to imagine how decline could gather momentum until it became unstoppable, how the heaviness could overwhelm our desire to lift and fly to a better place. And also how, after a length of time, much of the previous culture could become unrecoverable.

I wandered around trying to show Eve's picture to people who represented the final expression of America's fast three-century westward movement from the Outer Banks to here, jammed up against the end of the line, the last frontier. People with almost nothing, no assets, gathered in hundreds of shacks and lean-tos—maybe as many as five hundred tiny improvised structures, if the local papers were close to right—scattered over about ten acres of lowland at the edge of Elliott Bay.

People had built shanties out of scrap materials and held them together with whatever they could scavenge, used nails and wire. The walls might be sided with three or four different materials on the same structure—wide boards, cupped delaminating plywood, layers of cardboard. Anything flat and manageable and at least temporarily waterproof. Glass windows were scarce, but jute sacking served to cover window openings and could be rolled up and down. Roofs, ideally, were tar paper over the same materials as the walls, but tin cans stomped flat made fair shingles. Heating and cooking came from stoves fabricated from oilcans and dented, cast-aside stovepipe. Outhouses were situated at the ends of narrow piers extending into the water past the tide line, so it didn't smell as overwhelmingly human as I had expected.

The neighborhood hadn't been planned on a city grid. It emerged piece by piece on whatever open spot of dirt hadn't already been claimed. To follow the lanes from one side of the village to the other was a wander. You curved and made random lefts and rights. Most of the Hoovervilleans were older men, not teenage freight jumpers and hitchhikers. They'd settled into a world they likely couldn't have imagined ten years before, trying to ride through the current misery until better times rolled back around.

People sat beside little fires warming cans of beans and making soup out of over-the-hill vegetables donated by churches and relief organizations. A couple of ambitious optimists squatted at the edge of the bay doing laundry, trying to rinse dirt out of shirts with dirty salt water. Flat-palmed, they beat road dust out of worn wool sport coats and pants to look their best in case some magical opportunity for a real job arose. Maybe some millionaire would take notice and, like in a movie, walk up and offer to pay their way through college.

In general, the people I met were friendly enough. I'd brought painter clothes for just this occasion, so they took me as a fellow. They told me the real hobos, mostly younger people migrating with the seasons across the continent like flocks of birds, stayed north of the city in a place simply called the Camp. It's rougher, one man said.

One teenager, trying to shave looking at a broken mirror, said, The only jobs are at logging camps and mills and canneries and on fishing boats. But if you're seventeen and dirty and haven't done that particular work before, it's no good. Plenty of people waiting for jobs are willing but haven't done any of those things. He paused and said, It would help if I could tie a tie. He dangled one out toward me. Like all his clothes, it was precrash.

I took it and tied it loosely around my neck and then pulled it over my head and handed it to him. He looked at it like I'd performed a magic trick.

I gestured and said, Just snug it up. Don't start messing with it.

I saw very few women in Hooverville. One woman looked to be about fifty and slim as a girl. She wore very clean faded sky blue overalls and a man's white business shirt. She sat on an upturned five-gallon zinc bucket feeding a smoky fire in front of her shanty, almost a tent, patched together from gray scrap lumber and olive drab canvas. The woman's hair was pulled back into a short ponytail. Blond streaks about equaled the gray. I sat on the ground to get my head lower than hers and reached out Eve's photo.

—Have you seen her? I asked.

The woman tipped her head a few degrees in tiny increments, as if fine gears adjusted her face away from plumb and then back. She studied the photo and looked at me and said, What are you pumping me for? Are you a husband? Boyfriend? Cop? Probably hit her, didn't you, and then she ran off?

The woman's eyes were clear blue.

—None of those, I said. I'm a friend trying to find her.

—Sure. Course you are.

—I hoped you might have seen her.

—And what if I had? You ask too many questions. If this girl is missing, maybe you're what she wants to be missing from. Leave her alone.

—What if she's in trouble?

—I don't know that. Maybe she's in trouble and trying to get away from it and you're the trouble. I don't like meddling. People make their own choices, and after that, it's all on them. Free will, God's gift to mankind. He uses it to play with us. Mostly he punishes us with it.

I slightly shook the photo and said, But you've seen this woman or you haven't?

She took a cigarette out of the chest pocket of her overalls and scratched a match on the heel of her shoe to light it. She puffed and raised both hands and paddled two strokes my way in dismissal.

MY SECOND DAY IN HOOVERVILLE, I carried a few tinkling half-pints in my pockets, and a bag with treats like saltines and peanuts and little cans of sweetened condensed milk. People got happier to have me join them at their fires. One man, maybe sixty, chatted a summary of his life, said he couldn't even begin to figure out his ancestry. Best he could pin it down, equal parts Salish and Japanese, also some Irish and Scot. He looked at Eve's picture and whistled faintly. He said, If I'd of seen a hot dame like her, I'd not soon forget it. Guess you don't have an extra one of those?

I shook my head.

—Too bad, he said.

I went back to try again with the woman in overalls, but as soon as she saw me, she pointed her finger at me and shook it angrily and turned to go into her shanty. As she entered the doorway, over her shoulder, she gave me the middle finger.

After lunchtime I sat awhile with a couple of men in their forties, Sam and Randolph, roommates in an entirely tar-paper-encased shack with a strong list to the east. Nailheads fixing the faded black paper to the roof and walls had rusted. Reddish stains descended tapering and irregular like icicles or stalactites from each of many nails staggered all over the structure. I made a quick note in my pocket sketchbook to paint that charcoal-and-umber abstract someday.

I sat by the little outdoor campfire with the two men, and reached them a bottle of cheap bourbon, its color the only kinship to the real thing, and asked about their lives, which they were happy to talk about. They had known each other only two years, but their stories matched. They had both gone to college, Sam to Berkeley and Randolph to University of Arizona. Both had been teachers, English and history. Their jobs went away a few years after '29, when so many of their students left high school to hunt for work. Sam and Randolph spent some time trying to find work too, but the older you get, the harder it becomes. They met in Portland and ended up here in Seattle, hoping for different times than these.

—Not just different, Sam said. The correct word is *better*.

Since I was interested, they showed me the inside of their place. Two cots on opposite walls, two armchairs with stuffing coming out of the arms angled toward a woodstove made from a ten-gallon oilcan and a length of downspout, a braided rag rug in the colors of farm clothes—tans and browns and faded denim. A ripple-pattern afghan, blues and grays and a touch of maroon, draped over the arm of one of the chairs. I wondered who had crocheted it, what journeys it made to land here.

Pressed against all the walls, hundreds of books rose in horizontal stacks from floorboards to the joists of the shed roof. They said the books made good insulation in winter, and they'd bought them by the wheelbarrow load for little more than the work of hauling them away from big houses where hard times had caught up with the people who had lived there and were on their way elsewhere.

—In terms of cash, books aren't worth shit in hard times, Sam said.

Once they had stacked them, spines out, Sam and Randolph started searching for treasures. They found the majority of a once complete set of Dickens, a great deal of Byron and Tennyson and Wordsworth, and all seven volumes of Francis Parkman's *France and*

England in North America. There were travel books by the dozens—the Arctic, the Congo, the architectural marvels of Egypt and Peru, the ecclesiastical architecture of France and Italy.

Randolph said, Chilly rainy days, you build a bright fire in the oilcan and pull out a piece of wall and start reading.

Sam agreed, said, Not the worst way to spend a day.

Then he said, I made a crystal radio wave detector last year. Wound copper wire around and around an oatmeal-tube cylinder and hooked an antenna wire to my bedsprings to pick up faraway stations. No need for batteries. It finds electric waves in the air and catches them, and we listen to hissing and scratching on earphones until a station comes in. KOMO and KJR are so strong and close you could probably pick them up by sticking a nail in your mouth and clamping it between your teeth. Those two stations keep us busy. It's where we get news and the correct time and the Metropolitan Opera on Saturday afternoons. But once last winter, a clear night, when the signal must have bounced off the moon, we picked up WLW out of Ohio for almost an hour.

—Yeah, that was a thrill, Randolph said dryly.

—A novelty, let's call it, Sam said.

The men told me that government workers had passed the word that distribution of relief money in Hooverville would be easier and faster if the shanties had numbers. They'd also held out the further incentive that establishing an address was a crucial step in being regarded as a citizen of Seattle and getting mail delivery and being able to vote. So in the days afterward, many residents painted numbers on their doors.

Randolph said, Eight was particularly popular. There must have been at least fifteen or twenty eights scattered around, but we're starting to get that straightened out. A while back the city declared they'd tolerate us if we elected a committee to represent us and help enforce regulations. There's a young black man on the committee named Jesse who pretty much runs the show—we call him Mayor—and he's been especially enthusiastic about the numbering system.

Sam added, Of course the inevitable fervid minority refuses to number their homes on the theory that it would somehow make eviction easier. And maybe they're right in the sense that outliers like all of us can get overlooked or, worse, targeted, when bad times come falling down.

When I finally got around to asking about Eve and showing them her photo, they agreed that if she had been around, they would remember. But they hadn't seen anybody that matched the picture.

Sam held the picture and studied. He said, Her cheeks look smooth as a white ceramic teapot.

—This is a professional publicity photo for a band she sang with, I said. She's in stage makeup. Imagine her less polished.

Sam said, Pretend she's a real person? Then maybe I did see her.

He handed the photo to Randolph, saying, Remember, two weeks ago, about? She was looking for somebody?

Randolph said, No.

—Yes, you do, Sam said. The one you thought stole two dollars from us, but then later you found it?

Randolph looked at the photo again and said, Maybe.

Sam said to me, We made her a cup of tea and she stuck her head in the door to see our library.

—Was she with anyone? I said.

Sam paused and looked off in the direction of the water and thought. He said, Maybe, but I can't picture that. I see one young woman by herself. I think she was looking for someone who might have been living here a while back.

Randolph said, I think whoever she was looking for was her age, and we told her she ought to try the Camp. We told her to be careful.

—I hear it's maybe dangerous, I said.

—It's a different world, Randolph said. Here, we're hoping to get as close as we can to what we had. Up there, maybe they've given up.

Sam said, Wait, I remember now, real clearly. She said once she found her friend, she was on the way up to Bellingham. Might have been to do with a job. If she's a singer, why couldn't she have been looking for a job up that way?

—Well, why not? I said.

At the hotel that night, I stayed up late sketching page after page. Faces of people in Hooverville and the geometry of their shelters. Sam and Randolph's library and oilcan hearth. I spent a lot of time on the angled face of a man who had said very proudly, If I wanted to sell out, I could get as high as fifteen dollars for my house.

FROM BELLINGHAM I WROTE A postcard to Long in a tiny hand. Travel-book stuff. *About a hundred miles north of Seattle—less than twenty miles from Canada—town mostly stretching along the waterfront—much logging to the east toward Cascades—old forests cut down to bare dirt. Checking out a somewhat believable lead concerning Eve.*

A couple of days later on another card, I informed Long about possible clues I'd found in Bellingham and had followed to little towns farther east toward the Cascades like Marblemount and Darrington, where walking down the street you'd hear voices straight from the southern Appalachians, the same accents and expressions, *They Lord* and *I swan* to convey mild amazement. Those mountaineers had followed jobs diagonal across the continent to equally wet and mountainous terrain that felt a lot like home. Dark woods and fog, rich smells of wet black dirt and rot, moss and the mineral scent of rushing rocky creeks. Next thing to a jungle, a rainforest.

Sam and Randolph had seemed moderately sure about Eve going to Bellingham for a job, so I thought there was a fair chance she'd picked up gigs singing with bands at weekend dances out in the logging towns. And maybe she had done exactly that, but showing people a photograph and asking if they'd seen that woman singing at a dance in the past couple weeks ago didn't turn up solid information. Mostly they couldn't be positive matching the picture with memory. As the hotel clerk in Nebraska had said, those girl singers look a lot alike. Usually the hotel and bus station clerks I talked to couldn't even remember the name of the band clearly. Only that their music sounded like something on the radio, the Northwest Highwaymen or the Pacific Ramblers.

After several fruitless days, I finally acknowledged I'd reached another dead end. Either Eve had been up that way and left or she hadn't been there at all. No way to tell. Discouraged, I drove back to Seattle to try my luck north of town.

◇

THE CAMP WAS NEAR AN INLET, WOODS AND WATER.
It was quiet. The northern parts of the city lay nearby, but without
the occasional sound of a distant truck, it could have seemed like
green wilderness. People in congregation stink, it's the nature of
the beast, and this encampment held every possible human fragrance, plus cabbage cooking and campfires.

I had hardly gotten there when a skinny teenager pulled a blackjack and hit a man across the wrist—a hard flash of black leather
shaped like a fat spoon heavy with lead shot. The man's hand
drooped limp. He grabbed his hurt wrist and pulled the arm tight
against his chest.

The teenager said, Probably ain't broke. The feeling'll come
back before long. But get less than ten feet from me again and I'll
go for your head.

The man didn't say anything but kept holding his arm tight like
hugging himself.

The boy slipped the blackjack into his back pocket with the
handle sticking out and walked away.

Unlike Hooverville, the Camp made no attempt at structure
or order, no semblance of a neighborhood with houses and streets.

Geometry abandoned. Random jigsaw pieces of tarps and lean-tos, stacks of collected sticks for fires, tree-to-tree ropes with drying clothes rinsed in the waterway. Teenagers, a great many, faces shiny with grease and hair the same, sheltering under canvas rigging. Fires sent up acrid smoke from wood supplemented by old tar paper and garbage. Hooverville was an attempt to maintain some element of normality, but the Camp let wildness loose.

Girls so young living on the road looked either forlorn, like prey for the nearest predator, or so hard and self-contained they could put a knapped flint blade through the rib cage of a wolf. I crossed paths with two of the latter type, maybe sixteen, dressed like boys in oversized cast-off coats and baggy denim pants and work boots. They were almost the same height, and both had brown hair cut very short. One wore a beat-up porkpie hat and the other a newsboy cap. When I approached, they both put their right hands in their jacket pockets, almost choreographed, probably ready to pull knives. Identical sprays of pimples on pale cheeks.

I said, A simple question. I'm looking for a friend. Have you seen her?

I showed them the picture, and they both laughed at the same time.

The one in the porkpie said, Sorry. So many movie stars wander through here it's hard to remember.

I said, Come on, really look at the picture. It would have been a couple of weeks ago. Less makeup. Somebody downtown told me she was coming up here trying to find somebody. I drove all the way from Wyoming. Can you help me?

Porkpie said, And all you've got is somebody somewhere said something?

Newsboy laughed and said, Wife or girlfriend run away?

—Neither one, I said. A friend.

—I'd call that a pretty good friend, Newsboy said.

Porkpie said, Maybe we could aim you toward somebody somewhere who knows just about everybody out on the road and a little bit about everything going on.

—Sure, I said.

Newsboy said, We hear you've been handing out quarters like spreading chicken feed. Empty your pockets and we'll tell you where to find this guy. I mean, turn them inside out.

I thought, What the hell, and I unloaded about five dollars' worth of quarters into their hands. People worked a week for less. A wheelbarrow full of pork and beans and little paper-wrapped deviled ham tins.

Porkpie said, Not too far away, but on the other side of the inlet. A redhead guy. Last I heard he's squatting in an abandoned mansion on Duval. You'll find it. No guarantees, but if anybody knows anything, it'll be him.

—What's his name?

—You'll have to ask him. All I'm saying is redhead.

A TWENTIES PLASTER MANSION WITH vertical streaks of dark mildew dragging in stripes from the eaves down the cream walls. A strip of lawn between sidewalk and front door had been mowed recently, but at the sides the grass had begun reverting to nature, following the early stages of plant succession on the way back to wildness. I knocked at the door and waited and then walked around back past a clay tennis court growing flat plates of plantain and tall ragweed. The net was rotting, and the mildewed headband drooped almost to the ground. A swimming pool, empty except for a foot or two of dull black liquid vibrating with tadpoles. Something larger moved under the surface, and the liquid churned viscous as Karo syrup. Even if the tadpoles lived long enough, they'd never be able to climb out of the pit unless a tree limb fell exactly right and the newly transformed frogs could use it to climb out. But probably that larger thing under the surface would eat its fill of tadpoles and then lie in the black water waiting for the next thing to fall in.

At the deep end, a diving board had gone missing, only its metal frame and springs and hinges and fulcrums left behind like a squat industrial sculpture. The last time someone bounced and arced happily from that board into a blue chlorine splash might have been end of summer 1929. After that, a lot of people probably became too depressed to maintain a pool, not to mention running out of money for it. Two redwood lounge chairs, one tipped on its side, lacked cushions. The upper surfaces of wood had faded almost pink, graying along the edges. Off to the west, a charcoal bit of distant bay water wedged between two other big plaster houses.

At the back of the house, up three steps, a shaded back porch. The rusting screen bellied out from the frame. Down in the pool, black murk stirred again.

A latch clicked and the porch door opened. A pale hazed figure moved toward the screen and peered out.

—Hey, you can't be here. You have to go away. Go be somewhere else.

The voice had no determinate age or gender.

The sky was all gray, but bright enough that I needed to visor my hand to see the figure more clearly through the mesh. It was a plump man, maybe young. Tall with a large head. White bare chest and round belly. Reddish hair, pale thick legs falling chunky out of baggy white undershorts. He held one arm folded behind his back.

—Hey, he said. You hear me? You have to go somewhere else.

—I do hear you.

—Then go away. You woke me up.

—Are you supposed to be here?

—Caretaker. I'm looking after this mess.

—Yeah? Great job on the pool. A masterpiece.

He shrugged his folded arm around front and raised a little stubby pistol toward me. His fist enveloped it, and the black hole of the barrel barely peeped out like he was clutching a one-eyed pet hamster. Still, when somebody points a gun at you, even a tiny, silly gun, you tend to raise your hands.

I said, Whoa, whoa. Easy down. All I'm doing is looking for someone.

—Not here you're not.

—A woman named Eve. I'm trying to find her.

He paused and lowered the pistol.

—Who?

Slowly, two-fingered, I pulled the photo of Eve from my jacket pocket and held it up. He motioned me closer and looked at the photo through the screen for an instant.

—Eve, she's gone, he said.

—But was here? I said.

—Go away, he said. She's none of my business. None of yours either.

—She was here, though?

After a long pause, he said, Give me fifteen minutes and then come around front. Knock like a normal person.

—I already did that.

—What? You show up unannounced and knock on the door and I'm supposed to drop everything and run to see what you want? I'm not at your beck and call. I doubt your list of what's important matches mine at all. You want coffee?

HE HAD PUT ON A wrinkled flannel shirt and khaki work pants and a pair of heavy wool socks but still no shoes. He waved me toward a parlor, furniture upholstered in deep blue and maroon velvet. Heavy, dark curtains, and no paintings on the walls, but empty spaces and hooks where paintings must have been. Two mismatched mugs of steaming black coffee sat on side tables, and he motioned me toward one. I sat and sipped. It was the best coffee I'd ever tasted, and I said so.

—Cooking coffee's not that hard. Finding good fresh beans roasted right is. I've got a guy.

I told him my name and asked his. He said, I'm not required to give you my identity.

—Oh come on. Play along.

—It's Donal.

—Donald?

—No.

—How do you spell it, then?

—One *d*. Don't know many Irish people, do you?

—No.

—Neither do I, but that was my grandfather's name.

When I finished my cup, Donal said, There's more if you want it. You can't be all bad if you appreciate my coffee.

While he was gone, I looked around the room. On a tabletop in a corner, several open boxes of business cards, hundreds of them altogether. Cards for insurance companies, automobile paint and bodywork, diners, fresh seafood shops, men's and ladies' clothing shops. Donal came back with the refilled mugs and saw me looking and said, I get paid by the hundred to drop them off all over town.

On the coffee table, I noticed one business card by itself and picked it up. It was cheaply printed like the rest, just the name of the business and a street name—*Pacific Acceptance Company, Second Avenue South.* No specific address or office number or phone number. I turned it over and found a penciled note, *9 a.m. Friday.* No date. The handwriting looked like Eve's, but also like a million others', uniform script angling across the card.

The only acceptance businesses I had ever heard of were for car financing. If you wanted a new Chevrolet or Buick or Cadillac, the General Motors Acceptance Corporation would probably see that you drove away from the dealership in a new car.

Donal asked where I knew Eve from and I said Wyoming.

He said, I knew her from Kansas City. Then we went somewhere else together, maybe St. Louis or Memphis. I remember a big-ass brown river. Course a lot of towns have brown rivers. They all look the same after a while. She moved on in that one-river town. She was a runner. Get fed up and go. She always wanted the head guy. Tallest, best-looking. The quarterback, the captain.

—And you weren't that guy?

—No. We were friends.

—You've seen her lately?

—She came by.

—When?

—I don't know.

—Recently?

—Time seems so fluid these days. A year ago feels like yesterday and also like ten years ago. Not like I keep a diary.

—OK, let's go at it another way. Is there a Second Avenue South anywhere around here?

—Sure. Down around Pioneer Square.

—Do you have any idea why Eve would be interested in financing something there or having business there?

I held up the card and showed him the back.

—Looks a little like her writing, I said.

—Probably not. Or maybe a scribble that has nothing to do with what's on the front. A convenient scrap of paper.

—Maybe, I said. Any chance her visit had anything to do with her late husband, Jake?

—Late like dead?

—Identical to dead.

—Yeah, you hear all kinds of things. What I'm saying is, Eve was here a half hour at most, whenever that was. Had somewhere she had to be. Maybe heading eastward or southward.

—Almost everything is eastward or southward from here.

—Point of fact, Vancouver and Alaska aren't. And they're kind of a big deal around here. What happened was, I told her she didn't look so good and needed to take better care of herself. And she said—exact quote—*I'm trying to*. She gave me a long hug for old times and headed out. Here and gone.

Donal and I sat and finished our coffee.

I said, That's some good coffee. I wish I had a guy like your guy.

—He's an artist.

I said, I heard Jake might have been from here.

—Here like . . . Seattle?

I sat and waited.

Donal said, No. Somewhere way, way south. Gulf Coast. He said he grew up in a swamp with alligators and snakes.

—And his name's Jake what? Ar-something? Like Arnold?

—Orson's the name I knew. You're always so focused on the trivialities.

—And what was Jake Orson to Eve?

—I thought he was just another boyfriend, but at some point she started calling him husband.

—Did she say when they got married and where?

—Could have been anywhere. If it happened at all, it had to have been a great long while ago. Three years minimum.

—Did either one of them ever mention a divorce?

Donal said, The premise of your question is so far off I don't know where to start. They didn't hardly bother to mention a marriage, so I doubt they'd be featuring a divorce in casual conversation.

—But did they?

—Have to get back to you on that if you need your certainties. Hard to believe they'd have bothered making it legal to start with, much less going through the mess and cost of divorce. Besides, that kind of thing requires you to be in one place for more than a few days at a time. And maybe have documents. You know, certificates, licenses. And none of us carried around that shit. But why are you asking about all this anyway?

—About a month ago, Eve got a postcard, sent from Seattle. It said something about back in the days, something about helping. Eve's current husband wants to know if it might've had something to do with Jake.

Donal said, Eve had a lot of friends in Seattle. Could've been from anyone.

—Could it have been from you?

—I'm not much of a letter writer. All I know is there was a knock at the door one day, and when I answered, there Eve stood. Short visit and she was gone again.

It went on like this until I'd gotten about all I could get and started to leave. He said, Can I have that picture of Eve?

—Sure.

He took it and looked at it and said, People float. Come and go. See them awhile out on the road and then in a few months you're in Atlanta or Baltimore and they're not. Last time I heard anything about Eve, sounded like she had an old man on the string. Somebody with money. I'm guessing that's the current husband.

Then he handed the photo back and said, Second thought, I don't really need to hang on to this. It wouldn't be so good to keep around.

THE BUILDING WAS ONLY A half dozen blocks from the edge of Hooverville, and it matched most of the buildings in that area near Pioneer Square—brick, a few stories tall. On the directory in the lobby, names of accountants, insurance agents, a couple of dentists, and six import businesses, not surprising in a port city. And also the Pacific Acceptance Company on the third floor. I had spent almost three hours wandering around the area, showing the card to people, asking questions to find my way there.

The third floor was dim, lit only by light filtered through the rectangle of Florex privacy glass in each door. The doors were identical except for the business names stenciled in black paint. I found the acceptance company and tried the knob, but it was locked. Immediately after I knocked, a woman's voice said, Yes?

—I only need a moment of your time, I said.

The dead bolt clicked, and the door opened four inches before the chain tightened. I could see a brown suit with a silver pin on a lapel, a swipe of heavily powdered cheek and forehead, the arc of one severely plucked eyebrow, the corner of a dark red mouth.

—Yes? the woman said again.

I held the business card up to the door crack and said, A friend of mine had this. I wanted to ask about your company.

—Our cards are all over town. Anybody can come across one.

—She's gone missing. Her name's Eve.

Immediately the woman said, We only deal directly with the customer.

—And what is your acceptance service? I get that you loan money, but what does it pertain to? Cars?

The door closed.

I knocked again. The door opened an inch. The woman said, I promise, you don't want to do that again. Go away while it's still your choice how you go.

I walked a couple of blocks to a diner and ate a grilled cheese, beating myself up for my questions. Too straightforward. Too much assumption of goodwill on the other side. Like everyone's going to hand you what you need just because you ask politely. I needed to be more clever. Subtle. Come at questions sideways like Faro turning his back on a horse until eventually it came right to him.

I BANGED ON THE DOOR until Donal opened it a crack.

—Coffee? I said.

He let me in and said, I knew I wasn't done with you.

Someone farther back in the house played the largo from *New World* Symphony on a poorly tuned piano. Thanksgiving music. I remembered an older cousin, a teenage girl when I was ten, playing the part that sounds like you could sing *Once upon a time* or *I'll be going home* to it. She had played it over and over in the drowsy hour after all the holiday eating was finished and the living room fire had built a deep bed of coals and the logs were checked and hissing but nobody wanted to get up from their chair or sofa cushion and add more wood. I had a crush on her and didn't know what to do about it. But at some point, after many repetitions of the figure, I yelled, You've got those five notes down pat. Move on.

Donal made coffee and we sat. The light was dim, maroon and heavy. Motes drifted in sunbeams.

I took a wild stab and said, You saw her for a lot more than half an hour when she was here.

—What if I did?

—I went to the address on that card. Why would Eve be interested in an acceptance company?

—None of my business, Donal said.

I reminded him that along the road, singing in a band, Eve had found her head guy. He has plenty of money and power and perhaps more of both to come. And yet she ran anyway. So what was she looking for here in Seattle?

—I don't know. Might be she was interested in that acceptance place and went to check out the office. Maybe she wanted to buy a car, who knows. Probably nothing but a scam, a hustle. She was here for a few days and then floated on away.

I sat a minute and couldn't think of another question. I said, That convertible sitting outside is already hers.

Donal shrugged and said, Hey man, I like you. Do you like bourbon from back before Prohibition? Or even older scotch? Champagne?

—Sure. Any of that. But champagne particularly.

—Then I have a treat.

From the next room, the piano player said, Damn, Donal, you're going to run out if you keep giving it away.

Donal looked at me and smiled and then walked toward the back of the house. A few minutes later, he returned with two bot-

tles. I recognized them as very good only because Long had opened
a bottle one night and made a special occasion of it.

—You ought to see the cellar, Donal said. Guy ran off and left
it. He owes money all over Seattle, owes me a few bucks too. So a
basement full of wine and liquor is the least of his worries.

—He pays you to watch the place?

—Past tense. And precious little even then. The checks have
gotten sporadic, and one of them bounced. I don't do anything I
don't want to around here anymore. I keep expecting the bank to
run me out any day, but so far so good. Still have phone and power,
even.

We drank like rich people. The pianist came and sat on the
other end of the sofa from me with her feet together on the cushion
and her knees under her chin, oversized pajamas and gray ragg
wool socks flopping out past her toes. Round-faced, dark hair
pulled into a stub of ponytail, very pale skin like she hadn't been
out of the house for months. Her pajamas were dingy cream with
big red polka dots.

Donal said, Hey, Fawn, want a glass?

She said, Oh hell no. How do you drink that shit? It's not sweet
at all.

Donal shrugged and turned to me and said, All your questions
have me thinking about the past. About being almost a kid, out
on the road. It was like war must be. You had to have been there to
understand. Terrible, but not only.

—Eve described some beautiful moments, I said.

—Not exactly the word I would use.

—What was she like back then?

—Same. You could kind of count on her. However bad it got,
you knew Eve'd be the last man standing.

—And Jake?

Donal scrubbed his palm from hairline to chin. He said, This again. I don't have much to say about Jake.

—I'm mostly trying to find out if he's dead or alive.

—Like a wanted poster?

—Not really, I said. I've heard convincing stories both ways.

—I get it. Almost everybody has a list of people they wish were dead. I don't know anything for a fact about Jake.

—When's the last time you saw him?

—Long time.

—Before you got off the road?

—Possibly.

—Try to remember. Where did you see him last?

Donal looked up to the high ceiling. He said, Crystal ball says West Coast. Could have been here or Portland or Bakersfield. Definitely not San Diego. I'm positive about that. LA unlikely.

I said, Maybe somewhere around Frisco?

Into her knees, without looking at me, Fawn said, Man, only rubes call it Frisco. Don't embarrass yourself.

She reached for my glass and took a delicate sip and pursed her lips and very softly said, Whoa.

—Jake, dead or alive? Donal said. I never knew for sure. A lot of us thought he was dead.

—Thought or think? I said. Wished or wish?

—Semantics.

—Not really. I need to know if he's alive, if he might have something to do with Eve leaving home.

—The answer is I don't know and never did know and probably never will. OK? On the road one of the things you learn to do without is certainty.

—And straight answers to questions?

Donal laughed.

Fawn, looking at her socks, muttered, Fucking comedian.

After a pause Donal said, I don't want anything to do with Jake, not ever again. After a few years on the road, he changed a lot. If you want to poke around in his life story, don't talk to me. Go talk to his folks in Florida. If anybody knows, it's probably them. County with a Spanish name. Esta-something. You know, Florida shit.

I said, Damn, two days and I finally get something specific out of you.

Donal said, Pleasure doing business with you, Detective.

Then Fawn looked up and said, She could be anywhere. She didn't know where to go next. She seemed sort of mixed up. But part of her wanted to go back to Wyoming.

She never said that to me, Donal said.

Fawn said, Of course she didn't. But she said exactly that to me—*Some days I want to go straight back to Wyoming.* We were talking upstairs. You were gone somewhere, doing something. You think everybody's world stops till you get back from doing what nobody can ask you about? Like all information needs to flow through you?

To Fawn, I said, Where do you think she might have gone?

—Anyone's guess. I tried to get her to stay here until she figured it out, but she wouldn't do it. She was pushing to move on, or else something was pushing her.

We sat in silence. Light fell through the tall windows like smudges of pencil lead on your fingertips. I could hear the refrigerator humming all the way from the back of the house. Light rain in the trees and on the slate roof sounded like a slow, deep in-breath.

Donal finally said, Truth, man. I don't know where Eve went. I don't know what Jake's story is. All I can say is, if you're so desperate for information about him, try Florida.

THE NIGHT BEFORE I LEFT Seattle, I sent a telegram to Long— *MAYBE IMPORTANT STOP LAST NAME ORSON STOP FLORIDA COUNTY ESTA SOMETHING STOP RETURNING DAWES*

ON THE DRIVE BACK, I rehearsed ways to fill Long in on my time in Seattle. I tried to anticipate his questions about Eve and about Jake, about what little I'd found out and all I'd failed to find. Questions about whether I'd spent my time—measured in dollars—well or poorly. Donal had called me Detective as a joke, but that was part of what Long expected me to do, to be. Track and find a missing person. Why me instead of, for instance, hiring the Pinkertons? Probably the same reason he didn't want to call the sheriff's department and report a missing person. Apparently a great deal of my value was what I was not.

I started early and drove late, trying to make it in two days. Every couple of hours, I twiddled the knobs on the little circular radio dial in the dash, searching for music bright and jangly enough to keep me awake. Somewhere down in the southern half of Washington, a news bulletin reported still no trace of Amelia Earhart, sixty-three naval airplanes called back from their search. An hour later, an announcement that the Senate in their infinite wisdom had voted down Roosevelt's proposal to expand the Supreme Court and dilute the power of the current bunch of ancient shills for big business. A disappointment, but not at all unexpected.

By the time I reached the northeast corner of Oregon, I decided my best strategy was to emphasize Florida. And I decided the word *lead* worked better than *clue*. The Florida Lead. And really, the information I'd gotten about Jake's background was a big step beyond where we'd been when I left Dawes. I also wanted to emphasize Fawn's belief that Eve was confused and wanted, maybe, to come back to the ranch. *Yearning* might be a good word to use there. But something held her back, and Fawn didn't know what that was, and neither did I.

I kept thinking about Eve beyond my report to Long. The sense of something like desperation that Fawn had felt, like something was pushing Eve. I wanted to know what.

Second day of the drive, one big question remained—tell Long about the Pacific Acceptance Company or not? I had nothing concrete, only that something felt shady. Maybe Eve had simply changed her mind about needing a car after she ditched hers in Dawes. Or maybe she needed immediate cash without having to sell the painting. And maybe the woman who answered the door wasn't shady at all, just had talents other than dealing with the public. I was almost to the Wyoming line before I let intuition or whim or chance decide the matter. Could have been the flip of a coin. Heads tell, tails not. It came up not.

LONG AND I SAT SIDE BY SIDE WITH A CREASED, colorful gas station map spread on the dining room table. He said, I've never been to Florida and don't plan to go. When I want to see palm trees, it's Cuba. From studying the map, looks like they mostly name counties for confederates and conquistadors and fruit. He touched a finger to the middle of the dangling state.

—Estafa, he said. The county seat, Lee City, is the only town of any size, and the population is under four thousand.

He laid out my mission, saying, There are plenty of cheaper ways to accomplish what I'm after, but all of them would involve more people and slow things down. I want answers about Jake and Eve fast, before I make a fool of myself getting any deeper into politics. I want a buffer so that I'm not the one asking the questions. And I need to trust that buffer.

—Thus me? I said.

—Well, yeah, he said. It's simple. You drive to Denver, park the car at Denver Municipal. Then fly halfway across the country—a big adventure in itself. From Tampa go north to Estafa County and find this Orson family. They don't appear to live in Lee City. No phone.

I said, Outside of town sounds right. Donal told me that Jake grew up in a swamp.

—I bet he did. Makes sense. I'll keep trying to get you an exact address before you fly, but I'm not optimistic. You may have to beat the bushes to find them, but when you do, see if these Orsons know anything about Eve's whereabouts. See where it leads. Then ask if their son is alive. It would be convenient if he's dead like Eve led me to believe, but I'm beginning to wonder about that. If he's alive, ask what they know about his marriage, if in fact there was one. And if they believe so, then did it conclude in a legal divorce? And where did both formalities take place? That information is crucial because we'll need papers.

—If I get through all that, do you want to know where he might be?

—Of course. Last thing I want is trouble from a not-fully-divorced and not-yet-deceased husband erupting in the middle of a campaign. Or, nearly as bad, just before I get appointed to the US Senate. And timing may be important. Old Senator Philson isn't doing so well. People I know in Cheyenne are starting to take bets on whether he makes it past Christmas. Most places, a politician with a divorced wife is poison. But out here in what is still some-what the Wild West, it's looser. Bigamy, though, that's a different story. It would be a fatal problem. And if it comes down to her running off to be back with him, well, I wouldn't at all like being the butt of those jokes.

I said nothing.

Long quickly added, All that's hypothetical, of course. Let's focus on a few basic questions in order to decide what move to make next. And of course I want to know where I stand with my wife. I'm saying, question those Orsons hard about Eve, really dig in. You don't have to get personal about her, but I do need to know anything a newspaper reporter might find interesting. You find out the who, what, when, where. I'll figure the why for myself. In other words, do the boring due-diligence shit I should have done before I married her but was too crazy in love to think about. Then come back and tell me all the stories you heard, and we'll start sorting out from there. You'll be gone less than a week. Clear?

Fumblingly, I said, I mean, finding out where Eve is, why she's gone, if she's safe? Those are also important questions, right?

—Of course, Long said. Goes without saying that beyond anything else my main purpose is finding Eve. Realize, though, nobody except an idiot would expect to marry Eve with too many illusions of guaranteed permanence. But if you find her, and if any part of her has feelings for me and wants to come back, flowers and champagne to welcome her home.

I paused and thought a beat. Still early in knowing Long, I already didn't want to know everything he was telling me. I told him, I might start out a little more indirectly with the Orsons. Maybe not a good idea to muddy things up with mentioning a well-to-do fellow. They might pull out a protractor and start plotting their own angles.

—I disagree, Long said. Go straight at them. Dump it all in their laps first thing. Element of surprise. They'll have less time to think out their response.

—If you think that's the best way.

—Yes, I do. Quit worrying. Think about fine hotels in Denver and St. Petersburg, cocktails on the beach. Almost a vacation. And by the way, I trust you or I wouldn't be asking you to do this for me.

—Why would you do either?

Long seemed puzzled by the question. After a pause he said, Well, you haven't screwed up so far.

—OK, then. But I will need more prints of Eve's pictures. They were helpful in Seattle, but I used most of them.

—Done by tomorrow afternoon, even if Smiley has to stay up all night printing them. He lives right above his photo shop anyway.

—I'm planning to work on the mural tomorrow, so I can pick up the prints whenever they're ready.

Before I got up from the table, Long gave me a pistol, a tidy little semiautomatic, and a small box of cartridges.

He said, This is a Browning 1910, the smaller .32 model. Fits in a jacket pocket or, in a pinch, under your belt. I carried one of these with me all the way through the war as a last resort. And back then it had the ironic value of being the exact model that killed Archduke Franz Ferdinand and started that whole wasteful, crazy shitstorm. This isn't the one I carried, of course, so don't worry about it having particular sentimental value. I've got a dozen of them.

I said, I don't plan on needing a pistol.

—Of course you don't plan on it. Take it anyway.

On the way back to my cabin, I ran into Faro. He looked at the little pistol in my hand and said, Not that I'd know from personal experience, but I always heard that gunfighters don't watch the other man's hand. They watch the eyes.

—My next gunfight, I'll keep that in mind.

He said, Do you know enough about that old husband yet to know if he'd hurt her? I mean, good Lord, husbands and wives kill each other every day.

I said, I'm still not even sure he's alive, but that's all part of what I'm flying to Florida to find out.

—Good, Faro said.

RUST AND CHARTREUSE

~M~

AS I WALKED THROUGH THE LOBBY OF THE BROWN
Palace to catch my flight out of Denver Municipal, a bellhop
stopped me and said, Mr. Welch? He reached out a folded sheet
of hotel notepaper. The note read, *Call Long.* Triple underlined.

I carried it to the desk and started jotting Long's name and
number on the bottom, but the clerk waved me off and said, No
need. Mr. Long and Mrs. Long are regular guests. Should only be
a few minutes. Wait close by and I'll let you know.

Ten minutes later, he came over and said, Third booth.

Long said, You have a pencil and paper?

—Yes.

—This is the best I've been able to come up with in terms of
an address. Orson place, southwest Estafa County, near Withlacoochee River, Florida.

I said, Planet Earth, Solar System, Milky Way Galaxy, the
Universe.

—Third grade wisdom, Long said.

—Right around then.

Long said, I'm still making calls. If I find anything more specific, I'll send word.

YOU FLEW LOW TOWARD TAMPA from the east like you were going to land on Main Street. But then you veered south and crossed a patch of waterway toward a pale spit of sand, the tip of an island. The runway began as soon as the water stopped. At the far end of the pavement, nothing but Tampa Bay. Little room for error.

Like almost every human in the world, I'd never flown before, so those moments of rushing low over the city and then toward open water felt like the foyer to death. When the wheels touched down and the brakes caught and juddered the plane to a nonfatal speed, more than a few passengers cheered and applauded in relief and one man shouted, Oh, hell yes. When the door opened, I wobbled down the metal ladder to the ground, fragrant from a day and night of sweat and fear and proximity to eighteen other people—mostly full flights—many of whom had vomited into the useful metal bowls beneath every seat. With all the refueling stops, there had been more terrifying takeoffs and landings than I could count. I'd had all of the sounds and smells of people, including myself, that I could handle.

Passengers milled near the baggage hold, all shaky and dazed. The wings close overhead cast a band of shade that we huddled into. A man up in the belly handed down bags to another man, passengers claimed them, and like at a train station, porters rolled the bags away on carts. Passengers walked along behind, forlorn and shaky from the beating they'd taken by the wild currents of thin air up at nearly ten thousand feet. Everybody left, and my bag never showed. After Wyoming the air felt too hot and thick and wet to breathe, worse even than Norfolk in July.

The baggage man stepped down from the hold and looked at me like I might jump him and steal the plane.

I said, It's a small Gladstone. Scuffed brown leather.

He said, Well, I've unloaded every case on board. But if you don't believe me, feel free to check for yourself.

I climbed through the hatch into the belly of the plane and crawled around in the dim, metallic light until I found my little bag tucked behind a structural member, sort of like a rafter, or maybe a rib if the airplane had been a dinosaur. I dug through the bag, and everything was there, including Long's pistol. When I climbed down and held up the Gladstone, the baggage man shrugged his shoulders and walked away toward the main building.

The Tampa airport was a recently opened WPA project, a handsome, sand-colored building meant to convey modern angular functionality and strength. It already looked like a part of the landscape and stood solid against the water and the humid blue sky. The low brick city rose a couple of miles eastward. Inside, the building still smelled new, limerock and pinewood. In a few years, tens of thousands of us mammals would override its crisp fragrance with our dank animal funk like the inside of somebody else's shoe, as demonstrated by walking through any New York or Washington train station.

I carried my little bag out front and raised my hand for a cab, and when I opened the front passenger door instead of back, the driver looked surprised and had to forearm-sweep a half dozen pulp magazines and a wax-paper-wrapped sandwich to the middle of the seat.

He was a little younger than I was, early twenties. When I gave him the name of my hotel, he whistled.

—What? I said.

—Ritzy, he said. And a bit of a drive. It's over in St. Petersburg.

—Too far?

—Not at all. Except we'll either have to go up and around the bay and back down or else across the Gandy Bridge. Steep toll on the Gandy. Fifty-five cents, plus ten cents per passenger. But it saves a lot of miles, and it's an experience to drive straight across the bay right over the water.

I thought about my stack of Long's bills and said, Gandy it is.

On the way, I told him I needed to get up to Estafa County the next morning and come back by end of day. I asked the best way to do it.

He said, Bus is cheapest, but it takes forever. That way, you'd better plan on two days.

I said, What's fastest?

—A car.

—Could I arrange that at the hotel?

—Yes, but also right here. I can drive you up and back. And give you a better price for all day.

—I'm Val, I said, and reached over with my right hand.

—Raúl, he said, and we shook.

LONG HAD INSISTED ON ME staying at the Don CeSar, though it was a little inconvenient since I'd be traveling north in the morning to get to Estafa County. The hotel rose directly from the beach, a lavish, slightly sad remnant of the Roaring Twenties, an amazing leftover, like running into a famous almost forgotten silent movie star at a gas station and having her offer you a place to spend the night.

I dumped my bag in the room and showered away the nastiness and glamour and physical assault of air travel. Then I walked outside and sat at a table looking toward the Gulf and opened a book and breathed air that hadn't been filtered through eighteen other sets of lungs before it got to me.

I'd optimistically brought a couple of recent novels thinking I'd have time to read on my several flights, but all I had been able to concentrate on was the roar of the engines and propellers and the misery of being flung about. So I started fresh on *The Postman Always Rings Twice*, and the first sentence struck me as the best in the history of literature.

A waiter, much more dressed up than I was, stopped by. I ordered a gin and tonic, a double, and gave him my room number. He asked if I'd care for a half dozen oysters, and I said, Absolutely. When he came back, I handed him a couple of ones as a tip, and he thanked me with earnest surprise at my lavish secondhand generosity.

Long had said, A place like the Don CeSar, you need to have a pocket full of singles and hand a dollar to whoever does anything for you so they'll remember you.

A dime would have been a reasonable tip in most other situations I'd been in. Maybe a quarter if you happened to be at the bar in the Cavalier in Virginia Beach or the Jefferson in Richmond and you wanted the bartender to like you or wanted to impress a girl. But Long insisted on a dollar for everyone, so I randomly doubled it just to watch the reaction.

I read and drank and slurped oysters dashed with Tabasco and left the saltines on the plate. The oysters tasted different from Chesapeake oysters but good, an expression of local waters.

The daylight dimmed. A dirigible drifted over silently, like a great gray whale against the milky sky. It floated out over the Gulf and then very slowly turned south and followed the coast until it faded out of sight. A wealthy middle-aged couple walked by arm in arm like ghosts from the previous decade. He wore a dove gray suit and a yellow straw hat with a pink silk band, and she wore a straw-colored suit with a ham-colored hat shaped like an upturned bucket. Their outfits seemed coordinated, but maybe they had become so synchronous that such things happened naturally. Sunset swelled over the water in a preposterous gradation of pinks and oranges and reds.

I read a few more pages but couldn't concentrate any more than if I were still riding the tilt-a-whirl airplane. I watched the calm progression of sunset. When the colors went to mostly gray and blue, I thought about Long seeming to like me and to trust me with information I did not need to know. If Long's wary entry into politics went somewhere, then someone knowing details of his complicated marriage could be a problem. And yet he was telling me all about it. So he might already think of me as a sort of aide-de-camp. I couldn't imagine precisely what functions of value an artist might perform for a US senator, but Long would need someone who could do things and be discreet. Be a good Boy Scout. Loyal, trustworthy, helpful, brave, clean, and reverent. It looked slightly like a direction forward for me.

After dark I went inside and sat at the bar and charged to the room a beer in a tall, graceful pilsner glass and a grilled ham sandwich. I slid the bartender two ones.

Upstairs I sat on the edge of the bed and studied the new prints of Eve's photos. I tried to find some hint of her thoughts, some message expressed by image alone, but she refused to communicate back. So I absorbed the symmetries and asymmetries of her features and the light on her cheekbones until I finally gave up and flopped over in bed and fell asleep.

AT SEVEN THE WAKE-UP KNOCK I'd arranged at the front desk pounded like a police raid. I cracked the door and said, Awake. I handed the bellboy two dollars.

Raúl was set to pick me up at nine. I showered and shaved and went downstairs to eat an astonishingly expensive breakfast. While I ate, a bellboy brought over a telegram from Long that read, *RFD 2 WCOOCHIE ROAD SOUTHWEST ESTAFA STOP BEST COULD DO REGRETS*

I roughly knew or at least guessed what he meant, and the only new information was the road name and Rural Free Delivery route number. The money Long had saved with his telegraph shorthand would have been far less than one of his lavish tips. So after breakfast, on the way out to meet Raúl, I tipped everybody I encountered with crisp new dollars, including a confused fellow guest standing outside the front door waiting for his own taxi. I'd spent twelve hours in that opulent hotel, and wished Long had given me a per diem instead. I'd have stayed in a tourist cottage three rows back from the Gulf and kept the change.

WE DROVE A COUPLE OF hours north through long stretches of empty cattle land, pine and palmetto scrub, citrus groves, blackwater swamp. The air coming in the windows became steamier as the morning went on.

Raúl said, This country in here, this curve of Gulf Coast all the way around to New Orleans and Houston, was the frontier before white people got much past the Mississippi River. Cowboys and horses and herds of cattle. Outlaws. The reputation is, it was lawless way back then and hasn't changed much. They treat tourists like highwaymen treated stagecoach passengers. If you're never going to see them again, why not clean out their wallets before they go back north?

Raúl spoke with an accent, and I asked where he was from. He said he was born and raised in Tampa. His family had come from

Cuba, but he'd only spent a few summers there as a boy visiting his *abuela* before she died. As a child in Tampa, he had learned Spanish and English equally, but in Havana, people had a hard time understanding his accent. Also he couldn't always remember which word belonged in which language. He worked in the Ybor City part of Tampa, at Cuesta-Rey. He said it proudly, the finest cigar factory in the world. He'd started there when his age could still be expressed in one numeral. Over time he'd held every job from sweeping floors to stripping out the stems, and then he became a *bonchero* and then selected wrappers. After that he became the youngest *tabaquero* anyone could remember, which was the last and most august part of making a cigar, the wrapping and finishing. The position came with a significant perquisite. You got to take three cigars home with you every day and be a big man.

—Seventeen years old, he said, walking around the neighborhood passing out Cuesta-Rey cigars identical to those the king of Spain smoked.

As we traveled on toward Estafa, Raúl told me that he was only driving a couple of days a week to make extra money because he was thinking about quitting the cigar business and going to school. He couldn't decide whether to become a teacher or a lawyer. He pulled a picture from under the sun visor—him in a dark suit standing beside a small young woman in a large white dress. She seemed very serious. The photograph made her look like she had dark circles under her eyes. Raúl said, I know it looks like this could have been her *quinceañera*, but Alicia is almost my age.

He had been careful about expressing any opinions until he realized we shared a lot of them, and then he cut loose. He told me he had dreams for the future beyond making cigars, and he was certain those kinds of dreams were sacred here in the United States. Hard work and equal opportunity. I listened and worried that he actually believed the ideal rather than the reality, believed all the *bring me your tired huddled masses*, the *pull yourself up by your bootstraps*, and all that Hutch stuff about education and effort being the sure path to a better life, that if every generation helped lift the next generation a single step higher, who knew where we'd end up. I tried to believe all that too, but here was someone with more obstacles in his way than I'd ever had, yet still putting all his chips on hope, and it made me nervous.

I set in to warn him, telling him that in New York and the other wealth centers of the nation, they use those convenient dreams to mash lower classes flat and build personal fortunes on that foundation. They slap their knees laughing at the naivete, wipe their asses on trust and ignorance. According to the wealthy, if we let those dreams become reality, we'd end up with some nightmare of egalitarianism that would drag the handful who run the country down to some frightening level of mediocrity, which was not what they believe our founders in their gray wigs had in mind. And lately the old reptilian Supreme Court justices had been defending the final citadel walls against the New Deal and the downtrodden poor who'd been crushed by the Depression to the extent that the justices had declared that an industry as geographically and economically wide-flung as coal, its tentacles reaching into nearly every town in every state in the country, didn't qualify as interstate commerce. A ruling almost as far from reality as declaring that air didn't exist. Thus, in their opinion, the federal government had no power over the coal industry and no power to regulate the humane treatment or safety or pay of miners. So apparently, at least according to the Supreme Court, interstate commerce did not exist. And in response to rulings like that, Roosevelt had been trying to pack the court with new extra justices to counterbalance the old corrupt justices, but the Senate had recently voted down that plan. And also, I said, the weirdest thing about the Constitution was that apparently the founding fathers had wanted a third of the government to be unelected and lifelong and therefore uncorrectably corrupt. Or else they'd been optimistic flower-sniffers when it came to human nature and its primary tendencies toward raw self-interest.

I finally paused for breath and Raúl turned his face to me, looking equal parts alarmed and sad.

I cut off my rant. Part of me wanted to press on, to set him straight about his land of dreams, but the other part of me decided against it. After all, the nation's big, beautiful strength had always been dreaming forward against the brutal, ugly undertow of reality, the violence in the heart of the human animal, the gluttony and greed.

Finally I said, I guess what I mean is be careful not to jump too soon. This could be a very rough time to quit a good job.

Raúl waited a long quiet minute before he finally said, For people like me and my family, it's almost always a rough time to quit a good job. You think I don't know what hard work and equal opportunity really means? Means I have to work twice as hard, and it still might not be enough. Sounds like you probably understand that already. I know what I'm up against, and I'll give you an example. People say the Klan runs all of Tampa—police and firemen and city clerks, all members. And this past winter they had a big ceremony in a city park. Four hundred in hoods and robes swearing in a hundred new members. Newspaper said the cross they burned was twenty-five feet tall. That's just one part of what I'm up against, but I'm not about to quit.

I said, Man, I'm sorry. I probably shouldn't have . . .

—Probably not, Raúl said.

ON MAIN STREET OF A town named for a conquistador, a man at a country store with one gas pump said, You want to go about five miles north and you'll cross the Withlacoochee on a low wood bridge. There's a fish camp on the far side, and then about two hundred feet farther you'll want to make a left onto a sandy road. After that, I don't know what to tell you. That road follows the river and goes halfway across the county. You'll have to ask around.

Raúl drove slowly out of necessity, dodging swales and humps and sinkholes. Much of the time we traveled at no more than a brisk walk. Spanish moss nearly dragged the ground from live oaks six feet thick through the trunks. Lower limbs fat as normal trees stretched almost horizontal, and a thick carpet of dead leathery leaves covered the dirt underneath. When we could see the river, it lay flat black and moved too slow to tell which direction it flowed unless you sat awhile and studied the things that floated on it. Now and then we saw a black and motionless alligator lying armored on a sand bank, soaking up sun.

Not a lot of people wandered Withlacoochee Road, and those few didn't respond to my questions by telling me how far it was to the Orson place and how many turnings and significant landmarks to watch for and that I should have a good day. Instead they universally communicated, vocally or otherwise, one simple message—*What shitting business is it of yours where anybody around here lives?*

We kept going anyway. Soon we came to two men, wet to the elbows with blood, skinning a gator. When I asked about the Orson place, they looked up simultaneously and stared until we drove on. A bald eagle glared yellow-eyed at us from a high limb. A little ways on, we stopped to watch a very large water moccasin move with great effort across the roadway. It had evidently eaten something large, and its body was stretched and swollen, a dark, heavy cylinder about to split open from just past its wedge of head to its comically twig-like tail. It moved slow and flaccid, like it needed to grunt with every few inches of forward progress. We watched it cross the road in disgust and fascination, aware that if it were fully charged up with venom it could kill us both.

Raúl said, Crazy state. This kind of thing is why I don't like getting far outside Ybor City. But since I'm a lifelong Floridian, I don't really know what living in a sane state would be like. No point of comparison.

Finally, a mile or two later, a man with a fishing rod over his shoulder and a pistol on his hip said, Orsons?

—Yes.

—About three miles on. When the road starts getting bad, look for a house on the river side of the road.

—Starts? Raúl said.

I DIDN'T KNOW WHAT TO CALL THE PLACE. IN VIR-
ginia, even a small subsistence farm would have had some grazing
for a plow horse and a few cattle. The house stood alongside the
black river, raised about six feet on stilts above sandy ground. If the
house had ever been painted, the color had weathered away long
ago to mineral gray. There were elements of a farm, but with little
evidence of edible animals or plants beyond three or four brown
chickens pecking in the sand and a weedy kitchen garden with
tomato vines gone black and withered. Two split-log hog pens sat
empty, and a small barn leaned so far toward the river that the next
tropical storm might push it over. The most accurate description,
rather than farm, might be a house and an indeterminate piece of
land out in the country.

I sat in the car several minutes until Raúl said, You're going in?

—Yes.

—I'll wait right here.

I eased Long's little pistol out of my jacket pocket and tucked
it under the passenger seat. The air was so hot and wet my back
stuck to the seat when I got out of the car.

I walked slowly and said hello to the house a few times before I climbed the porch steps. A purple mass of bougainvillea grew up lattice between the ground and the porch boards, and the screen door was rusty and hazed with pale green algae, a shade shy of chartreuse. Those were the only blasts of color not an earthy variant of gray, green, brown, or black. The room inside was dark, but I could see all the way through the darkness to a bright back door looking out on the river. I knocked, and soon a vague woman in a pale dress moved out of the dark and stopped about ten feet from the door.

She said, There's a loaded shotgun right to hand with birdshot in one barrel and buckshot in the other. The first is to send you running with your ass on fire and the second is to cut you in half. I can fire before you could open the screen. This close, that second barrel would be bad.

—A big mess to clean up. You'd be picking up chunks and mopping floors the rest of the day, yes?

The woman started to laugh and then took a draw off her cigarette. Her eyes were nearly the color of the house.

I said, Are you Mrs. Orson?

She waved her cigarette in response, a wordless message to get on with it.

—My name's Valentine Welch, and I'm hoping you can help me. I'm looking for a missing woman, or at least information that might lead to her.

—Plenty of people these days have family they haven't heard from in a long time. What can any of us do but hope for the best and wait? Sometimes girls are smart to run off and disappear. If you've got a bad boyfriend or husband, then a new life is a good dream to have.

—True, but you might know the particular woman I'm looking for. She might have come around with your son Jake.

—I know his name. You don't have to tell me.

Mrs. Orson took a couple of steps to a table and stabbed her cigarette out in an ashtray, then came over and lifted the hook from the eyelet to open the screen door and motioned me in.

I stopped only a few steps inside the door. The place smelled of mildew, damp wood, full ashtrays, pork fat. Out the back door, the river might as well have been a skinny lake, and its smell of rotting leaves and wet black dirt and reptiles drifted through the house. Mrs. Orson lit another cigarette and rested it between her middle finger and ring finger where she didn't have to exert any pressure to keep it from falling. It could lodge there unassisted until she remembered to take a puff or until it burned down to the webs of her relaxed, drooping hand.

Times in my life, it was unusual to talk to a woman with no makeup on at all. Seemed like Mrs. Orson might never have applied more than a tap on the cheeks from a powder puff. Her skin was a degree of color between honey and milk. There was a magnetism to her that I couldn't quite sort out.

She squinted at me and said, I just remembered my husband's out of the house. We need to be out in the open.

—Of course.

—You go sit there on the porch steps so anybody walking down the road can see us, and I'll get you a glass of water.

She faded so smoothly back into the brown dark that she might have been on wheels.

Through palmetto fronds and live oak boughs and hanging moss I could barely make out Raúl slouched down in the car, probably reading a *Black Mask* or *Dime Detective*.

THE WATER MRS. ORSON BROUGHT was a shade off clear. It tasted like sulfur and rust, a little like sucking a cut finger. She sat down three feet away and looked off toward the road.

Inside she had looked confusingly too young to have a son Jake's age, but up close in the daylight I could see she must have been early forties. Her skin was dry, parched, thirsty, and I could see the pleats in her lips and the hollows in her cheeks, which I guessed came from dragging hard on Chesterfields two dozen times a day since she was about fourteen. The skin around her eyes webbed fine in delicate and sunken arcs above the high cheekbones.

—What's that out in the car?

—His name's Raúl, Mrs. Orson. I flew from Denver to Tampa. He's driving me up here to talk to you and then back to Tampa.

—Gotten to be little but Cubans down there. And just call me April.

She paused and said, Flew? Meaning drove real fast? Or flapping your arms?

She reached and touched me on the knee to make sure I knew she was joking.

—Airplane, I said. Rough trip, or at least it seemed like it to me. I'd never done it before.

—Just to come here?

—Yes, to talk to you.

—About some girl Jake might've known?

—Her name is Eve.

—What about that pretty little bitch?

—She's the one who's missing.

—Well shit, she said. Right from the start, she walked in here and looked like trouble.

Her voice had the flutter of a dirty carburetor struggling for air. It took Mrs. Orson three limp paper matches to light another cigarette, and then she talked as she smoked, pausing to inhale and then speaking on the out-breath so that her words emerged visible in threads and blossoms of smoke barely rising in the heavy air.

She said, Around here there's two kinds of land. Sandy ground that drains well and don't hardly want to grow anything but pine and palmetto and scrub oak, and black ground that's rich but doesn't drain and turns to swamp in a heartbeat. Everything you plant grows fast, but blight and mold and scale and every kind of bug and snail grows faster than a tomato vine. Fat, beautiful tomatoes ripen from hard green almost to the point where they're red as a rare steak when you slice them, three days away at most. Then nasty green worms big around as your thumb eat from one side to the other overnight. Leave a brown hole like a dog's ass.

She took another draw on the Chesterfield and said, But you're not here for gardening advice.

—Like I said, I need to ask about your son and about Eve.

She said, People take off all the time nowadays. Who knows where they go. The world's all wrong. Everything's broken up and not likely to hook back together again. I wouldn't make too much of one stray if I was you.

—Even if I agree, I can't tell that to Eve's husband.

—Far as I know, Jake's her husband. And if he's not worried, I'm not.

April tried to act like what I'd said didn't concern her at all, but she looked puzzled.

I arranged my face bland and still as a cup of milk so as not to let on that April's confusion surprised me.

I said, How do you know he's not worried?

—I just do.

—Because you've talked to him recently?

April sat silent, dragged on her cigarette, and thought. The air and the river and the land rested so still I could hear her suck air through the cigarette and then the sizzle of tobacco leaves kindling.

I changed tacks and said, You mentioned that Eve visited here. What do you remember about her?

—I remember she left the bathroom clean. And she could sing. Sat out by the river and sang the songs you hear on the radio and sounded exactly like them. That's all. I might not even know her if she walked over from the road right now. Does she still have mouse-colored hair?

—Blond, I said.

—Of course.

I pulled one of Eve's photos from my pocket and reached it to April.

She didn't touch it, but she looked briefly and said, Trowel on that much makeup and almost everybody looks good.

I set the photo between us on the step and asked if she knew where Jake and Eve had been married, and April rambled awhile about how Jake's life had gone from bad to worse when Eve came along. Eventually, she guessed they probably married in one of those places they migrated through from late winter to fall picking fruit, which could have been almost anywhere between Florida and upstate New York. But she guessed that most likely it happened in a state that didn't much care who married who and didn't expect you to give the act of marriage more than a moment's contemplation.

April said, First guess, South Carolina. Or here in Florida, especially if they had a few spare bills to slide to a judge or a preacher. We're noted for how easy we are about getting married or unmarried.

She talked on about Jake like she was describing a dream or vision, a memory vividly reimagined past the point of reality and yet ultimately disappointing. Jake was meant to be her primary contribution in life. The masterpiece she'd given the world. He'd been the smartest kid in school, which April admitted wasn't saying much in Estafa County, but she'd been proud anyway. He left when times got hard, and then he got lost out on the road. Gone from her life. Now and then he sent a letter with a little money, always vague about what he was up to. The only real information was the postmark on the envelope. But by the time a letter arrived, she assumed he was long gone from whatever town the postmark showed.

—When was the last time? I said. And where was the letter posted?

—A good while back. I don't remember exactly.

—Could you look for the letter? Surely you saved it?

—Threw it in the fireplace. It made me mad.

—Why mad?

—The waste of his life.

—Did he mention Eve in the letter?

—Look, I can't keep track of her, don't want to, don't have to. It's in the Bible. You can't worry about every sparrow that falls. Look it up. Besides, maybe that girl's better off for running, or maybe she's dead and better off for it. There's worse things than dying. Who knows?

—She wasn't dead a few weeks ago. I ate dinner with her at her husband's house.

She looked confused again and said, At Jake's house?

I saw no clear way to sidestep such a direct question, so I said, No. Her current husband's. What I need to know is if she and Jake actually got married, and if so, I need to know where he is so I can sort out whether or not they ever got divorced. Trouble is, Eve has given the impression that he's dead.

I should have held that last bit back. April looked like I'd slapped her face. She didn't speak for a while, only looked off toward the road.

She said, I don't believe it. I'd feel it if he was dead. That little whore is lying for some purpose of her own. That's what you ought to be looking into. I doubt she'd even get out of bed in the morning if it didn't lead to some benefit to her.

—I'm sorry to upset you, but I can't believe she would lie to me about that.

April perked up and said, So you're doin' her too?

—No ma'am, I said.

It just popped out.

April laughed and said, I'm not even going to get insulted by you speaking to me like I'm your schoolteacher or your granny. Besides, she'd have gnawed you down to the knees by now.

I wanted to get back to the subject, so I said, I'm trying to find out the truth.

—Truth? God bless you, but you'll die looking for it. Can you prove to me Jake's dead? No. And you can't prove they're married or that they're not. And you can't prove they divorced or that they didn't. You ought to go home and quit bothering me.

—Mrs. Orson . . .

—April.

—I don't know what's going on. I've traveled thousands of miles doing a job, trying to find Eve for her husband. First Seattle and then here. I didn't come to upset you. The man paying me loves Eve and wants her back, but he also needs answers about Eve's marriage to Jake.

—Seattle? I thought you said Denver.

—I went to Seattle first. Not the point.

April seemed tired from all this. Her face looked as if a bucket of sorrows, soft as concrete dust, had drenched her. She said, Maybe that rich man paying you ought to wave a stack of money in the air, dangle it on a string for bait. That'll draw her back.

—I'm sure he'd be willing to give that a try.

—That little whore didn't fool me one bit, but she sure fooled Jake. I've seen many like her long before he was born, ready to trade their little nook for whatever they want. Sometimes that's simply cash money, but not always. She was that second kind. Hard to figure. They stopped here a week on their way from picking strawberries down near Plant City to picking something else farther north. Peaches in Georgia, maybe.

She tapped a finger on the photo between us.

—Look in that girl's face and you'd see she had big wants that couldn't be met easy anywhere. And not ever around here.

April raised her chin and looked at the lowering sun, a hazed disk behind the humidity, and said, About half a moon tonight. Then she flipped the butt out into the sandy yard and stared out at the live oaks. Their fallen leathery leaves and their shade killed off other growth in a circle corresponding with the drip line.

—Do you know where they met? I said.

—Maybe in a boxcar, or wallowing pumpkins out of a field. In a peach orchard or a strawberry patch. And I'm not talking them down. Most of those kids hit the road partly for their families, to make their own way and ease the burden. Jake didn't run off intending to be a bum. He left to find work and, like I said, every now and then he sent money to help us out. Less often lately, though. Somebody like you wouldn't know anything about the past eight years, how hard it's been to keep going.

—I know something about it.

She said, Hard times in college? Some teacher being mean to you?

She paused and then said, I've got a question for you. How did you know how to find us?

—A friend of Jake and Eve.

—Uh-huh.

She shook the last cigarette out of the Chesterfield pack and lit it and then balled up the paper and cellophane and threw it overhand toward a nearby palmetto trunk. It hit the sand halfway there and began slowly uncrumpling itself like a wounded dying creature. We both watched until it was done.

NOISE FROM THE ROAD, A car door slamming, men shouting. Whatever happened was happening on the far side of Raúl's car. I saw vague distorted shapes moving through two sets of windows. Heads bobbed above the roof and ducked down.

I stood and hurried off the steps, heading to the car. But I stopped when I saw a man and a teenage boy coming toward the house. The boy prodded Raúl in the back with a shotgun, and the man ranted in the volume and rhythm of a preacher winding up to ask for money.

The man shouted to April, This one was sitting out in the road looking to rob us. And probably kill us. He had a pistol under his car seat.

He held up Long's pistol as evidence.

The boy, sixteen maybe, poked at Raúl again with the barrel and said, A fucking Cuban from fucking Tampa, he said. I don't know why we ever let them in. I thank God I've never even been to Tampa. Couldn't pay me to go to Tampa. Surprised I didn't find a straight razor on him. That's how they do things down there.

The boy was blond and had on khaki pants and went shirtless, his skin a strange matte color like charcoal dust blown over chalk.

There was no fat whatsoever on his torso and arms—clenched muscles plated and fused, ribs countable as an anatomy illustration. His pants hung by a narrow belt from the juts of his hip bones. Pale gray eyes looked out from the upper corners of his rectangular head.

Man and boy registered my presence at the same time. They stopped and the man pulled back the slide on the Browning. The boy couldn't figure whether to aim the shotgun at Raúl or me, so he shuffled his feet awkwardly and looked back and forth at us as if trying to figure which of us needed shooting first.

I said, Whoa, whoa. Nobody's looking for problems here. He's with me. His name's Raúl. I hired him to drive me up here from Tampa.

The man kept Long's pistol on me and said, That's no letter of recommendation saying he's with you. And who the fuck are you to say whoa to me on my own land? You're nobody I know, sitting there on my front steps with my wife like you own the place.

April sat with her right elbow in her left palm and held her relaxed cigarette hand a couple of inches out from her mouth so that she talked around it. All those bony limbs arranged for defense, and her hand with the cigarette in front of her face like it provided deniability for what she said since Orson couldn't see her mouth actually saying the words. Either that or protection from a slap.

—This one here's been full of questions, April said to her husband. He's looking for Jake. That Cuban boy has been in the car all the time. This is the first I've seen of him.

Then she said, Timmy, lower that shotgun before you hurt somebody.

The boy drooped the barrel a few inches.

Orson gave the situation some thought and then said to Raúl, If I was to cut you loose, would you run and get in your car and drive real fast back to Tampa and not come back and make me shoot you? Cause that's what I would do.

Timmy said, Bud, I was you I'd take that deal.

—Yes, I will, Raúl said.

Orson flipped the back of his hand toward the road. Raúl didn't run, but he went at a brisk walk. Nobody spoke until the car fired up and drove away.

April looked at me very sad and said, I believe your ride's gone off.

Orson tucked the pistol under his belt and said, Let's go have a sit-down in the house and talk.

I listened as Raúl's car faded out down the road. I was abandoned, shipwrecked, now afoot. I looked at April and said, Do you have a phone?

—Sad but true, we don't.

INSIDE, APRIL MOTIONED ME INTO the living room. The first thing I noticed was a big braided rag rug, an oval spiral, a vortex, every band of its dizzying structure a color of earth and bark and fur. Floors and walls were old heart pine, dark as low-quality honey. April twisted a switch to an overhead bulb, but its harsh light only intensified the brownness. She sat on the sofa and motioned for me to sit next to her.

Orson grabbed a fairly full bottle of brown liquor from its place on the big wooden slab of mantel and then scrubbed the inside of his other wrist against his forehead until his hat sat pitched back, revealing a fish-belly inch of skin below the hairline. He took a drink from the bottle and then paused and took another. He sat in a stuffed chair and rested the pistol on the chair arm, watching me.

I waited for Orson to speak, but he seemed content to make me wait.

In front of the dark fireplace, a pale brown dog, blocky through the chest with a head shaped like a pumpkin and its ears torn to scraps, lay stretched across the limestone hearth. It watched every movement with its yellow eyes, but otherwise embodied stillness itself. Timmy sat next to it. The dog growled a wavelike note lower than the fattest string on a double bass, maybe even the fattest pipe on a pipe organ, a subterranean sound.

—Don't worry about Timmy. He's harmless, April said.

I looked confused, and Timmy said, Dog's named in honor of me.

I said, So it's Timmy the dog and Timmy the boy?

—Fuck you're stupid, Timmy the boy said.

Boy and dog sat together on the limestone hearth staring at me.

—You police? the boy said.

—No, I said.

—If you are you have to tell me. It's the law.

—I already said I'm not.

—I don't believe a damn word you say to me.

April looked at me and shook her head very slowly twice, as if submerged in heavy water, her closed eyelids so thin I could imagine her seeing shapes through them, like underexposed film or figures in a dream.

—Two boys was all I had, she said. And Jake's gone. He was the most like me, and who knows if he'll ever come back.

Then April stood and said, How about a cup of coffee, Mr. Valentine?

—That would be perfect. Black please.

—I don't know how you drink it without a lot of cream and sugar.

—Well, make it like you're doing it for yourself, and I'm sure it will be perfect.

Orson said, Anybody give a shit how I want mine?

—I know how you want yours, April said. I've been making it the way you want it for twenty years.

—Going on twenty-five, Orson said.

When she was out of the room, Orson laid his hand on Long's pistol and finally said, Tell me what you told her about why you're here, and don't leave anything out.

So I did, dumped it all in his lap like Long had told me to. When I finished Orson said, There's not a word to describe that level of bullshit. If you believe it, God help you, but I'm not getting paid by your damn rich man.

—Look, it's very simple, and a lot of it's boring legal stuff Eve's current husband hired me to find out. I'm not trying to get your son in trouble or say he did anything illegal. I'm just trying to find Jake, if he's alive. If he is, I need to know whether he and Eve were ever legally married and, if so, were they legally divorced. And besides, maybe he's seen her or heard from her. She's been missing over a month now.

—Let's set the dead shit aside a minute. How do you know she's not with Jake anymore?

—She's been married to her current husband for a year or more and she's told him Jake died.

Orson said, So you believe anything some girl says?

—Do you know something different?

—You don't cross-question me in my own house. I question you. You don't seem to know much about this girl. Do you even know her real name, back before she married Jake and this rancher?

—It might have been Eve Miles.

—Might. But you can't prove it. Can't even prove *Eve*. She called herself that when she was here, but who knows? Maybe you ought to start by answering that before you come in here messing with my wife and saying my son's dead. I don't know anything about this girl. She was a looker, and she was here a few days, and then she was gone. Her real name could have been Greta Garbo for all I know. Your rich rancher could have fixed up whatever documents and whatever name he needed to get married if he was in such a hot rush. Here in Estafa, twenty dollars could get you a birth certificate saying your name is J. Edgar Hoover.

APRIL BROUGHT OUT CUPS OF coffee with two soggy vanilla wafers on each saucer, and we sat a few minutes enjoying. The radio was playing *The Jack Benny Program*, but too low to really appreciate the dry comments.

Timmy the boy, out of nowhere, said, When the news came down that the war was lost, our governor told the legislature he didn't care to live under Yankee rule. A couple of days later, true to his word, bullet to his head. That's a man. And that's what kind of state we are. Florida. We have our honor.

I didn't bother responding.

After coffee, Orson began sharing the brown liquor, pouring us all a couple of shots. I didn't recognize the label and thought it had a faint taste of fish.

At some point of drunkenness, Orson pointed Long's pistol at April and said, Everybody ought to have to say what their first French kiss was. You start.

April said, You, dear. Who else?

Orson pointed at Timmy, who said, Some whore in Lee City, I guess.

When Orson pointed to me, I smirked and said, What's a French kiss?

April laughed, which was my intention, and Orson said, Don't think I won't shoot you just because my wife thinks you're cute, you little shit.

Orson set the pistol on the chair arm, which seemed to indicate the game was over.

I said, It's your game, but you haven't answered yet.

Orson said, Fuck you.

After a pause, sort of hangdog, he said, April.

ALL THREE ORSONS HARDLY MOVED, perfectly happy to sit in total silence for minutes at a time in between short bursts of questioning me. Time dragged forward reluctantly. On the radio, Duke Ellington played Caravan through a veil of static. I stood by a back window and looked at the river, attempting to compose my thoughts. The light had fallen into the live oaks and become choked out by the hanging moss. Venus stood over the treetops, bright yellow and immense. I asked to use the bathroom. Inside, a whisper of sound came from behind the moldy shower curtain. I pulled it back a few inches and saw a badly injured hen turkey lying half alive in the bathtub, breathing but not much more. One leg broke at a wrong angle and one wing too. Back in the living room, I asked about the bird.

Orson said, Weather's hot. I don't need it dead until tomorrow, and they can be fuck hard to catch.

Timmy studied a small homemade tattoo on the web of skin between his thumb and forefinger, a blurred gray-blue spider or coiled snake or girlfriend's initials, two of the rounder letters. He licked it to make it darker and shiny, and then he watched it fade back to the same matte as his skin.

The night was so still you could hear every frog and owl. Everybody sat and listened to an engine in the distance. Orson said to Timmy, That sounds like Ricky's truck. Go out and catch a ride to town and call that number Jake sent us. Go in the kitchen. The number's in the drawer with the change. Get a fistful of it, could be a costly call. Hurry.

Timmy said, I say we take it off him. It's his fault we have to call so far away. You hold his pistol on him, and I'll dig around in his pockets.

Timmy seemed a little disappointed when I dug around in my own pockets and reached out one of Long's fives.

I said, Where's the call to?

Orson said, Oh, shut the fuck up.

Timmy took the five and looked at the front and back like he hadn't personally handled too many bills that large.

—Wonder what else he's got on him if he's pulling out fives for a telephone call?

April said, We're not robbers, Timmy. Her voice carried a weariness that I guessed dated back to a choice she'd made when she was maybe seventeen.

Orson, his voice rising again into barking preacher pitches and intensities, said, No, we're not, but let's see what Jake says, if we can find him. If somebody comes to our place to rob or swindle us, that's another story. I'll strip him clean of everything he has and throw him in the river.

April said, flat and bored, We're not murderers either.

—I've not ever been pushed all the way to it, but come after my family and it could go real bad for you.

I said, I'm not coming after any of you. And I'm not saying Jake's dead, I'm saying that Eve told her husband that Jake was dead. I'm trying to find out what's true, and I'm trying to find Eve. This is not complicated.

The truck grew louder, and Timmy waved the five and ran out

the door and down the steps. The truck stopped and then started back up.

Timmy the dog lifted his head an inch off the hearth stones and looked at Orson and then at me. His head seemed so large and heavy that he conserved energy by not moving it much while remaining electrically alert to the current moment in the room.

Calmer now, Orson said, So this husband needs to know he has a clean slate?

—Except Val wouldn't have flown on an airplane all the way from Denver to talk to us if the husband didn't think there was a good chance Eve was lying, April said.

—That's one way of looking at it, Mrs. Orson. But the last thing he said to me, straight out, was that he loves her and wants me to find her and bring her back.

—At gunpoint? April said.

—Of course not, I said.

Now that there were just the two of us men and April, Orson made a show of checking Long's Browning for the third or fourth time to see how many cartridges the magazine held and working the slide as if the very simple mechanism had vexed him in the past but now he had mastered it. When he was done with his display, he settled the pistol in his lap. Outside, nature screeched, and the radio murmured tunes that bled into each other.

Real weary, April said, This isn't even a state road we live on. It's county.

—Good Lord, you bring that up about once a month, Orson said.

SOME VAGUE TIME LATER, AN hour or two, Timmy showed back up with the law, a pair of them.

—Jake didn't answer the phone, he said. But look who I ran into.

Orson stood to shake hands with the sheriff, and then said, Nice of you to come out, but I hate to bother you. Nothing here that I couldn't handle. He vaguely waved the Browning in my direction.

The sheriff was barely older than me, and he was short enough to make the pistol in its holster running from hip almost to knee look huge. The older man with him didn't carry a gun, and his uniform was simply pants and shirt, both khaki, with a deputy badge pinned to the flap of the shirt pocket. He held a long billy club relaxed down by his right leg. I was on the sofa and the deputy stood next to me. The sheriff and Orson talked in low voices by the fireplace.

After a minute, the deputy raised the end of the club an inch, and real soft, almost a whisper, said, Son, I hope you're not aiming to test me.

—Nope.

—That's good. Give a stocky five-year-old or a smart monkey the right stick and he can hurt you bad with it.

—I believe it.

—After teeth and claws, a good stick was the first weapon. This one has a lead core thicker than a carpenter pencil. I'd reach it to you and let you feel the weight of it, but not quite yet. Kind of fun when somebody with a pistol thinks he has the upper hand and then all of a sudden realizes his wrist is broken and his gun is laying on the ground. Funny thing I've observed is, they never go for the gun with the other hand. They grab their wrist. A stick like this can really mess up a knee. Crack a head like an egg, but that move's ugly to do. Troubling.

—Happens a lot?

—Twice in thirty years. But no worries, I can already tell we're likely to get on fine.

Orson and the sheriff came over, and I told the sheriff a terse, wholesome version of my story. Brought out the well-to-do Western ranch gentleman and the runaway young bride. Stepped lightly around the possibility of bigamy, which I'd begun to think could have been an invention of Long's jealousy, but I did mention Cheyenne connections.

Orson and the sheriff overlapped each other saying, What's Cheyenne?

Before I could answer, April said to the sheriff, He had a picture of that girl Jake brought around. I still can't believe Jake ever had anything to do with a girl like that.

Her tone was perfectly neutral.

She picked up the photo of Eve from the side table, thumb and forefinger touching only a corner like she might get soiled.

The sheriff took it from April and said, Is this girl Jake's wife that we're talking about?

Orson said, That time he brought her around here, they claimed they were married.

—When was that? the sheriff said.

—Couple of years, Orson said.

April said, Maybe longer. Sometimes it feels like a hundred years, and sometimes it feels like yesterday.

I thought about quoting Donal on the fluidity of time, but it didn't seem like the right audience. I sat and tried to construct a calendar of Eve's marriage to Long in my head so that Eve might have been in Florida only two years before with Jake Orson, but I couldn't make it add up. From her stories, it seemed to me that her hobo days had ended several years ago, before she got into show business and then married Long. Maybe that was one of those areas Long mentioned where looseness in regard to fact was a feature, not a flaw.

I said, Are you sure about your date, Mr. Orson?

Everybody looked at me. The sheriff said, You don't ask questions.

The old man with the stick made a sucking sound through his teeth and then whispered, There's your first mistake.

The little sheriff said, I'm not much liking you coming around here bothering people that don't deserve it. And you've got nothing but your bullshit story and a picture that looks like what comes in a cheap new wallet. That and your word, which amounts to nothing. Know what I think? I think you're running some kind of scam. You're going to say Jake's missing and then offer to find him through this girl, for a fee. She's probably in some dingy tourist court in Crystal Springs waiting. And then you bring her here and she tells some sad story about Jake being in big trouble and needing money to get out of it and get home. And when Orson here gives you the money, you and this girl drive all night to get out of state, Georgia or Alabama. You can't fool me.

He came to a dramatic pause, and then he said, Where did you come up with these folks' whereabouts so you could come around with your flimflam shit?

—Like I told Mrs. Orson, a friend of Jake's said I should come here if I wanted help finding Eve.

I'd been sitting there thinking these loudmouth rubes were amusing, but realized that, in fact, I had very little to back up my story, and whatever monetary and political power Long controlled two thousand miles away meant nothing here. Maybe the muddy bottom of the Withlacoochee River really was layered with bodies as a result of people like the Orsons and the sheriff getting riled enough to blink out someone's existence.

I looked at April, and she wouldn't meet my eyes. I said, We could call my employer out in Wyoming. He'll back me up.

—Sure, the sheriff said. Like I was born yesterday. You give me a phone number, and I call it and get a voice telling me every word you say is true.

Orson said, Fuck yeah.

Timmy piped up and said, That one he was with that got away was a Cuban.

The sheriff looked at me and smiled. He said, Cuban? In this county, if your skin's darker than the peel on a Irish potato, you'd better not be in Estafa after dark.

—He drove off before sunset, I said. And anyway, he has a good job and a family. He's going to school.

As soon as those words erupted from my mouth, I felt idiotic.

The sheriff said, Don't mean shit.

And then I made the mistake of standing up to argue.

Before I could say a word, the deputy hit me across my lower ass with his leaded stick. It didn't immediately hurt, but my knees collapsed. A nerve thing, like throwing a switch to off. I slumped down with my elbows on the sofa cushion to hold me up instead of curling into a ball on the floor like I desperately wanted to do. I felt like my legs had gone dead, and then they started hurting like the baton had been a glowing-hot branding iron.

The deputy sat on the sofa beside me and touched me on the shoulder and said, I hope you appreciate I wasn't aiming to hurt you much. Since we're friends and all, I didn't take a full swing and aimed for the meat of your ass so I wouldn't hit bone. Ten minutes and the feeling will come back and you'll be walking again. You'll limp tomorrow, but give it a week and you'll be fine. Don't be surprised by twin bruises big as saucers.

April said, None of this is necessary. He hasn't mentioned a word about money since he got here, and hasn't accused Jake of anything. I believe he's telling the truth. He's trying to find that girl for some man with more money than sense. There wasn't any reason to bring in the law.

The sheriff said, Just because you think he hasn't committed a crime doesn't mean I can't hold him in a cell for a few days to make sure.

—That's right, Orson said.

April said, I'm about fed up here. Y'all go on back to town and do whatever you do in the middle of the night.

—At least we can drive him back toward town a ways and make a point about him not ever coming back to Estafa County, the sheriff said.

—I know what that means, April said.

I said, I can swear on the Holy Bible that I'll never be back.

The deputy patted me on the shoulder as if to say, Good job.

April looked at Orson very intently. Sort of mopey, he said to the sheriff, We'll get him on his way at daybreak.

Timmy, sunk down in a chair in the corner, lifted his head and said, He comes back, I believe this little asswipe's time will have come. We crack his head open and throw him in the river. Next week he won't be nothing but greasy alligator shit settling to the bottom of the Withlacoochee.

The sheriff laughed and moved toward the door. He said, Yep, we can make that happen.

April looked at me and turned her palms up. I couldn't tell if any one of them, April included, was bluffing or not. I had no interest in hanging around there until dawn, but I couldn't calculate a way to bust out without Orson or Timmy taking the opportunity to shoot me right there in the living room.

Shortly, I managed to get up and sit on the sofa. My legs hurt but held weight. Timmy made one quick clicking sound from the corner of his mouth, and the dog moved low and soundless and very fast. He bit the calf of my right leg in the middle of the muscle. He gave one shake, only hard enough to suggest what he could do if he got angry. April snapped her fingers. The dog let go and backed off to the center of the rag rug and lay still and stared at me.

I pulled my pant cuff up, thinking I'd find blood, but the carefully calibrated bite had only left red tooth marks on either side of my calf. I figured I'd have a bruise there to match the pair I'd have on my ass.

ON PAST MIDNIGHT, ORSON SLEPT in an armchair with Long's Browning loose in his hand, and April dozed in and out on the sofa beside me. An hour or so before, Timmy the boy, apparently fatigued by his vibrating aggression, had said, Fuck it, I'm laying down, and wandered off. Timmy the dog stretched out on the cold hearth with his head between his front paws, relaxed but still looking yellow-eyed right at me every second. The radio played music that could have been the Paul Whiteman Orchestra, and then Bix Beiderbecke.

I said, mostly to myself, Why wait until morning? I'm heading out.

April heard me and stood, then stepped over to Orson. She eased the pistol out of his hand and sat again, sliding it under her thigh. She whispered to me, I might have just saved your life.

She leaned very close. In the firelight, she looked like an old woman and a young one flowing together at the same time with nothing in between, and her voice struck me like a drug. She barely brushed the back of my wrist with her fingertips. Her lips almost touched my face, and she whispered, If you'll be nice, I'll tell you a secret. It's something you really want to know, but I'm not sure whether I should tell you.

The only thing I could think to say was, I can't imagine ever being anything but nice to you.

That moment, April angling into me, tingled like lying pitched back in a barber's chair, the paper tape tight around your neck, the white foam faintly sizzling up to your ears, the barber leaning over with the blue steel blade of the straight razor freshly stropped on leather, and then beginning to etch clean swaths, sleek tracks from your cheekbones to the nape of your neck, lines of great precision because a miscalculation more than the thickness of airmail paper would lead to blood. The kind of moment that differs only by intent from the seconds before an execution.

April breathed her words more than whispered them. She could have been alone in a room making up a love song. Her words, though, were, I want that shiny little bitch out of my life and out of Jake's life. I don't want him getting in trouble over her. She's the kind that could tear you down to the ground and walk away humming a happy tune, no looking back.

I said, Will you tell me where he is?

—I shouldn't, but if it'll help get her gone for good, I'm willing. And besides, you're so sweet. About a month or two ago, he was heading out to Oregon for some government handout job near Portland. Building something. But that's it. Don't ask for more. You need to get going.

She stood and pulled me up close and tucked the pistol under my belt. She touched two fingers to her lips and then touched my face and said, So long.

Orson roused up awake and roaring drunk. He looked for the

pistol and then grabbed a stick of kindling from the hearth and yelled, Get the hell off my wife.

He rushed over, wobbly and still fighting gravity from his drunk sleep, but fast enough nevertheless. I was stepping onto the porch, and he hit me three times hard on the side of my head. Then I was down the steps and gone in the dark.

᭡

A BLACK NIGHT, MOONLESS STILL AND HALF THE
sky clouded. Limping and wiping blood from my ear, I walked
down the road beside the dark river trying to feel directions, as if
the rotation of the planet, the great east-to-west sweep, ought to
be discernible if you made yourself tingling sensitive enough. The
night pressed down so dark you could hardly tell where the road
was sometimes, except that if you walked in leaves and needles
more than a few steps, you were probably off the track. Insects and
reptiles roared all around. Shortly, the moon April had predicted,
not quite last quarter, began rising as if through a layer of gauze,
milky and vague behind the ghost moss. Get east-west sorted out,
and north-south comes easy, so wherever I was heading was mostly
west.

Off in the jungle, something sounded like dogs crunching
chicken bones. The soggy warm air smelled like soured laundry
and acted like a lens magnifying the moon beyond reasonable pro-
portions. Humidity thickened the longer I walked, as if the air was
in process of becoming gelatin. An enormous pale owl sat motionless on a fence post except for swiveling its head very slowly to watch
my passage.

I walked along the sand road thinking about fields of magnetism or gravity dragging at us and shoving at us, blind forces we like to believe have meaning and sometimes call fate or destiny, like poker players believing the random deal of cards has personal meaning, a judgment of the player's worth, a manifestation of a god called Luck. But the longer I stumbled through the dark, the angrier I became with Long for being unwilling to do his own dirty work, though neither of us had thought of this trip as dirty work when we planned it. Clearly, though, I'd been naive to believe as firmly as Long that the golden light of his influence protected me.

SOMETIME BEFORE DAWN, NOT A shimmer of light to the east, a rooster crowed, more a yawn than a shrill. A car came up from behind, and I eased over to the edge between sand and weeds to let it pass, but it hovered there, two yellow beams of light. Finally it pulled up alongside and stopped, a squad car. The uniformed man inside sat silently and studied me. He was younger even than the sheriff. Finally he said, I don't know you, and that makes me suspicious. I know everybody around here.

—I've been to see the Orsons, and my ride went off without me.

—And you know the Orsons how?

—I didn't know them. I was looking for their son Jake.

The deputy pondered and finally said, Get what you were looking for?

—Not really. They say they haven't seen him in a while.

—Just a tip, if you do find him, you might wish you hadn't.

—Why's that?

—Might not be what you're bargaining for. Anyway, he's not here. And I make a point of knowing when that mean little bastard's around.

He drove away without offering me a ride.

I walked on, and in half an hour, I passed through what felt like a ghost town. Random frame buildings spaced out by live oaks and palmetto. A few houses, a church, a couple of citrus-shipping buildings closed for the season. No lights in the windows, no one in sight.

FINALLY THE SUN BEGAN RISING, a vague luminosity across half the thick sky. The river lay flat as glass, its muddy surface sheened by early light, a black ribbon between the pale sand road and flared thick cypress trunks on the far bank.

From behind me, a flatbed truck came up and drove past and then stopped, angled across the road as if to block me. The driver sat with his elbow cocked on the windowsill. He looked at me with no expression. His possum-colored hair was cut an inch long and stood in oily points all over his head. Nose like a big pink wad of chewed bubble gum.

Eventually he said, Can I help you?

I said, I'm a little lost.

—Hell yeah.

—I'm trying to get to the Tampa airport.

He laughed one bark and said, I'm not swallowing that.

I revised and said, Is there a bus station close by? I need to get to St. Petersburg.

The man considered his answer, figuring the vectors of profit. He finally said, Have to go all the way to Lee City. And then who knows when the next bus to Tampa leaves. It'll stop in every little two-store shithole. Might get you to Tampa by midnight.

I looked at the sky, still cupping the light of dawn. In twenty-four hours, I needed to be ready for the rigors of a long day of flying back to Denver.

—Forget Lee City, I said. How much for you to drive me all the way to Tampa?

—That's a hundred miles at least. He paused to do the arithmetic and then said, So two hundred round trip. Seven hours driving. I'd have to charge seven dollars.

I said, Get me there by noon and I'll give you twenty.

The driver waved me in and said, Call me Huey.

We rode along in happy silence for nearly a mile, and then he said, That Roosevelt, I can't believe he's running the country. I mean, listen to him talk his sissy talk and smoke his cigarettes out of a fancy long holder. And that Communist wife of his thinking she's running the show. All they want to do is give everything to the negroes—he said the word heavy with sarcasm—them and anybody else too lazy to work except on the public dole.

—People building airports and train stations? Skyscrapers and bridges and post offices?

Huey said, I mean people drawing federal money that comes out of my pocket.

I didn't respond. We passed through a town with a few houses and a gas station and three stores. Through palmetto fronds, fragile light reflecting silver-blue from a still lake.

Eventually he said, How do you make your money?

—I'm an artist. Right now my job is painting a mural in a new post office building.

—Good God. You're on the dole finger painting while I'm working my ass off every day?

—Different kinds of work, maybe? How do you make your money? Right now you're driving me in a truck and I'm paying you a lot more than the going rate.

Huey said, Around here, we're somebody, my family and me. We've got three hundred acres and we've sold rights to dig phosphate out of our ground. Plus, there's a barge canal about to get dug all the way across Florida from the Atlantic to the Gulf. It'll save cargo aiming for Mobile or New Orleans or Houston having to go all the way down around the Keys and back up. It's going to cut Florida in half, which is not a damn bad idea given what the south half is like. The canal runs right through Estafa County, and me and my neighbors get to sell some of our land at a good price. We'll be living high. This time next year, I might be retired.

—And who would be writing that fat check? The government? And that's OK for you, but not for me?

He slammed the brakes, and the truck jerked to a stop.

—Get out. I'm not driving you anywhere. And I want my twenty dollars.

I stepped out of the truck and swung the door closed. Through the open window I said, We've gone ten miles. I'll give you fifty cents.

I reached in my pocket and held out two quarters and rubbed them together between my thumb and forefinger.

He leaned almost horizontal across the seat and snatched the coins and then pulled a revolver from under the seat and leveled it at me. He said, Look around, asswipe. I could lay you down in the road right now and never serve a day. Then he tried to spit on me through the window but failed. He slammed the long shifter into first and popped the clutch and roared away.

I started limping down the road again. As I walked I thought, Florida is an exhausting state. And Estafa County might be the bellwether of the entire country. If the Depression never ends, if everything keeps falling apart, crumbling like watching the geometry of the Pyramids dissolve grain by grain into smooth humps of sand dune, then maybe Estafa is already one step further into the future than the rest of us. Maybe its purpose is to demonstrate how foolish we've been to put so much effort into all the physical work and the airy ideas of building the nation, all the sweat and science and poetry and philosophy gone back to dust and mud. Estafa looks at the rest of the country like God judging your best works and saying, Not good enough. And then wiping it all away backhanded.

I'D WALKED ANOTHER MILE WHEN Raúl drove up. He leaned out the window and started asking questions. Telling me how bad he felt about running out on me, asking who beat me up.

I said, I'll be all right. No telling what those assholes might have done to you if you'd stayed.

—I've been driving up and down these river roads looking for you. I slept a little in the car.

—Never been as happy to see anyone in my life.

I walked around to the passenger door and climbed in and said, Let's get the hell out of this place.

THE GULF DROPPED AWAY AND the airplane pitched and creaked and rattled. Once we leveled out, the air hostess staggered down the aisle and looked at me and said, Oh my. Are you all right?

I patted the side of my face where Orson had clobbered me to see if it had continued expanding. The earlobe felt like a rotting tomato.

—Train wreck in Estafa County, Florida, I said.

—I didn't hear about it. Must have been awful. In my job, you lose track of news.

—I'll be OK.

She leaned in and whispered loudly over the propeller noise, We can't sell liquor, but if a drink would help you be more comfortable, there's gin up in the cockpit.

Up close, she smelled strange. Shampoo and clean high-altitude air and the slight airline fragrance of human vomit.

I said, Yes please. Gin aplenty.

She laughed and patted my shoulder and said, Don't worry, the pilots wouldn't miss anything under a quart, and besides, we have another bottle they don't even know about.

—I'm Val, I said. What's your name?

—Lulu. And I'm a registered nurse. A lot of passengers take great comfort in that.

STILL DAZED FROM AIRPLANE GIN, I walked into the Brown Palace in the middle of the night. I looked at a clock on the wall, and it seemed wrong. The hour felt vague, and not just because of time zone changes. The lights in the lobby were dimmed, and when I looked up into the high, vertiginous void of the amazing architecture, I wobbled seasick for a second.

I angled my hat brim low to shadow the messed-up side of my face. At the desk, I said my name and that I had a reservation. The clerk looked through his papers and said, Welcome back to the Brown, Mr. Welch. I hope you enjoyed your trip to Florida.

—Not in the least, I said.

I lifted my hat and let him take in my bruised face before I turned to reveal the ear. I could hear his intake of breath.

I wrote numbers on the hotel notepad and said, Need to call Wyoming.

The clerk said, It's very late. Or should I say early?

—Absolutely it is, I said. But I'm sure he'll take the call.

The clerk said, The circuits aren't busy at this hour, so it should get through fast. Go ahead and sit in booth three.

The telephone rang in a matter of minutes. Long didn't sound sleepy, and he didn't even say hello. He said, What's wrong?

I rushed out my anger and said, Whatever's going on with you and Eve and her husband and his awful people in Florida and your ambitions, I didn't sign up for this. I took a goddamn beating by the Orsons and Estafa County law, and I'm dog-bit. Nearly everybody I met offered to kill me and throw me in a damn blackwater swamp. I'm done. I'm coming up to get my car and my pay and to put the last touches of paint on the PO wall, and then I'm over and out. You can track Eve and figure out why she ran and anything else you need to know about her husband and his criminal family on your own. Seems to me you don't have a clue what this is all about.

Long left a drawn-out silence. I waited for an explosion of threats. Instead he said, Take a breath, Val, and some aspirin. Get some sleep, as much as you can. Don't worry about how late you get in tomorrow. Your cabin's ready when you get here. And keep in mind, I need what you're doing for me, and I'm guessing Eve does too. Also, no worries about the last bit of work on the mural for now. I talked to Hutch again and told him you're helping me track down a stolen Renoir and will be back to finish up at the PO very soon. And I also sort of agreed to fund a pet project of his.

The line went dead.

I'D SLEPT SO MUCH DURING the flights that I knew it would take a while to ease down to sleep again. I showered off the filth of air travel, and while I was still bare, I looked over my shoulder at the mirror. My ass displayed twin purple bruises as the deputy had predicted, and the calf on my right leg blazed blue and yellow in shades like propane flames. I took three aspirins and sat in bed with my sketchbook. I made angry notes about the trip, writing most of the time, but sketching some too. I noted Raúl's comment that Florida was the original frontier. Now that the mural was nearly finished, I had apparently wrapped around to the origin of the West to learn something essential about it, its core of lawlessness that spread across the continent all the way from the Gulf to the Pacific. The mood I was in, I saw the large sweep of American history as Florida's assault on civilization. If Raúl was right, and Estafa *was* the Wild West, painting what I was feeling about it right that minute, pain throbbing all over, wouldn't make an acceptably optimistic post office mural. But it was what I wanted to paint.

I jotted a note about what I had learned in Florida—*Jake alive, possibly in Portland, marital status unclear, crazy-violent family heritage.*

But it seemed that however much I learned, Eve still receded before me, fading into distant perspective. I couldn't hold a clear image of her in my mind, not long enough to sketch her, much less understand the paths of her wanderings and how she intersected with the Orsons, either for a brief time or all the way until now. I tried to draw a map of all her crisscrossing continental travels— railroad bum and cowgirl singer—but realized that I only knew a fraction. Probably she couldn't remember it all either. She'd said one night, I don't think about the past much. I try to take each day as it presents itself and let sleep put it away before the next sunrise.

Until she married Long, she had mostly lived on the road, possibly for as many as five years. I'd already crossed the continent on the diagonal from Seattle to Florida trying to find her, tracking her through her past. I thought maybe I should also go look around in San Diego and Bangor and then draw converging lines from all four corners of the country and look for her somewhere near the intersection. *X* marks the spot. Omaha, Wichita, Dodge City.

I wanted to figure her out, find her, answer the question of why she ran away from Long. Having lived fifty feet from their back windows for nearly two months, I could testify under oath that I never heard a fight. Even angry as I was at Long, from what I'd seen, I figured you could find a million worse husbands. And apparently Eve had done exactly that the first time around. But still, something had made her run from every kind of security money can buy, right in the middle of hard times that stretched back for years and had no sure end in sight. I wanted to know what that something was.

Dawn began to spread across the sky. I looked at everything I'd written, and it seemed obvious. I needed to quit trying to believe that Long's interests and mine were the same. They couldn't be. His were complicated and mine were simple.

Last thing before nodding off, I wrote in my sketchbook, *April said Eve sat by the river and sang songs. I've never heard her sing a note at the ranch.*

LATE AFTERNOON, I TURNED DOWN THE DRIVE TO Long Shot prepared to blow up. Most of the way up from Denver, I had imagined expanding on my call from the Brown Palace. I wanted to quit and quit mad. After all, it wasn't like I needed a letter of recommendation from Long. A good Kodachrome photograph of *The Trackers*, once I was finally able to finish it, was the ground I was willing to stand on, not Long's opinion of me and my work. I considered tracking Eve on my own, but wasn't sure I could manage it without Long's funding.

I hadn't even gotten my bag out of the car, though, when Long came out to welcome me back and worry over my wounds and thank me for what I was doing for him and for Eve. I went ahead and said what I'd planned to say. Except maybe less angry and more sad. More than anything, I felt deflated.

Long said, I understand how you might feel, Val. But Julia is going out of her way to cook that boeuf bourguignon you like so much. So let's talk this out over dinner. Come over the usual time. Faro's coming too.

And then he was gone into the house.

After Florida—a state equivalent to a hot towel from somebody else's bath flung sopping across your face—Wyoming felt clean and brittle, the light fragile as a flake of mica, the high air rare enough to be measured in the lungs and appreciated in its thinness, its lack of substance.

When I carried my bag from Eve's car to the blue-door cabin, the cowboys, especially Wiltson and Faro, thought I was hilarious, walking short-strided on my billy-clubbed, dog-bit legs and buttocks, the side of my face swollen and demonstrating every color bruises can be. The earlobe delighted them most. It was a fat red grape about to burst open.

At a lull in the jokes, I said, Wiltson, you looked worse when Faro finished with you.

Faro said, Apples and oranges. Yours was an amateur job. I can go for either instruction or for damage. Wiltson was instruction. I knew he had a cowboy in him, and I wanted to bring it out.

—Goddamn, Wiltson said. It took me a month to heal up. How bad would it have been if you'd been serious?

—How bad's dead? Faro said.

All the cowboys laughed, and Wiltson laughed, and I laughed too.

Faro said, Hey, what happened with that little Browning?

—About like I expected, not much help. It's in my bag. I had it taken away from me, but I got it back.

Wiltson said, Did you have to shoot him when you took it back?

—It was a she. Her husband fell asleep, and she eased it out of his hand and slid it down the front of my pants.

I got the big whoop from the cowboys I was expecting.

—Best way to retrieve a pistol I've ever heard, Faro said.

Wiltson said, Was she good-looking enough to paint her picture?

—I plan to do it someday.

—Whoo! I want to see it. I hope she'll be buck neckid.

Faro said, Wiltson, every time you open your mouth, it's like you're competing against yourself to say something stupider than yesterday. And you always win.

—Thank you, sir, Wiltson said. I'll mark this on my calendar. Red-letter day. Faro says I'm special.

WHEN I WALKED INTO THE dining room later, Long and Faro both sat waiting, three bottles of very good Burgundy already opened and breathing on the table.

First thing I said when I sat down was, I understand why you don't want to take this to the sheriff as a missing person case. The one in Estafa opened my eyes. He was as corrupt as they come.

Long said, The sheriff here knows my politics and I know his. He wouldn't be looking for Eve, he'd be looking for something he could use against me. Every detail would be in the paper here in a week, and in Cheyenne the week after. Not good for her, and especially not good for me.

—Yeah, Faro said. Our sheriff's a piece of work.

—You could hire a professional investigator, I said.

—Of course I could, Long said. But a lot of them are essentially criminals themselves. The Pinkertons aren't much better than a private army you hire to work on your side. Tell those guys who's causing you trouble and they'll go take care of them. Sometimes by killing them. Angry as I am with Eve, I'm not turning this case over to anyone like the Pinkertons.

I said, The problem is, I'm beginning to worry that we've been on the wrong case all along. Jake's family acted like they'd only heard from him a handful of times the past few years, acted confused that he wasn't still with Eve. They only met her one time. Whatever happened between her and Jake, I don't think he bothered to tell his folks. All I've got is that his mother told me he might be in Portland working a WPA job. Something's not adding up, though, and I can't figure where to go from here.

Long said, My point is, when it comes to finding her and answering all these questions, I trust you more than the sheriff or the Pinkertons. You don't really know what you're doing, but I can tell you have Eve's best interests in mind. And mine too, I think. I'm still trying to believe my interests and hers overlap to a great degree. I want her here instead of somewhere else, so I can't throw up my hands and say, To hell with you.

—Which kind of makes me wonder if you wouldn't be better off looking for her yourself, or at least coming with me, I said.

Long raised his hand and made a vague circling gesture and said, She might have run away from me and from all this, and she might have stolen my favorite painting, but not my most valuable painting. There's a message in that. She took the Renoir to hurt me, and she succeeded. I am hurt. That painting is an important part of my life, the end of the horrible war, a time when I couldn't imagine anything but death and violence ever existing again. But then, the surviving beauty of Paris and art and culture. The little painting sums that up for me, and in my mind the cash and the canvas are not at all equivalent. Eve knows that too. Still, I have a little pride left, so I'm not going to chase all over the country for her.

Frustrated and sore and tired, I said, So instead you'll just keep hiring me to do it?

—As long as you keep letting me pay you, Long said.

Faro reached for the wine and poured himself only an inch, and then Long filled his own glass nearly to the brim. Faro lifted his glass and breathed in deep and said, That by itself takes you off somewhere else from here.

Long and I agreed.

Then Faro said, Y'all can be delicate about why the pieces aren't fitting together, but this might be simpler than you want it to be. The assumption so far has been if Eve's husband's alive, maybe she ran off to find him. Could be she just learned he's alive and she left to divorce him. But what if she found him and it didn't work out the way she planned? I knew a woman in Tulsa who married and divorced the same man two or three times. Get divorced, marry somebody else, and then in a couple of years she'd run back to her first husband and he'd take her in and marry her again. Couldn't help himself. Their craziness was a perfect match.

—That's a lot of speculation, I said. What I'm trying to tell y'all is that I don't think Eve running had anything to do with the husband at all. I can't prove the negative, but I also haven't found one shred of evidence suggesting he's why she left.

Long said, Look, I'm sick of her secrets and evasions. What you may not know yet, Val, is that she lies whenever it's convenient. I've heard a dozen conflicting stories about their marriage. And if I pushed her to admit Jake never drowned in that river, I guess she could come up with just as many tales about a divorce. One minute she talks like he was the sweetest man in the world, and then the next she's saying he tried to whore her out in Houston or Albuquerque. She tells whatever story suits her at that minute. I don't know whether she convinces herself it's the truth or not.

I said, There's another thing we're leaving out—all your political business. It may factor in. The night those gas guys were here, she was really upset. Said she was sick of being used to get what you want.

—Val, name me a marriage that doesn't involve using. I've never seen one. Fact is, my chances of getting appointed to the Senate, or even winning an election, are fairly good. But not if I'm married to a bigamist.

—Wouldn't that sort of make you a bigamist too? Faro said.

—I'm no more a lawyer than you are, but I'm positive it doesn't count if she was lying to me, and I didn't know about it.

—And you didn't know? And you've checked with a lawyer about the ignorance part? Faro said.

—Of course I have. If she'd told me the truth about Jake from the start, before we got married, I could have taken care of it. But now that gets much harder. The thing is, while suspicions don't count for much in law, they rub off all over you in politics.

It aggravated me that Long was still more concerned about a presumed threat to his political ambitions than about where Eve was and if she was safe. I glanced over at Faro, and his face changed as it had done in the barn when he walked in and found Eve introducing me to the horses, a reaction not really of anger but something more complex. It was like something rising from inside Faro, a predator fish materializing mouth-first out of a muddy pond to swallow a frog swimming across the surface, a motion as effortless as taking a sip of water.

Not seeming to notice Faro's brief transformation, Long said, It's simple. The way I understand it, if you marry someone who never got divorced from a previous marriage, then your marriage to that person is invalid due to bigamy laws, which honor priority. If you don't know your wife is committing bigamy, then your own intent and knowledge become very important. But if your wife's first spouse dies or simply disappears, then you'd either have to prove death or wait seven years before he could be legally presumed dead.

Long paused and twiddled the stem of his wineglass.

Faro said, I'm nothing but an old cattle drover, but what I'm hearing is, like they say, Death cures all.

A long silence followed, and then Faro said, Don't people say something like that? Death heals all wounds.

—It's time, isn't it? Long said. Time heals all wounds?

—Same difference, Faro said. They say all kinds of stupid things about death. They act like a baby dying is unnatural, but there's no such thing as too young to die. Go walk around a graveyard and look at the dates on the stones.

We sat there a few more minutes, thinking.

Faro said, I'm not making shit up. I'm just saying, what you're talking about is pretty clear. If this Jake guy's not living, none of what we're talking about matters.

Long paused and then said, Well, yes. That is the bare fact of the matter.

Then he smiled very unhumorously at me and said, Now do you understand the differences between your skills and Faro's?

Another glass of wine later, Long said, Those Orsons down in Estafa must have been very different from what Eve's become used to here.

I half expected him to spread his fingers and hands and arms in a globular gesture like a king suggesting the vast scope of his holdings.

I said, They're more feral, at least. Almost every one of them ready to blow up mad at the slightest provocation. I took the dog bite and the billy club strokes to the ass in their living room. The ear occurred on the porch. Mr. Orson woke up and thought I was kissing his wife, and he hit me with a stick of kindling on the way out the door.

—Were you? Faro said.

—Not exactly. But she was leaning a little close.

I told Long what I had inferred from the young deputy cruising the swamp roads, that Jake was at least as dangerous as his family, possibly more.

—Do you believe it? Long said.

—Maybe. The deputy seemed to have strong feelings behind what he said. He and the husband would be roughly the same age, so possibly some old grudges echoing around between them.

—I wish you two would stop calling him *the husband*, Long said.

—Would *first husband* soothe your feelings? Faro said.

—Call him whatever you want. I want him out of my life.

—Jake's mother said the same thing about Eve.

Long and Faro both sat silent.

Eventually I said, What would the next step be?

—Let's think about it for a day or two while you heal, Long said.

LATE THAT NIGHT, I SAT in the dark of the cabin. The bunkhouse was dark too, and the only glow of light came from one lit window in the big house. I walked over to the barn and looked in on Pálida. Half asleep standing, but immediately alert when I spoke her name. She smelled an apple I'd brought from the kitchen and stretched her neck out over the stall door to eat it. I reached and moved the forelock out of her eyes and scratched her forehead, hard as a slab of walnut. I tried to imagine the movement of power on Long Shot as something like the electric and telephone lines drooping pole to pole. Sometimes that power ran directly between Long and Eve, and sometimes it tangled among Eve and Long and Faro. I had become tangled too in their paths of force running across the high plains, which maybe explained how Long had managed to cool me down and make me a tracker again.

AFTER WORK THE NEXT DAY, I sat on the cabin porch reading. Long walked up and said, As long as you're not doing anything, we'll ride. Little outing. The horses are being tacked up now, so get dressed. I've been calibrating the scope on my old rifle, and I'm almost there. We'll ride awhile and then fire a few rounds to test it and come back. Two hours, at most. I know your ass won't take more saddle time than that.

We headed south, open hills and the Winds at our right shoulders, even the highest peaks almost bare of snow in the heat of August. An entity all its own, the sniper rifle rode in a leather scabbard on the mount side of Long's horse. Long talked about nothing but ranch business, how to rotate the herds to keep the grass growing, how spurge was becoming a problem and how it would take over grassland as cattle avoided it and it spread. How, luckily, most of them recognized it was poisonous and wouldn't eat a lethal dose. Same with horses, except you couldn't always trust a horse not to do something stupid and fatal when they get bored.

Long said, You can try to burn spurge out, but a year or two later it grows back. Deep roots. Nothing but goats eat it, and I have no interest in being a goat rancher.

At some point he said, Hey, Val, I haven't seen you grab the saddle horn once so far. That's progress.

I said, Oh, I thought grabbing is what they're made for.

We came to the top of a rise with a broad view. To the east and the west, two widely spaced herds of cattle drifted along like cloud shadows. Even at a distance, now that I had learned to look for it,

I could see yellow-green stains of spurge here and there like algae blooms in bay water. We rode down into a draw and stopped at a pitiful, scrubby pine.

Long said, We'll shade up the horses here.

He drew the rifle from its scabbard and handed me a pair of binoculars. We walked downhill toward a thread of creek and then stopped at an almost level spot and stomped down the grass. He pointed across the draw and said, Spot for me.

I looked where he pointed and found a prairie dog town on the opposite slope. Naked eye, you could hardly identify animal life, but through binoculars the prairie dog hills and holes and the animals themselves—moving around and ducking down and standing straight up to scout around—became alive, a community. Long attached the bipod to the rifle and stretched out on the ground and settled.

He said, The recoil keeps me from spotting my own shots, so your job is to say whether I hit the target or not, and if I miss to see which direction I went wrong.

Except he didn't miss. Through the binoculars the prairie dogs dematerialized in quick red puffs, a magician's trick. I had a grandfather I loved deeply who died a hard old-age death, and I wished he could have gone in an instant, vaporized, instead of three bad years of doctors and hospitals and confusion and pain until he hardly knew who he was or where he was except that he desperately didn't want to be there.

Long fired a half dozen times and then took out a tiny screwdriver like you'd use on the hinge of eyeglasses and made one minute adjustment and fired three more rounds, all on target.

He said, Close enough. I'm done.

Then he paused and said, You want to fire it? There's a kick, though.

I said, I used to bird hunt in Virginia with my grandfather's twelve-gauge Parker Brothers, which I still own but haven't fired in nearly five years.

—Comparable, he said.

Long handed over the rifle and took the binoculars. I sprawled in the dirt and looked through the circle of light with the crosshairs and then, with no expectations, fired. It kicked, but less than the Parker. I didn't hit a tiny faraway mammal and cause it to disappear, but Long seemed satisfied. He said, Low and to the right. Couple of feet.

On the way back, Long rode silent. I tried to imagine a deeper purpose behind our outing, a connection to some emotion or experience central to Long's being. I kept to the few facts I knew and the stories he told, and only those bleak years of war and the glow of Paris immediately after felt right, felt like the central movement of his life. He'd never talked about some doomed early love consuming and darkening his life ever after. He'd inherited the ranch, hadn't built his wealth from nothing but brains and hard work. So, for him, just the Great War and then comfortable days ever since.

It seemed to me that Long was more driven by the beautiful present and the powerful past of his life than Eve was. Their memories, the horrors they had witnessed, must have echoed one another, but they reacted quite differently to them. Long seemed to live mostly in the space between now and then, while Eve craved forward motion right now, as little past as possible.

We were almost back to the house when Long said, In that stupid European war, I must have killed at least a couple of dozen better people than any of my siblings. Took a breath, held it, tripped the trigger, my spotter watching through binoculars as a life collapsed, came apart, disintegrated. Some optimistic fool once called it the war to end all wars, as if that were possible. Case in point, right now, those madmen overseas pushing us ever closer to the brink of a new war. I hope I'm wrong.

He paused and then said, Statistically, some of the people I killed over there must have been honorable people, certainly more so than my siblings. If any of them had any honor at all, I never saw it.

It felt like Long had more to say, like he was holding something back. I said nothing, but was reminded of his dinner table thought experiment from my first week in Dawes. Would I pull the trigger if someone evil needed killing, if I were called to make that decision? Does the good of the one outweigh the good of the many? I hadn't ever answered him, and he hadn't asked again. Now it occurred to me that Long apparently thought often about arbitrating who deserved to live or die in any given situation, and who got to be the arbiter. It also occurred to me that, in a way, after Eve ran off, Long had entrenched himself there on the ranch like a sniper—remote, hidden, keeping his hands clean.

At the barn, he handed the reins to one of the cowboys and walked into the house without a word. I wondered again why Long had invited me to reenact the war on a minuscule scale, whether his thoughts about Jake had begun to tilt toward Faro's simple solution.

TIRED OF WAITING FOR LONG to decide on the next step, I suggested calling Donal to see if he could clear anything up. I called from Long's office. The operator said the circuits were pretty busy so not to worry if it took a while before the call went through. Maybe half an hour, maybe more. She talked about the circuits like the weather, uncertain and beyond the ken of mortals.

Long waited with me until he got bored and left.

When we connected and I told Donal who I was, he said, God-damn, man, you can't be calling me here.

—You gave me this number.

—Oh, yeah, I forgot.

—I'm still looking for Eve. I've been to Florida, and Jake's family damn near killed me. All I learned is he's alive and might be in Portland. Seems like you sent me on a snipe hunt, so maybe you want to revise what you told me before.

Donal paused a long time, and then he said, Shit, I shouldn't have sent you down there. Now it's blowing back on me too. Jake's family told him a friend of his and Eve's in Seattle sent you to Florida to cross-question them. They told Jake about Eve's rich husband—idiot move on your part—and he's been here threatening me for information I don't have, but he doesn't believe me and figures he can beat it out of me. He keeps threatening to cut me. Already busted my lip so bad I probably need stitches.

I said, Jake's there? Maybe I'll show up at your front door in a few days to talk some of this over.

—No don't. The mood he's been in, I'm scared of him. About all I can tell you is that when Eve left here, she was on her way to find a gig singing in a nightclub or a bar in San Francisco or maybe Sausalito. Didn't tell you before because I wanted to keep you off Eve's back. But now Jake's about the worst I've ever seen him be. He's ranting that as soon as he gets some money together he's going down to find her and sort her out. And you and that rich guy too.

—You told him where she is?

—I couldn't tell how far he was willing to take things with me. I've seen him go too far before. I was scared. But all I said to him was Bay Area. That's a lot of space and about a million bars and clubs.

—Is that the truth?

—I swear. You can't see it over the phone, but I'm holding my hand to my heart like singing the national anthem at a ball game. So I'm telling absolute truth.

—Yeah, kiss my ass, Donal.

—Hey, you're the one told his folks there's money to be had out of this. Now he's mad and mixed up and he doesn't have a plan, but he smells a big payday. Bad combination.

—What does he mean by *sort her out*?

—Shit, Donal said, and the line went dead.

LONG WANDERED BACK INTO THE office, and I relayed what Donal had told me. I was worried and, in truth, a little scared at what I'd gotten into.

But Long, very cool, said, I fail to understand your trust in this Donal. He has not once provided any real clarity in this situation.

—I think he just did. I've never fully believed anything Donal says, but some of it has proven to be the truth. I believe him when he says Jake's planning to go after Eve and that he could be dangerous. Donal has known Jake about as long as Eve has, and he was shaken up. He may or may not know exactly where Eve is, but he told me somewhere in San Francisco. A singing gig. Look, Jake's after a payday. He's so broke I bet it wouldn't take much cash to impress him. I mean, if it kept Eve safe and got this guy off your back . . . ?

—I won't be blackmailed, Long said. Especially not until I know more. For example, you and this clown in Seattle and Jake and Eve could be working together.

I started to protest, but he put up his hand and said, Only a concrete hypothetical. I'm sure I can rule you out of that scheme, but I'm not as certain about the other three.

I said, There's no certainty anywhere in all this except that you don't know where Eve is, and you don't know whether she's in danger. In your position, I'd want to know.

Long sighed and flipped both his hands at me and said, Go find her and some answers too. I'll make a reservation at the Clift. It's central and convenient. If you run into Jake, try to get his perspective on whether he's still married to my wife or not. That's simple enough. But I won't be paying him. Not for information, not for silence, not for anything. As the cowboys would say, I don't owe him shit.

—I'll leave first thing, I said.

I PACKED THE CAR AND went to bed, planning to wake up before dawn and head out, drive hard, and be in San Francisco in thirty-six hours. But that night I couldn't get to sleep. Donal's warnings had unsettled me, and Long had too. He mostly seemed annoyed, like any threat to Eve hadn't registered.

My mind rolled over and over thinking, What next, what next? Find Eve, ask her how we ought to handle Jake, find out if she even wants to come home. But after that, what then? I should have finished the mural weeks before and moved on to the next thing. But what was that? Go to the beach shack and live like Sam and Randolph in Seattle except completely alone?

When I was twenty, I had thought there was a clear path through the world for me. Go to art school and meet interesting, useful people. Hutch had been more than that and would be again someday, but he had hundreds like me pulling at him for a commission. No telling where my next steady pay might come from, so I figured I ought to be more intentional about socking away the cash Long paid me, make it last, because his generosity could end at any moment. But it might not. If he considered me successful in answering his questions about Eve and Jake, if I brought her home all happy and settled, he might want to keep being generous. Particularly if the old senator cashed out. But what would continued entanglement in his life mean for me? What would it cost?

I jotted a note to Long saying I'd left early, and I drove away from the ranch into Dawes.

MIDNIGHT, THE FRONT DOOR OF the PO was unlocked as Don Ray had said. Only a couple of dim lights on. I sat cross-legged on the floor and looked up at my work, at what was done and the little left to do. It seemed at that moment to have missed the mark I had aimed at, but I wasn't sure exactly how. Hutch and his people wouldn't have approved the plan if they didn't see promise, and I hadn't really deviated from it. With creative work, surely doubt and disappointment are inevitable. If you have ambitions, the thing you create will always fall short of what you intended. The PO in Dawes, Wyoming, was not the ceiling of the Sistine Chapel, but still, something else needed doing.

I stood up and headed west.

IV

—

CINNABAR
AND AZURE

I SAT IN A DARK BACK CORNER WITH A GIMLET, but the Rose's had gone bad. The taste of vinegar instead of sweet lime overwhelmed the gin. There wasn't a stage, so no stage lights. A bulb under a flat metal shade hovered over the combo and cast a dim yellow circle. I held my glass to it, and the gimlet looked brownish.

Eve and two men in rumpled black suits—a bent-over piano player and a double bass player who touched the strings of a beat stand-up bass as soft and careful as if they might be searing hot—worked through a very quiet and sleepy version of a Cole Porter song from a movie I'd seen but couldn't remember anything about except this particular song, All Through the Night. Eve wore a black cocktail dress and held a cigarette like a stage prop, part of the show. Sometimes she paused and watched the smoke curl up into the light. She sang the song almost like a lullaby, slow enough that she could smoke with little interruption and so quiet I could hear the calluses of the bass player's fingers scrubbing the windings of the fat strings. She looked tired and beautiful. I'd never heard her sing, much less perform, but this sleepy late-night gig bore no resemblance to the rollicking shows she'd described from her cowboy band days.

Altogether a scatter of maybe forty people sat drinking and listening around the room, couples at tiny round tables and lonely solo men at the bar. Eve never seemed to look at the audience, so I wasn't convinced she knew I was there. For a long stretch, while the piano and the bass improvised beautiful sounds too dreamy to be called a song, Eve sat and sipped from a martini glass. Her dress looked elegant in the dim light, but I guessed that in daylight it would be shabby. They dreamed on with All Through the Night for as much as twenty minutes. It was a mood more than a song, and everybody in the room shared it. I tipped my wristwatch to the light and it showed two thirty. When they came to a halt, a dozen of us applauded.

Eve said, Thanks so much. Short break and we'll be right back.

She walked straight to my table and stood nearly behind me so that I had to twist around in my chair to talk to her.

—I've been wondering when you'd show up, she said.

I turned my palms up and said, You ran off without a word. People worried.

—People?

—Long, of course. And all of us. You could've been kidnapped or gotten on the bus with a cowboy band or something. First thing, Faro and I trailed bands all over three states looking for you.

Eve said, Ha. Probably didn't take you two days to rule out kidnapping by pirates or a cowboy band and lay it off on *something*. Donal told me John was paying you to nose around for me.

I said, Could you sit down for a minute?

She had to think about it, but finally she sat and a waitress immediately came over and said to me, A drink for the lady? Eve waved her away, but I held up my tainted gimlet and said, Could you bring me just gin and a slice of lime?

—No lime today.

—So, a martini glass of gin?

Eve held up two fingers to the waitress, then turned and said, Tell me, Detective, how'd you find me?

—Spoke to Donal and he mentioned you might be singing in San Francisco. I've spent the better part of a week searching bars and nightclubs. Finally tonight, jackpot.

—You must be exhausted. All that hard work. Though I'm sure John's cash helped make the task at least a little bit enjoyable.

I said, You've been in touch with Donal since you left Seattle?

She shifted and, annoyed, said, I have. He told me that all this shit has to do with Jake. That John sent you to Seattle and then to Florida and now here. Donal told me all about your journeys. My first year on the road, I traveled that far, maybe farther. Wears on you, doesn't it, Val? Except I was doing it riding boxcars and hitching rides and sleeping on the ground, not sleeping in expensive hotels and taking hot baths and flying in airplanes. So I know for real it's a damn long way from Seattle to Florida, across a continent the long way. What I don't know is why you and John are that interested in Jake.

I didn't say anything. She was angry, like she thought I'd wronged her for the fun of it.

She said, I mean it. What for?

Sheepishly, I said, Long found a postcard from Seattle that said something about back in the days, and then he started connecting dots, wondering if Jake was alive, trying to sort out what that might mean for him.

—If that postcard had been some deep secret, I'd have cut it in a hundred pieces and burned it. Talk straight, Val.

—He thought you had run off to meet Jake. Maybe because you're not divorced. Still in love or whatever.

Eve shook her head wearily and said, Idiots.

—Didn't Donal tell you any of that?

She said, Of course he did, some of it. But I wanted to hear you say it.

—It was a theory.

Eve said, No, it was the sun in the center of the solar system that you and John created. All I can tell you, Detective Welch, is you've been on the wrong case if you think I was running to find Jake for any reason. Not because he's my one true love. Not because John might be embarrassed by my first marriage if he sinks himself even deeper in the outhouse pit of state politics. And that postcard, by the way, was from Donal.

I felt foolish for not pressing Donal harder on that, for taking him at his word. I'd given Long's theory too much credit for too long, let it narrow my focus like a horse wearing blinders. Finally I said, So if we were on the wrong case, what was the right case?

—Oh, fuck you. I'm not telling you that. I thought you were a friend, but John's paying you to try to haul me back to the ranch.

—I'm not trying to make you do anything, and Long didn't hire me to do that. If he had, I'd have walked away. And I kind of wish you hadn't thought that about me.

—Oh, golly, hurt feelings, Eve said, holding both hands toward me and wiggling her fingers. I don't spend much time worrying about feelings. They don't amount to much, mine included.

—Yeah, well.

Our drinks showed up and we drank in silence. The pianist and bassist watched us from the bar, and I raised a finger in recognition to them.

Eve said, They're wondering what's happening. Not used to seeing me talk more than a minute with the drinkers. Or maybe they're just wondering if they have time for another shot before we start back.

—Look, I said, I need to know when you last spoke to Donal. Jake has been up there with him.

She said, I know. I called him a few days ago to tell him I'd found a gig, and he said I ought to keep an eye out for Jake, and also for you. Said you had somehow tipped Jake's parents off about my new rich husband, and now Jake wants a big piece of the pie.

—Donal sounded scared when I talked to him. Said Jake hit him and was planning to come sort you out. I was afraid he might find you before I could.

—Poor Donal's always been so sensitive. Probably Jake grabbed him too hard by his shirt is all. And for the record, Val, I don't need you saving me.

—Point taken, I said. Do you at least think Donal's right, that Jake's looking for a payday?

—Of course he is. Everybody is. And whose fault is it that he knows there's money to be had?

—Yeah, well. Either way, Long told me he won't be black-mailed. I couldn't convince him otherwise before I left.

—That would hurt his pride too much, Eve said.

She looked off for a moment and then said, John told me about how much the little Renoir would be worth. Maybe more now that rich people are spending so much on the bigger ones. I could sell it and pay Jake off that way. Simple.

—Not necessarily simple, I said.

—Oh, I'm sure John wants his little picture back. Losing that would have stung.

—All he's said about the painting is that if you've sold it, I should arrange for him to buy it back.

—Yep. Buy it. That's always worked for him.

—Eve, I don't know much of anything about the inside of your marriage or anybody else's. What I can tell you is that he sent me out here to find you and to find out if you're still married to Jake. The way Long sees it, you packed your bag, took a valuable painting, and hit the road without a word. He wants to know if it's because there's something back there in your past that would be very bad, fatal, if the governor is possibly going to appoint him to the Senate. He wants to avoid stumbling into a public mess and looking like a fool. Those are the kinds of questions he's paying me to get answered, not to drag you back.

Eve said, I don't give a shit about any of that. I've done my part to help him get what he wants so bad. He'll have to get the rest for himself. If we had a partnership—which, well, he doesn't know what that is—things might be different. The goddamn Senate. I wish we could be like couples who quarrel over buying a new car or having meatloaf too often for dinner.

She stood and threw back the last of her drink and said, I've got to get back to work.

FOR HALF AN HOUR OR so, the trio played two more dreamy songs to a dwindling audience. Then Eve whispered in the piano player's ear, and he touched a few keys almost randomly and then started a slow version of St. James Infirmary, which soon became a long solo improvisation. While he invented new music on top of the old—and groaned now and then with the effort—Eve came back and sat down.

She said, I thought of something. Where are you staying?

—The Clift.

—Up above Union Square? I bet John got you a nice room.

—Yes.

—Does it have a sofa or a stuffed chair?

—Both.

—Where I'm staying, it's a dingy rooming house down on the Embarcadero, two roommates and a gray, stinky bathroom down the hall. One cut above a flophouse. It's always bad, but it might be a really bad place now that Jake's trying to track me down.

—I found this club in a few days with only a vague tip from Donal. He claims he told Jake you were headed toward the Bay Area, nothing more specific, but who knows. That was a week ago now, so he could show up here anytime.

Eve said, The club's different from my room. Here I have Art, a real good bouncer, and he likes me. If I'd given him a signal, you'd have already gone skidding across the pavement on your chin. Plus, it feels good to perform again. I don't want to quit yet. Jake doesn't get to decide that.

—So what are you asking me to do?

—I'm talking about a few days, or however long it takes to figure out enough money to get Jake out of my life again. You have a sofa, so I could be gone from my rooming house and out of sight all day. By the time I finish singing here at the club, most people are about to wake up and start thinking about breakfast and going to work. I keep a little bag in back with a change of clothes, and I'm certain Art will give me a lift to the hotel. He helps clean up, so it'll be sunrise before we leave here. I'll show up at the hotel and take a slow hot bath in your big tub and go right to sleep. You'll wander around town and ponder the world and look at art and eat lunch. Go be you. I can tell you some good cheap places in Chinatown or seafood down at the water. I don't really start work until ten, but I can come to the club and hang around as soon as it opens at eight. So other than you maybe taking me out to supper and dropping me off here, you'll hardly know

I'm around. And we don't even have to have supper together. It's whatever you want.

I tried to tamp down my reaction to some of what she had said. *Hot bath. Whatever you want.*

I said, Another way would be for me to telephone Long. Let him know I found you, that you're safe, that it'll take a little while to sort Jake out before he sorts us. So you need your own room at the Clift.

Eve scoffed, almost a cough, and said, What a goddamn Eagle Scout.

—I don't want Long to get the wrong idea. And by the way, I wasn't an Eagle Scout. I was a Star Scout, just below Eagle back then.

She laughed and said, So quitting a notch below the very top makes you a wild rebel? You act like me sleeping on your sofa for a few hours during the day is going to make all the papers. Big scandal. Look around, Val, this is goddamn San Francisco.

Eve finished her drink and said, I'm serious. Can you do this for me without a lot of wheedling and questions? And without calling John to say, Hey, your wife wants to spend the week with me in the hotel room you're paying for, is that OK with you? Val, please step up and help me. I need this favor. I'm a little scared, and I need time.

There at the end, Eve seemed genuinely lost. Not acting.

I said, OK. Whatever you need.

She nodded and smoked, and I finished my gin. By then there were hardly a dozen people scattered at tables. The pianist and bassist were back at the bar, this time not watching us.

Shortly, the waitress arrived unbidden with another round. Lifting her glass an inch, Eve said, So you met April?

—She was the bright spot in my trip to Florida. Except for a couple of hours sitting by the beach at the Don CeSar baking my cuts and bruises in the sun.

—So she came on to you?

—Came on?

—You're not that stupid.

—Great God, no she didn't. She was charming, sort of sad and clever and a little sweet. Not a bit like the rest of the Orsons, or anybody else I met in Estafa County. I felt sorry for her, stuck in that awful place.

—So you *were* that stupid. All I can say about her is that she's held up to becoming an Orson better than I would have. I bet she gave you an earful about me.

—More or less, I said.

—And what do you know about Jake after all this luxury travel?

—Not much. April told me he's alive, that he's probably in Portland doing a WPA job. And then there's what you've said about him to factor in, that he's real sweet, which doesn't square up with what Donal said.

—Donal embellishes.

—Maybe, but Jake being sweet also doesn't square with the feeling I got down in Estafa. I'd been beat up and badgered by Orson and the two Timmys and the county sheriff. All of them except April and the dog had threatened to kill me. I was walking down the road away from the Orson place, middle of the night, pitch black, and a young deputy pulled up and warned me that if I found Jake Orson, I might wish I hadn't. Not like the deputy was threatening me too, but like he knew Jake from way back and was warning me, trying to keep me from getting hurt worse than I already was.

Eve sat very still. Eventually she said, Whatever I said about

Jake a long time ago isn't important now. And I'm sorry they beat you up, and someday I may explain what the right case was. But what's important now is how we deal with the wrong case, the one that John invented and you followed to right here, right now. I'd nearly forgotten about Jake, and he'd probably forgotten about me. All that year or two together floating away into the past. And then you and John had to dig it all back up. You went to Florida and told his family I'm married to a guy with money. With Orsons, that's like throwing chum into shark water. What in hell were you thinking?

—I guess Long was grasping at straws. And for the record, I told him it would be a bad idea to mention his money to the Orsons, but he insisted.

—He would. And you just went ahead and followed orders. Look, your job has been tracking me, and now you've found me. So, new assignment. Clean up the mess John paid you to make. But this time, I'm the boss.

—You paying, boss?

—It's a volunteer position.

After a long pause I said, Change of subject. This hotel where I'm staying is pretty nice.

—So you don't want me trashing it up, Star Scout?

And then that's when I made a leap. I said, I mean it could be a problem if you're in and out at all times of day and night. Long's paying the bills directly. You don't want him knowing I found you, so it's better all around for him not to suspect any of this. I'll have to tell the desk something. You're an assistant, maybe. Or my cousin who moved out here last year.

—Sure. I bet lying's your finest skill. Got the merit badge in a drawer back in old Virginia. And by the way, I think Timmy is really scary too.

She stood again and held up her index finger to indicate one last set, then walked slowly to the microphone. Nearly four in the morning, sitting there with a handful of other sleepy drunk folks, Eve singing lullabies in a pool of light in a dark room, I felt myself doing exactly what many had done before me. Falling.

THE FIRST DAY WITH EVE SLEEPING ON THE SOFA—
which really meant her climbing into my bed as I got ready to
leave—I asked where the Renoir was. She said it was safe, but I
pressed her. Annoyed, she finally gave me the address to the flophouse on the Embarcadero.

—It's under the bed, but don't go yet. The girls will be asleep
until noon at the earliest.

To kill time, I bought a more detailed city map than the one I
already had and walked for hours. I knew my way around a little
from tracking her down, knew the names of principal streets and
landmarks, but I wanted to be able to reorient myself if I got turned
around for a minute, to know a bigger and also more detailed picture of the city than I did, the kind of knowledge that comes from
walking miles and miles and staying alert to the cardinal directions. What I'd gathered so far was that San Francisco feels at first
like a fairly easy city to learn, so many landmarks and so many
angles of view toward the bay to reset your internal compass. But
then fog pushes in and you're lost.

After wandering awhile, I sat on a bench by the water looking
out at the brand-new Golden Gate Bridge, at the new configuration

of landscape that it invented. I counted back and reckoned it had opened for traffic not even three months ago. It seemed timeless already, a construction our age could put up in competition against the Acropolis and not be embarrassed. A geometry of steel girders and enormous sweeping cables somehow conveying lightness and strength at the same time. It stood out from the landscape, from the city and the open hills and the barrier of bay water widening into ocean, and it connected them with lines and curves, the geometry of the made thing, the force of art and imagination. In the larger sense, I was one of the first people to sit on this spot and be stunned by this brilliant construction.

My first thought was, how sad if it had been painted black or gray instead of a color in the range of cinnabar. The beauty and airy strength of the newly created bridge made me feel vastly and oddly hopeful. It was a bright counterweight to the darkness the Depression had cast over the country for so many years. Long had told me once that Michelangelo's Laurentian Library—the totality of its architecture, the stone and the air captured inside the stone shapes—created a powerful field of energy, like electricity but not electricity, and he sensed it immediately as he walked up the stairway, before he even entered. I'd never been to Europe, neither to fight a war nor to look at old masterpieces on my father's dime. But sitting in front of the Golden Gate made me think that if we, meaning our culture, could make this bridge-sculpture right now, bad off and broke as we were, then surely we could do almost anything, and we could do it gracefully, powerfully, beautifully, and functionally. Hope can sometimes be a sad thing, that or embarrassingly unhip, but I couldn't help myself. When I looked at that bridge, I felt hope in a simple and powerful form.

At a shop nearby, I bought two copies of a linen-textured picture postcard with an image of the bridge, cinnabar in front of a brilliant azure sky. On the first, I jotted a note to Hutch—*This may end up being our Acropolis. You ought to come see it sometime. Massive and airy all at once, an embodiment of this whole big project we're a part of, including a little PO in Dawes.*

On the second postcard, I wrote my first big lie to Long—*Searching every club with a singer. Lot of ground to cover. Will be in touch if/when there's news.*

EARLY AFTERNOON, I STOPPED BY Eve's room on the Embarcadero. Outside the building, a pair of longshoremen and a couple of maybe hookers stood by the front steps smoking and laughing. On the third floor, I knocked on a door and woke up one of Eve's roommates, bleached hair cut short, sleepy, wearing men's pajamas with the pants and sleeves rolled up.

I said, I'm a friend of Eve's. She sent me to pick up a few things.

She looked me up and down and let me right in, no questions asked. I was immediately glad Eve had convinced me to let her stay at the hotel.

The room was what you'd expect—three single metal-frame beds with sagged mattresses, a sink in the corner and a bathroom down the hall, clothes draped everywhere since there was no closet or wardrobe. I asked if anyone had come by looking for Eve, and the roommate said, Nobody but you.

I told her Eve wanted me to get her suitcase and clothes. The girl pulled a case from under a bed and picked through the scattered clothes. She reached me a rumpled pile and said, I think this is all hers.

When I opened the case to pack it, the little Renoir was right there for the taking, rolled up in a towel.

BACK AT THE CLIFT, EVE sat in the chair by the window holding a mirror in one hand, pressing powder onto her nose and forehead.

—Great hiding spot for the Renoir, I said. Loose in your suitcase?

Eve looked up and said, Where else was I supposed to put it?

—I don't know. Cut a slit in the lining and slide it in there?

—Oh, sure. That would fool anybody. Besides, who thieving from a flophouse would be interested or know it was worth anything? Not like it has a price tag on it. I told the girls it came out of my granny's farmhouse and had sentimental value. Some favorite half-blind aunt painted it.

She told me to stop worrying about hiding the painting, but I insisted we find a small box to pack it in, then put it in the hotel safe.

—I'll leave that to you, she said.

I sat on the far corner of the bed, not sure where to look. Eve balanced a little tin on her knee with something black and cakey inside. Looked like shoe polish. She scrubbed a tiny brush into the tin, then opened her mouth into an *O* and brushed her eyelashes dark.

Without stopping Eve said, You just gonna stare at me?

—Sorry. I've never seen a woman do all that before. Even my ex-fiancée refused to let me see her without her makeup done.

Eve jerked her head to look at me and said, *Fiancée?*

—Ex. Thought I'd mentioned that at some point. She eloped with someone else three days before our wedding. But before you start thinking I'm some sad sack, just know it was the best thing she could've done. Embarrassing at first, but ultimately better than if she'd gone ahead and married me.

—You are full of surprises, Valentine.

I TOOK EVE TO DINNER before driving her to the club, and I tried awkwardly to convey what I'd felt that morning looking at the Golden Gate Bridge, to explain the kind of hope that had led some of my friends to say that communism held the moral high ground over capitalism because it was based on ideas greater than greed and self-interest.

She said, I don't know, I'll have to think about that. Seems like about every system we've thought up contains enough loopholes for greed and self-interest to sneak in and spread like weeds. What I know is, people want what they want and they don't want to wait. Be great if they didn't, though. At least not all the time. Take Jake, for example. He wants the same thing everybody wants—money. Now that he knows John has a good bit of it, he wants a chunk for himself. Right now he won't know how much he wants because he doesn't know how big the pot is. But probably whatever I can get selling John's little painting will be enough.

I wanted badly to avoid helping her sell stolen art, so I said, There's still an option here that might be easier. Tell Long everything and maybe he'll change his mind. Pay Jake to go away. Get his painting back. Case closed. And if Jake won't let it stay closed, I suspect next time it will be Faro, not me, he'll have to deal with.

—Doesn't matter if John would change his mind. Case not closed, not as far as I'm concerned. I need to try it this way first, so quit trying to get me to call him.

I said, OK. We'll try it this way, then.

—I don't even know why I took the painting, Eve said. I don't like it. That girl looks like she'd survive about a day out on the road. A little delicate flower. I didn't intend to steal it, not at first. I was on my way out the door and noticed it. I hadn't had very much wine that night, but you and especially John had gone late at the table. I know what those bottles cost. A good portion of what I would have earned in months on the road got swallowed that night. I planned to leave the convertible in town and take as little of John's property as possible until I was sure what I was doing, but the little Renoir caught my eye. I knew it was worth something, and I knew I might need money at some point if I wasn't going to be back on the rails. To be truthful, I also took it because I knew it meant something to him, and I figured losing it might hurt him more than losing me. Besides, I figured if I sold it, he could probably buy it back. His misery wouldn't even be permanent.

—Sounds like partly you want to sell it so he's forced to buy it back.

—Maybe so. I didn't plan it that way when I took it, but yeah.

—That sounded genuine.

—It is. I've told John so many lies. He liked it when I told him Jake and I were living very hard and had been traveling together and taking care of each other from early spring to late fall. Winter was coming. It made sense at the time to get married. It would make getting a cheap room or staying together in a shelter easier. That part was true, but John liked the innocence of it so much that I started telling him some bullshit like Jake and I were Hansel and Gretel, lost in the dark, dangerous woods. Which maybe wasn't a total lie, but mostly. And then after that there was the showstopper, the tale of the big flood where Jake drowned. You heard that story.

—After you left, Long mentioned that you'd only ever said you *lost* Jake in the flood, never that he had died. That suspicion sharpened his focus.

—Not sure the choice of word was even intentional, she said. Either way, that story was nearly all true except, of course, Jake didn't drown. He washed up on the opposite bank and showed up at the remnants of the camp a couple of days later. He claimed he crawled out of the water in the middle of the night with the powerful thought in his head that he needed to go on alone. He said he nearly took straight off for Chicago to start his new better life but decided he ought to check and see if I'd survived that bad night. It wasn't like he'd had a revelation from God. It just seemed like the best thing to do. Show up and say, Hey, Eve, here I am alive. And you are too and now I'm gone. So long, see you later, good luck, goodbye. Which is exactly what he did. I was hurt, of course, but not bad hurt. At some point I had no choice but to keep going, moving forward, because you have to. Life is like watching a movie. It runs one way only.

NEXT MORNING, RIGHT ABOUT DAWN, Eve let herself into the room with the key I'd asked the desk to hold for my assistant. She stretched out next to me on the bed, and I got up and moved over to the sofa. Sleepy and blurred, she said, Hey, Star Scout, you'd never have made it in a tent full of dirty teenagers in a railroad jungle on a freezing night. Bet there's not a merit badge for that.

I lay there trying to convince myself I needed to stop falling for her. Then it dawned on me that I'd been doing it for months, since before she ran.

I said, Have you decided if you're going back to Long? Fawn said you weren't sure.

—Oh, you met Fawn. Sweet girl. But I don't know yet. Maybe. Possibly. When I left, I thought I'd be back home in a couple of weeks, but somehow I keep not going.

She rolled over and closed her eyes, end of conversation. I lay on the sofa another hour trying to piece together all she wasn't telling me, what the plan should be going forward. Eve had brushed off Donal's fear of how violent Jake had become, but even if she was right about that, the blackmail element remained, and I wasn't sure how to proceed. I went for a walk, hoping I'd come up with some other way to get Jake paid, but all I managed to do was convince myself that Eve might've been right, that selling the Renoir wouldn't necessarily be permanent. I felt stuck, caught in the middle—Long refusing to send money, Eve refusing to ask for his help, and no clear way to come out of it with both of them happy.

EARLY AFTERNOON, BACK AT THE hotel, I told Eve I wanted to take her to Coit Tower to see the new murals inside. I'd already visited them on my second day in San Francisco. Call it taking a break from searching.

I had walked first to see a Rivera fresco at the San Francisco Art Association up past North Beach, only a handful of blocks from the water. Rising high on a wall at the end of a long room, it was a disorienting picture within a picture titled *The Making of a Fresco*. Rivera himself was shown brush in hand, his back to the viewer, his wide ass at the center hanging off a scaffolding platform. The whole image a jumble of background and foreground— the subjects of the painting and the makers of it. Looming at the apex of it all, top center, the giant furrowed face of a worker in blue coveralls, one eyebrow raised wearily and maybe skeptically.

From there I'd walked uphill to Coit Tower, a beacon above me. My battered ear had mostly healed by then, but it throbbed afresh climbing that hill. Inside the tower, I quickly realized the thousands of square feet of murals were too much to take in at one go. I went ahead and sent Hutch a picture postcard immediately. On the front an image of the white tower, and on the back a breathless note—*Dear Hutch, Rivera fresco a bit jumbled but clever. Murals in Coit Tower overwhelming, dizzying. Could go back a hundred times and not exhaust their force. My dreams haunted by mass of faces in J. L. Howard's California Industrial Scenes. Can't wait to return to Dawes and finish up.*

Now that I'd found her, I was eager to show Eve a vaster display of what murals could be, for her to see that the small wall in Dawes linked up with a nationwide movement, that I was part of something important. I didn't give her the guided tour, explaining the influence of Rivera and Thomas Hart Benton on almost all the many painters, or tell her the history of murals back to cave painting. I hardly said anything, just wanted her to be immersed in the color and the images. Stunned by muscled factory workers massed together shoulder to shoulder, repeated monotone sepia faces dreamlike and powerful and frightening, and by the ways doors and deep-set windows of the tower had been folded into the images. Also farm workers in plaid and denim, and a prominently placed cowboy with hat and chaps and a pistol and lasso who would not look out of place working cattle at Long Shot.

We began climbing a steep, narrow spiral stairway barely wide enough for two people to pass. Eve stopped and looked back over her shoulder at me, on either side a twisting cityscape of Powell Street, crowds of people, faces everywhere, cars and buses, buildings stacked and layered up the hills. She said, I almost feel like I'm in the lobby at the ranch, except no space at all between the pictures here.

She faced forward, then turned back again and said, I can tell you the moment you fell for the power of John's money.

—I don't agree with your premise, I said. I didn't fall for his money. Turn the tables, when did you fall? Marrying him would be a clue.

—Asshole, Eve said, half laughing.

—When, then?

Eve climbed a few more steps up the spiral into the tight swirl of mural, surrounded by color and light. Without looking back she said, You fell before you met him, the minute you walked into the lobby at Long Shot and saw all those paintings and the house and all the other signals of money.

—Including you?

—Sure, if you need to be insulting. First-class ticket riding on the gravy train was what you saw. Maybe you and I both saw that. John has it to give, or for us to take. The difference is I have loved him, and you just have a boy crush. He has what you wish you had, the art and money and taste. And the experience. The stuff you thought was right there in front of you, almost close enough to touch before the crash.

—And you love him so much you packed a bag and ran, I said.

—You've tracked me thousands and thousands of miles, and you still don't know anything about why I left.

Without thought I said, Does it have anything to do with the Pacific Acceptance Company in Seattle?

Eve stopped and turned and looked at me with something new in her eyes, not panic or fear but something. She said again, You don't know anything. But this time she said it with uncertainty.

Four people came up behind us and pressed past in the tight space.

Eve said, I've got to get out of here.

She hurried up the last tight curve of the stairs and said, Where's the fucking elevator?

—It's over there. But we should go up the stairs to get to the top and see the view. Eve headed straight for the narrow doors.

She said, I can't breathe in here. It's like being buried in art.

When the elevator operator closed the scissor gate, she grabbed my hand and held it tight. I realized it was the first time she'd adjusted herself into even a slightly reliant posture to me. Every breath she drew, she nearly panted. The only word she said was the silver name on the metal threshold of the elevator—Otis. When we reached the bottom, she shouldered through the opening gate and rushed outside.

We sat on a bench and looked across the city and the bay. Eve closed her eyes and took breaths that became longer and deeper and slower. The sky was not blue and not cloudy, but bright and luminous like a pearl. Out past the Golden Gate at the edge of the Pacific, a wall of dark fog stood ominous as an approaching storm.

When she eased down, Eve said, What do you know about the acceptance thing? Don't be cagey. Tell me.

—If you'll do the same.

She touched my hand and said, I can't promise that yet.

I made no promises either, but I told her what I knew. That in Seattle I found a business card in Donal's squatter mansion that had what looked like her handwriting on the back. He said he didn't know anything about it, that he got paid to distribute all kinds of business cards around Seattle. I told her I assumed she'd been looking for a loan, maybe for a car. I told her about the strangeness of the office and the threat if I didn't leave. And that was all I knew. Questions but no answers. Donal had been entirely unhelpful.

Eve said, That's Donal. You can always trust him half the time.

—Exactly, but I like him fine, except when he had a pistol pointed at me.

—Don't take it personal. He's the same with everybody, gets excited and acts stupid.

—So what was that office?

She thought a minute and then said, Look, after I left Dawes and went to Seattle, I was there with Donal and Fawn for a week or so. I had something to do and I did it and then I left. That office isn't important. What's important is that you and John decided I ran off to find Jake, and then what? Accidentally fell back in love because I felt more at home with my hobo husband? Because I'm crude and not educated, not in on some kind of secret code like you and John and your kind of people are?

—No, Eve. I don't believe Long thinks you're crude or any of that, and I know I don't either. What he does care about is you being married to two people at the same time. Partially because there's a law against it.

—You can say the word. I know it.

I didn't say anything.

Eve said, It was more complicated than that.

—It would be.

—You want to hear or just be an asshole? I'm good either way.

I turned my palms up and said, Shoot.

—On second thought, I don't believe I will.

I backed down a bit and said, Look, Long found something that made sense to him and stuck with it. The longer I tracked you, though, the more I suspected you ran for a completely different reason. In particular, I've been wondering about that dinner with the gas guys. How upset you were. You kissed me that night and a week later you were gone.

—You remember that?

—I sure do.

She touched my hand and said, Of course you do. I'd had a

Nembutal and wine and then the whiskey I asked you to bring from the kitchen. And also, I'd really been wanting to kiss you. So I did. As for that night and also right now, all I'll say is that the first thing you learn as a hobo is never start looking way down the road. Take one problem at a time. Keep it simple. First problem we've got to solve is Jake. I'll deal with why I'm upset with John later, if I decide to go back to the ranch.

EVE STILL WASN'T TELLING THE whole truth, maybe not even half the truth, but I couldn't sort out why. So the next morning, I called Donal from a booth in the hotel lobby. When he realized it was me he said, Goddamn, why do I ever pick this son of a bitch up? I wish the phone company would cut it off, but it keeps on working.

I said, Turns out you're the one who sent that postcard to Eve. She told me. So now I've got a question, and don't lie to me. You know I'll find out if you do. I need to know, what did Eve need help with? The postcard said you could help.

—Yeah, hard to say. That was, what, two or three months ago now? Maybe last winter?

—Come on, Donal. Think.

—Shit, man. You are trouble to know.

—Don't make this complicated. When she got in touch, did she say specifically what she needed help with? Did it have anything to do with Jake, or was it something else entirely?

The line hissed a few seconds and then Donal said, Well, man, you know, sometimes it takes asking a question just the right way to get the answer you need. Buddha might of said that. Or Jesus, probably. So thinking back, Eve coming here had nothing to do with Jake. You're the one who brought him up, and I went along to keep you off Eve's back. I told you that already, but you never do believe me. As for what she needed help with, I can't recall exactly. But hey, you're there with her—why don't you ask her yourself? Straight from the source.

—I've asked, but she's not really answering, I said.

—Then maybe it's not my place or yours to speculate if she doesn't want to clarify things herself. Sometimes you've got to swing with it, but probably you won't. I guess I could look around for Eve's letter, but this place is a damn mess. The deal with Fawn was she would straighten things up a little now and then in exchange for a place to stay. But she sleeps and plays the piano about a fifty-fifty amount of time. We're OK, though. We sell stuff from the house to buy groceries, and there's still lots of stuff left. No worries. We're not even halfway into the wine and liquor.

I said, Save me a little of that champagne we had when I was there.

—Yeah, I'll do that. A case with your name on it. Come see me, OK?

—Maybe someday, I said.

—Oh hey, any sign of Jake yet?

—Nope.

—Huh, Donal said. Figured he'd be in a big hurry.

I sat in the booth awhile after we hung up. Seemed like Donal had landed on some wisdom in there about speculating Eve's reasons for running. After all, the whole mess with Jake had been brought on by Long's incorrect theory. Eve had seemed so close to explaining outside of Coit Tower, but I'd pushed too hard, and she clammed up. So I figured I ought to take a step back, get out of the way so Eve could run the show for a while. Quit playing Detective Welch.

~W~

IT HAPPENED LIKE FOOTFALLS BEHIND YOU IN the dark, the sense of being watched.

Third day with Eve, we took a cab instead of her car from a restaurant to the club. I had felt jangled and tense all day, and I wanted to wear myself out walking all the way back from the club in North Beach through Chinatown to Union Square and up Geary to the hotel.

I fell asleep on top of the covers with my clothes on and the radio playing sleepy nighttime voices and quiet music.

A brisk knock on the door woke me up, and immediately a voice said, Telegram for Mr. Welch.

I opened the door, and a man shoved me hard farther back into the room. He held a knife in his hand. He said, Go stretch out on that sofa right now.

I backed to the sofa and sat down and looked at him. He was a little thick across the brow and the bridge of his nose, just like both Timmys.

I said, Jake Orson? There's a family resemblance.

—I told you to lie goddamn down.

—When I was in Estafa, your father and little brother kept

telling me to do things or else they'd throw me in the river for the alligators.

Jake gave on the point of my lying down. He sat in the chair and rested the knife on the chair arm and studied me.

He said, Hard to believe. You fell for the oldest trick in the book. God, you're stupid. *Telegram for Mr. Welch.*

—You don't look a bit like your mother, I said.

—What about my mother? Don't talk about my goddamn mother. I hear you were kind of forward with her, but it could be she was kind of forward with you and you didn't crowd in on that and acted like a stupid fucking gentleman. So I'm giving you one pass for not making a move on my mother.

He held up one forefinger in illustration of his generosity.

I said, Get on to the blackmail business.

—OK, yeah. You can call it blackmailing, stealing, grifting, whatever. Or you could call it a normal sale of an item of information for a certain amount of cash. What do you call how you're getting money out of Long? How different is your way from my way? Or Eve's way? Are you two working together or playing each other?

I didn't answer that.

Jake said, You know what I think you are?

—It doesn't matter what you think I am.

—It will, buddy, it will. You keep pushing and being stupid in your speech, then there'll come a point where the only thing that matters is what I think you are. Picture yourself kissing my ass. Bad day, yeah? Then picture me taking you both—you and Eve—on a ride out to the desert. There's places out there nobody has ever been to. Very useful places. And if you're counting on my old feelings toward Eve to make me go easy, well, that won't happen. Not for either of you if you get in my way. I move on easy, and Eve made it even easier one time on the street in Gallup doing something stupid in front of a crowd before a show. I don't let go of somebody shaming me.

—So, you move on easy or you don't let go?

Jake looked confused for a beat, and then he said, Never can tell, buddy. That's my point.

He sat there awhile with his eyes down and his knife up. He said, Eve's real good at moving on. I don't know if it's a talent she was born with or if it's a skill she learned. Whatever feelings I felt about Eve came on strong, but I nearly died in a flood once, and when I crawled out of the water, I was sure that she would leave me behind someday and that I should go ahead and leave her first.

—Those are old grievances. Right now what are you wanting?

—You mean what will it take to get me out of the middle of your sweet little scam?

—Most people would see what I do for Long as a job. Pay for work.

—Yep. I don't have much experience with straight-up real jobs, but I hear most of them include fucking the boss's wife. Do you get overtime pay when she spends the night?

I wanted to take him apart like Faro did Wiltson. Instead I tried to stare him down but failed. He presented a blank predatory visage, no reasoning, no possibility of negotiation, just locked-in aggression. I realized he'd been watching us for days, learning our patterns.

Jake said, Eve was easy to track down but hard to get alone without causing a scene, so I went the other way, and you were stupid easy. You sure do walk around a lot. Tonight I trailed you all the way through Chinatown. I wasn't twenty feet back and you never looked around once, never even scratched the back of your neck to show you felt me following back there.

I had felt him following. All day, maybe. I just hadn't known what I was feeling.

I said, You planning to get to the point?

—Sure am, Jake said. Thanks to you and my old pal Donal, I know Eve's other husband has money, and I'm going after some of it just like you two. I can fuck up his life in all kinds of ways, and I have all kinds of stories, some of them even true. I could be awfully entertaining. Ask Eve.

I said, The way I've heard it, you got married in a hurry on the road. Probably no documents. So maybe not binding.

—Not how I remember it. Besides, even if the paperwork wasn't perfect, and who's to say it wasn't, it would still look bad printed in the papers. So a lot of questions remain. I think those questions get me a ticket to the big table. I'll let you two grifters sort it out with your boss until I get bored waiting, and then I'm cashing in that ticket. Tell that to Eve.

He folded his knife and walked out the door.

EVE GOT TO THE ROOM early, gray dawn. She knocked two taps as usual and then used her key. She'd barely closed the door before she said, all cheerful, Busy night tonight. Lots of tips. Crowd stayed awake later than normal. Wish you'd seen it.

She went straight to the bathroom and started running a hot bath. Through the open doorway she said, I need it scalding. I feel filthy.

Foggy sunrise filtered through the curtains.

Finally I said, Jake stopped by for a visit. Jake and his knife.

Eve didn't say anything.

—He wants money, of course. So we need to get serious about selling this painting if that's how you want to do it. Sounds like he's holding a grudge over something he thinks you did in New Mexico.

All she said was, Shit.

She kept getting ready for her bath. Heavy, wet air drifted into the room through the open door. I stretched out on the sofa, and Eve settled into the tub. I could see only the crown of her wet hair above the curved rim of porcelain.

She breathed deep and then said, I saw him once after he left me beside that flooded river. Not long before I met John. I've never told anybody this story. Gallup, New Mexico, on a Saturday night in summer. You have to see it to believe it. Route 66 goes roaring right through town, and the cars are bumper to bumper both directions, and the sidewalks are full of cowboys and Navajo and tourists. If you were playing there on a Saturday and your band was any good, the dances were huge. Shows like those, they're something else. A thousand people coupled up, moving all together like a big flock of birds to the music you're playing. If I was singing lead, I could take a step toward the front of the stage and look to one side or the other or sweep my arm one way and the dancers would move in that direction like a wave. No feeling like it.

One time right before one of those big shows, the band was getting off the bus from the hotel. People milled around on the sidewalk to see us unload. That didn't happen too much. When I got off in my fringed pink-and-white cowgirl outfit and my stage makeup on thick, I felt like a movie star. Teenage girls asked me to sign their autograph books. I didn't spot Jake in the crowd, wasn't looking for him. He didn't come running at me, thrilled to know me. He just lifted a finger to draw my eye as if to say, I'm here. He looked beat. I went over and hugged him and kissed him on the cheek like an old friend, leaving a big red lip-smear across the side of his face. A few of the teenagers applauded. Then I made the fool move of reaching into my little fringed purse and pulling out a twenty and shoving it at him. I was probably a little lit up with drinks and nerves before a big show. He waved the bill away and said, Slipping a couple of ones or maybe even a five would be welcome help from an old friend because things are rough right now. But a twenty? Fuck you, Eve. I'm not applying to be your full-time whore. I should have walked away and let you die in the desert that time. Remember in Arizona, you were sick and a bull threw us off the train? Twenty miles to the next town and a hundred degrees? All I had to do was walk away, and I'd have been done with you forever. He let that soak in, and then he turned around and disappeared into the crowds on the sidewalk.

Water splashed as Eve got out of the tub. She came into the room wrapped in towels, one for her and one for her hair. She stopped beside the couch and looked down at me. Her skin was pink and she smelled like lavender soap.

—Part of me knew what I was doing in front of that crowd, she said. So some of this is on me, and I'll claim my part. But it wouldn't have been enough reason to hunt me down if John hadn't sent you on Jake's trail.

She walked to the bed and pulled the covers back and climbed in. She said, Go and do for a few hours, Val, whatever it is you do. Then come back about two and take me to lunch and we can make some plans. Or just go back to sleep now.

I stayed where I was.

A few minutes later she said, I've got an idea. I might still go back to John, but not yet. Until I decide, let's pretend I'm your girlfriend. Except it will be real. It won't be hard for me to fall in love with you a little bit, and you're already in love with me. But if it's a love story, it's a very short love story. Every love story has an end. And when ours is done, when we've sold the painting and given

Jake what he wants, there's a chance I'll ask you to send John an urgent telegram that you found me and that I'm really sorry and want to come home. That I got nervous about not being good enough to be his wife if he ever became a senator. You know, stage fright. But that if he'll take me back, I'll try my best. And that's not a total lie. But you have to know right now that this is a short thing. If I decide to go back to Long Shot, it's done and we go back to being friends. Want to try that?

It was a terrible idea, and of course I agreed. Stood up from the couch and walked to her.

MIDDAY, ONCE WE'D GATHERED OURSELVES, I pulled the boxed-up painting from the hotel safe, and then Eve and I went down to the lobby and crowded together on a little sofa to study a telephone directory. On a piece of hotel stationery, she wrote gallery names and addresses in her tidy script, and I marked locations on my street map. Her plan was to drive around to every address and say, What will you give me for this very valuable picture? And then, after a couple of days, we'd be sitting in the hotel bar with a stack of cash celebrating the highest and best offer.

She saw San Francisco as a big city, but I tried to convince her that the art world would be more like a village. Gossip would travel fast. If we went barging gallery to gallery, in a couple of days everybody would know about a possibly shady minor Renoir making the rounds. We had to be careful—start with a short list, gauge interest and suspicion. And also, to avoid having to deal with a bank, which would mean handing over identifying paperwork that they'd file away, we'd need to find a dealer slippery enough to do a cash deal.

—Only identification I have is a driver's license, and that points straight back to John. So cash it is.

—The next problem, if you don't want to sell for the lowest dollar, is provenance.

Eve said, I never heard that particular word, but I had a year of Latin in high school, which is where they put me when I said—first day as a freshman, before I learned to be careful how much truth to share with people—that I wanted to go to college. I might as well have said I wanted to own a yacht and be president of the United States. But no regrets, because I liked Latin better than typing, and it made sense to me, like a secret code that—surprise—you already knew some of. So I can guess that the word might be like a question. *Where from?* Which is the first question out on the road if cops walk into camp and you have a half dozen ripe watermelons or a couple of chickens roasting over a fire or maybe a wooden apple crate of rusty wrenches and hammers and screwdrivers out of somebody's garage. Point being, I'm good at thinking that stuff up on the fly. The painting belonged to my dear dead husband, and now I've got to sell it because it makes me miss him so.

—Not bad, I said. Maybe work on the sincerity a bit.

—Noted.

I reminded her that if it were sold correctly, the painting, converted into cash, would be enough to buy a two-bedroom bungalow, or to start a business like a little neighborhood grocery or a beauty shop or a bakery.

—You think Jake's planning to open a beauty shop with this money?

—I meant more what it could represent for you. If you took the money to start a new life.

I wasn't sure why I'd said it, but there it was.

Eve explained to me as if talking to a child that she did not want to buy a house or open any kind of shop. She said those kinds of choices tie you down.

I said, What about school, then? You wanted to go to college when you were younger. You're smart enough and you'd have the money.

I wanted to pull those words back immediately.

Eve looked away for a long minute, and then she said, I've known a bunch of people who went to college, and some of them were on the road as busted as everybody else. So I don't put a lot of romance on college and it being a marker of who's smart and worth something and who's not. John went to Princeton and still can't get over it—calls it a magic place—but take away everything he didn't inherit, and what does he have left? Not much is what. The people that really made his money, dead in the ground. When I'm around him and most any college people I've ever known, I don't feel way dumber. Plenty of smart people didn't or couldn't go to college even before the crash. Mostly it's a fucking lottery, and I've seen the winners and the losers. So, Val, I don't need you telling me I'm smart enough for college. I don't need your endorsement. OK?

I nodded.

—One night with me and you're planning a future. Not part of the deal, Star Scout. Don't start muddying things. Let's go sell this pretty little painting.

Humbled, I followed her through the lobby and out to the car, the Renoir tucked under my arm, trying not to imagine all the ways the afternoon might go badly.

What I knew about the real business of how art was bought and sold was largely theoretical. The only pieces I had sold were mine at prices that maybe paid a couple of weeks' rent. And the few I had bought were painted by friends when I had a little cash and they needed rent money, with the stipulation I had to sell their art back to them if asked. So really, my direct knowledge of the commerce of art was more like hocking a watch than doing real business. And on top of that, I'd heard that selling art had changed drastically in the years since the crash, as had everything except the phases of the moon and the progression of seasons.

CLEAR SKIES, TOP DOWN ON Eve's roadster, we headed out to the first gallery on our list. I was on edge, but Eve chattered about strategy while I dodged traffic. She wanted to go into all the galleries with me. I told her I knew how to talk about art. Let me do it. Wait in the car. Don't worry.

—Nope, she said.

—Look, we're taking a risk doing this. I'm afraid you'll say something that might touch off a call to the police, and if Long has reported the painting stolen since I left Dawes, we'd be in big trouble. Grand theft. Prison time.

Based on nothing but her conviction that Long loved her and would back away from actually harming her no matter how mad he was, Eve said she couldn't believe Long would have her thrown in prison.

I couldn't fully endorse her logic, but all I said was, He might throw me, though.

Eve turned her palms up and made a weighing motion, then leaned and kissed me on the cheek and smiled.

We parked in front of the first gallery and went in. Eve asked a few vague questions about Renoir, I said a few standard things about the Impressionists, and we both feigned great cluelessness about the market. It went about as I expected.

Back in the car, Eve steamed.

—References, she said. They want to see *my* references? Maybe I want to see *their* references.

I tried to tell her this was more complicated than buying or selling a used car.

She said, How? He kept saying how little they might be able to offer. It feels exactly like my daddy dealing on a used car, except this salesman had on a better suit and a different brand of hair grease.

—It's more than that. A Renoir we can't prove is real, much less that it's yours, is a different thing entirely.

—You're so gullible. You walk around every day being a mark.

ALL AFTERNOON, AS I HAD predicted, dealers at four more galleries asked who we were, where we lived, and what references, preferably local ones, we could offer. Based on just our description of the painting and Eve's provenance story, two dealers were interested, but only if they had time to do things carefully, and they both told us it could take months to find the right buyer. Folks at the other two galleries sensed trouble right off and shooed us out the door, suggesting we try an auction house instead.

Early evening, only halfway through our list and both of us worn down to a nub, Eve said, That's it for me today. You forget I've got to work all night.

—You don't have to keep doing that, I said.

—No, but I *want* to. Let's go find some coffee.

Back at the Clift, Eve talked while she got ready.

—Tomorrow's Sunday, she said. All the galleries will be closed and we'll be able to sleep as late as we want, lie around here most of the day. You want to come with me tonight?

—Absolutely, I said. I'd love to hear you sing again.

At the club, I sat in my familiar dark corner sipping gin. The pianist and bassist recognized me and made a great show of winking at Eve and tipping their chins my way, to which I raised my glass and nodded.

MONDAY MORNING, FOG THROUGH THE curtains of the hotel room. Eve and I were in bed when I brought the topic up.

I told her I'd tried to adopt her attitude toward our deal. That it was like a game with a time limit, finite and without consequences. And yet I felt both guilt and jealousy. I knew I was in no position to be jealous when she talked about going back to Long, but I was jealous. And I also felt guilty regarding Long. I was, after all, sleeping with his wife.

Eve said, Guilt? Heavy word. And jealousy is heavy and stupid too. Isn't the whole reason you've been chasing after me that I'm probably not married? Or at least not legally and properly married to John? You and John can't have it both ways.

I rolled over and mashed my face into the pillow.

Eve patted the back of my head and said, Poor little Star Scout. This must be so difficult.

AN HOUR OR SO LATER, we wandered through tightly packed gaudy little French and Italian vases, Chinese vases six feet tall, lots of large, bad paintings from the previous century in heavy gold frames, and tables crammed with silver—flatware and platters and serving dishes. I asked a passing saleswoman about the function of two dozen small and very specific-looking tined eating utensils.

She said, Those are *repoussé* asparagus forks, of course.

As the saleswoman turned to walk away, Eve said to me, purposefully loud, I'm shocked you didn't know that, Valentine.

—Maybe my family didn't take asparagus seriously enough.

Eventually a wary old dealer with a monk's haircut and an expensive gray suit nearly worn out, waist measurement about double the inseam, came over to see what we wanted. He immediately sniffed out a hint of shadiness in the way we asked about the local market for Impressionists, and very brusquely he asked, What is it you're trying to sell?

Before I could wave her off, Eve said, A Renoir.

She gestured her hands side to side and top to bottom to shape its size and said, The frame's nice too.

The man smiled a strained smile.

He said, Dear, I'd either kick you out or call the cops without another word if you weren't so charming and naive. But you are both, so I'm not going to do that. I'm also not touching this picture that you think is a Renoir. Don't want to see it, don't want to know how you came by it. Neither of you look like criminals, but these days, who knows?

At the same time, Eve and I both said, But . . .

The man held up his thick right palm, the color of a ham steak, to stop us. He said, Every alarm bell rings. Renoir is having a heyday this summer. I'd bet you're well aware.

Eve shifted into another gear, winding up for her provenance tale. Very soft and vulnerable she said, We're not criminals, and the painting is really a Renoir and really mine. My husband died a year ago, and I inherited it. But it makes me unhappy to be in the same room with it since he passed. The girl looks so sad, and her eyes are wide-set and downturned. Problem is, I'm going to be traveling for a while and may not be back here anytime soon, so I don't have a lot of time. Surely there's a way we could help each other.

The monk looked at me and said, I could listen to her talk all day, but what I hear is a bell going jingle-jangle-jingle. Hear it? Now, let's walk outside.

On the way out, the names of a couple of galleries possibly better suited to our needs came up in a very vague and roundabout way. It was nothing but friendly chitchat, but I came away with the impression that a gallery called H. Gareth Windsor had become less than meticulous about the tedium of establishing ownership and authenticity of goods. And yet nothing the monk said conveyed any specificity that would stand up in court. His language involved lots of qualifiers and subjunctives.

Outside, embarrassed by every feature of the moment, I said, Thank you, sir, for your advice.

Too quietly for Eve to hear, he said, Careful. You may or may not already know it, but you're in over your head.

Then he turned and faded back into the dim, crowded space of the auction house.

Eve walked straight on without another word until we reached the car. Inside, she said, Fuck that old asshole.

—He was trying to help us. He mentioned the name of another gallery.

—What an idiot.

I didn't know whether she meant me or the monk who had tried to nudge us away from trouble and had taught me that I knew nothing when it came to selling stolen art. Maybe Eve was right in thinking that Long would not consider her walking out with the girl in a field of wildflowers actual theft, but if you throw love and rejection and retaliation into the mix, then who knows how anyone might react. Probably half of domestic murders arise from something called love or at least passion. Early on I had felt sure Long loved Eve in some way or another, but in my journeys tracking her around the country, I'd become fuzzier in my understanding of his feelings for her. And the past couple days with her had made matters much fuzzier, to say the least, about how

Eve really felt about Long. The monk was right—I was in over my head, but I had no vision for a way out except to keep moving through.

AFTER MUCH SEARCHING THAT AFTERNOON, we eventually found the shop called H. Gareth Windsor. It was the kind of place you had to know was there to find it. The sign was small and didn't share any information about the nature of business conducted inside. The building was slender and vertical and white on a narrow street pitched steep down to the bay. You could see a corner of the new Bay Bridge. Morning fog had burned off into an extremely sunny afternoon. People back East seem to believe that San Francisco is always gray and foggy, but the mid-afternoon light fell blue and sharp and brittle.

We stood there a minute looking at the view, and then I looked over at Eve—silk scarf tied like a cap around the back of her head, circular smoked-lens glasses, lips painted red, black knit top and high-waisted, wide-legged linen slacks. She'd been wearing variations of that same outfit for days, and only ever put on a dress to sing at the club. Since I'd found her, not once had she dressed like a pretend cowgirl or a rich future politician's wife.

—You look like a movie star, I said.

Eve lifted one corner of her mouth slightly and looked at me over the top of her glasses, then back at the view. She said the angles and elevations and all that jamming up of natural and man-made—the buildings, the bay, the hills, and especially the crazy bridges like optical illusions floating over the water—made her a little dizzy. She leaned over onto my shoulder to steady herself. I rested my chin on the top of her head for a moment, and then I put the top up and locked the doors. Eve and I walked into the gallery, leaving the painting wrapped in a quilt and hidden behind the spare in the trunk of the roadster.

Inside, there were a few minor Impressionists on the walls, and some of the painters who traveled in the same circles as Benton and Rivera. I'd have been happy—thrilled—to take any of them home with me.

A slender man came over and introduced himself simply as the gallery owner. He wore a crisp navy three-piece suit and a creamy yellow shirt. The loose bow tie was rose. He seemed young to be so bald and soft, at least after I'd become used to Faro and the cowboys for the past few months.

Eve said, Mr. Windsor?

He said, I'm Dr. Horowitz. If I can give you information about any of the paintings or about the gallery in general, I'll be glad to do so.

—Is Mr. Windsor here? Eve said.

—Mr. Windsor *non est*.

—Dead? Eve said to Horowitz. Or out to lunch?

Then she looked at me and said, Imagine, a chance to use Latin twice in one week.

Horowitz smiled and said, Dear girl, Mr. Windsor is a figment of my imagination.

I said something complimentary about his gallery, and then I said, We're mostly interested in the Impressionists. And out of that group we're particularly interested in Renoir.

—Interested in what way? he said.

—In every way. Looking, buying, selling.

—Exactly, Horowitz said. But I don't currently have Renoir in the gallery. So show me what you have to sell. He smiled faintly at his scored point.

I went to the car and brought it in. Horowitz propped the little painting on a shelf, and we all stood and looked at it. A flicker of something passed over his face, but then he stifled it. I guessed he could tell it was real.

—I can take only a certain amount of commerce at one time, he said. It's exhausting. Let me make tea, and we'll all sit and calm down. Breathe and talk a bit. No rush. So how do you take it?

—Take what? Eve said.

—Tea. I have Earl Grey and oolong.

—How do you take it? Eve asked the doctor.

—Earl Grey with plenty of cream but no sugar, he said.

—I'll have it both ways, Eve said.

—Meaning plenty of cream and plenty of sugar and very little tea? Dr. Horowitz said.

—Exactly, Eve said.

I said, Straight tea, either of them.

When Horowitz returned, we sipped and sat in the presence of the painting, all of us breathing.

Finally Dr. Horowitz said, You wouldn't mind if I asked how you came by this pretty little thing would you?

Eve said, It was part of my late husband's estate. He was older, and he passed a year ago.

—Understandable that it's become time to let a few things go, Horowitz said.

Eve improvised and said, There's a Matisse I'd never get rid of unless I was starving.

—So this one doesn't speak to you in the same way? Dr. Horowitz said.

—Exactly, Eve said.

—And how did your late husband acquire this painting?

—In Paris immediately after the Great War, Eve said.

Horowitz said, Mmm-hmm. Lots of people over there needed to sell art then.

He sipped and looked and breathed some more, and then he stood and stepped very close to the painting and studied. When he sat back down he said to Eve, You realize there are other ways to sell that would realize more for you?

Eve shot me a quick questioning look, and I said, We plan to be out of the country for a while. Possibly a year or more.

—So the sale is more a matter of convenience than necessity?

—Convenience, yes, Eve said. She gave me a glance like she was having fun.

A lull fell, and then Eve said, By the way, Dr. Horowitz, what kind of doctor are you?

—I have a doctorate in history, specifically of the Mediterranean region. From Berkeley.

—So not the kind of doctor who helps people, Eve said.

—Absolutely not, dear.

—That was a joke, Eve said.

Dr. Horowitz chuckled but didn't seem to know why.

Eventually he said, I know it can be hard to believe there's still enough money around that people are buying paintings, but some are.

Eve said, I do believe it. My late husband is an example.

—What sort of figure were you thinking? Dr. Horowitz said.

—Let's go the other direction, Eve said.

—In that case, I'd say that if we had a little time, say two weeks to work on this, you'll probably get at least double what you'll get rushing a sale.

He mentioned a number as a target and a number as a minimum. Several thousands in between the two.

—Before or after the commission? I asked.

—Before, of course.

Eve gave me a quick look and then decided not to ask her question.

Instead she said, I'm going to have to think this out. What are your normal hours?

—We open weekdays at ten. Well, to be safe, say ten thirty. Close by about four, give or take. Goes without saying that we're closed on weekends.

—Sweet work schedule, Eve said, smiling. We'll talk it over and maybe come see you in a few days.

Dr. Horowitz checked his watch and said, Goodness, nearly three thirty. May as well close up for the day after all this excitement.

Back outside getting in the car, I said, Nice touch saying late husband instead of dead husband.

—Thanks for noticing. I like that guy, the doctor. He's just shady enough to trust. In fact, I can't see a reason not to go ahead and make a deal right now.

—Maybe sleep on it?

—Nope, I'm ready now.

Back inside, though Horowitz seemed tired of us by then, we managed to settle on an arrangement for him to find a buyer for the painting. Eve and Horowitz signed some papers and Eve sweet-talked him into a good faith deposit, five percent of the target price.

—I think I can have something worked out in a couple of weeks, he said.

—Couple of weeks? Eve said.

—Yes, Horowitz said. Unless you want to give it away.

—Not a problem, I said.

Eve drove away slow, both hands gripping the wheel, staring straight ahead, silent. I wasn't sure how we ought to proceed, how we could possibly keep both Jake and Long strung along for two weeks while Horowitz worked.

—I haven't been in touch with Long in five days, I said. Sent a postcard saying I hadn't found you yet but was checking all the clubs. I feel like I need to send a telegram, maybe say I've found you.

—I don't know, Eve said.

—Something vague like, *Found Eve's club, will update once I talk to her.* That might buy us a few days.

—Not yet, Eve said.

THAT NIGHT I STARTED TO feel hopeless. I wasn't sure what I was doing. I kept worrying about all the ways that Long might retaliate against one or both of us, especially if he ever suspected Eve and I had gotten involved.

Eve said, No need to mope. What's done is done. How about taking me to dinner in Chinatown on the way to the club? There's a place I want to go in and sit down and eat at a table for sentimental reasons. I was panhandling one afternoon near this restaurant, maybe almost five years ago. An older man, older than John, gave me a box of leftovers instead of pocket change. He said, Good luck to you, sweetie. And then he walked on. Didn't try to talk me up. The box was still warm, rice and a heap of vegetables and dark sauce and shreds of beef. I went around a corner into an alley and ate it with my fingers, and at that moment I thought it was the best food I'd ever had. Let's go eat there.

—Deal, I said.

WHEN WE'D NEARLY FINISHED OUR meals, our table crowded with plates and tiny bowls and large serving bowls, I was ready to pull out my wallet and pay up. But Eve called the waiter over and said, Bring me one more little thing. Doesn't matter, one dumpling or something.

She turned to me and said, I'm not quite ready for this to end.

I said, Thinking about the alley?

—Yeah.

—Can you tell me how you felt that day? I can't imagine.

—Of course you can't. I already told you how I felt. I was panhandling, and it was the best damn meal of my life. Anything else, emotions or whatever, they're mine to sort out and carry with me or to leave behind.

THE NIGHT WAS MOSTLY CLEAR, the moon just past first quarter, and we had time before Eve needed to be at the club. She wanted to go down near the Ferry Building, walk out on a pier and enjoy the view toward Sausalito and see Treasure Island, the brand-new land mass being built of stone and sand and mud pumped from the bottom of the bay to house an airport and a world's fair in a couple of years.

We stood out there, me in the role of boyfriend, and she said, Feels like we're on a high school date. She asked what high school was like for me in Norfolk, and I talked about dances and drives over to the beach. I reached for her hand.

—How about you? What was high school like for you?

Eve said, I left home toward the end of my junior year. Didn't want to. I'd always enjoyed school. I remember liking chemistry a good bit, the big colorful chart of the elements rolling down from above the chalkboard and making so much sense. Geometry was my favorite class, the one I got nothing but A's in. I liked the tools—the protractor and compass—and mostly how concrete it is.

Squares and circles and triangles, a simple straight line being such an important thing.

She said, All that year my mother kept telling me how busted we were, how my little brothers and sisters were this close—pushing her thumb and forefinger an inch apart toward my face—from starving. I needed to contribute, needed a job. Quitting school was the first step. I looked but couldn't find anything but odd jobs making a quarter or two here and there. So, early spring, I went out on the road with a girlfriend in about the same situation. Our plan was to be fruit tramps for the months from strawberries to apples. Look after each other, see the country. But she met a fellow in a tomato field in early August and took off with him. I kept going, looking after myself.

I've only gone back home once, a year or so after I left, and I could tell I made them nervous, so I took off again. Not a good feeling to realize that the place you came from didn't really want you back. After that, I wrote home a few times to my mama, telling her I was doing fine. Migratory as a bird. But really, I didn't much care about home and family. Times were bad, but not everybody set their daughters out like unwanted puppies by the side of the road.

—I'm sorry, I said.

She leaned against me, and I wrapped an arm around her shoulder. We stayed like that awhile, standing silent together looking out over the water.

WALKING BACK TO THE CAR, a man came up from behind and whispered, Hey, look who's enjoying the evening.

We turned toward the voice, and Jake flicked open a straight razor and held it with the blade and pearl handle at an obtuse angle. He offered the blade to the nearest streetlight so we could see the reflection.

He grabbed Eve by her hair, gathered up in his left fist.

Eve froze.

He said to me, Don't be stupid, Mr. Welch. Or can I call you Val? I think I will. Stand there and listen, OK? Y'all haven't been taking me seriously.

He reached with the blade and flicked across her earlobe, like a fine pencil line. Blood didn't gush or run. It formed one drop from what wasn't much more than a briar scratch.

—Look at that, he said to me. Isn't that high-quality work? And really quick. That's control. Call it a warning, except it seems like I've already warned you, and you've ignored it.

Jake shoved Eve toward me. She stumbled and I leaned and reached out for her. When I did, Jake passed the razor along my collar line. I didn't feel anything until a trickle of blood began to run down my neck.

Eve didn't scream, but she yelled, You son of a bitch.

I grabbed at my neck, and Jake said, You're not hurt bad. The lesson to draw is simple. I want my money or both of you will get hurt real bad. And real soon.

He looked at Eve and said, Take him back to the hotel and give him a Band-Aid and fuck him good and he'll be in fine shape to start getting my money together right after breakfast. My advice, call the rich guy.

—How would we tell you we have it? Eve said.

—Not how *would* you, baby, it's how *will* you. And you don't get in touch with me. Whenever I get impatient, I'll be in touch with you. Like tonight except rough if you don't have some cash for me.

Jake walked off a few steps and stopped under a streetlight. He looked at his wristwatch and then over his shoulder to the clock tower of the Ferry Building. He twiddled the stem of his watch to synchronize it.

Eve said, You didn't say how much.

Jake laughed and said, I figure ten thousand seems fair.

He turned and walked away.

The night so clear, across the bay a gesture of hills against the sky, a spray of lights across black water from Sausalito, a faint smell of coffee from the big roasters near Fisherman's Wharf. Eve and I watched Jake fade into the dark.

We touched our wounds and looked at our fingers. Not nearly as much blood as we expected. Hardly any. Smears. Still rattled, jarred, shaken, we couldn't think of anything to say. When I tried to touch Eve's ear, she jerked back and said, It's nothing. She took my handkerchief out of my pocket and pulled my collar away from the cut and pressed the handkerchief against it. We weren't really hurt, but Jake had made his point. A quarter inch deeper would have made a great difference.

Eve said, I don't know what he might do.

—So Donal wasn't embellishing after all?

—Apparently not. It's just I've never seen Jake exactly like this.

—You're not singing tonight, I said.

—No, of course not.

I turned to walk to the car and told Eve it was time for a new plan, that I wasn't willing to be killed by a damn Orson.

—MAN, YOU GOT TO STOP THIS SHIT.

—Donal, this is important.

—Yeah, everything about everybody else's bullshit is supposed to be more important than mine.

—You hinted Jake might have killed somebody. Was it true?

—Why?

—Donal, no bullshit right now. He's threatened Eve. Threatened to kill her. I need to know exactly how scared to be. Need to know if he might be bluffing or if we ought to skip town.

Donal paused long enough that I thought he'd hung up.

—Donal? You gone? I said he threatened to kill Eve.

—Got that in its entirety. And I'd bet he threatened to kill you too.

—Yes.

—How drunk at the time?

—Jake?

—Keep up, man. I don't have time to do both our jobs.

—Seemed like not very drunk.

Another pause, and then Donal said, Possibility exists that he might mean what he's saying. Pass this story along to anybody else, and I'll deny I ever said it and claim I know naught about it. I'm already regretting picking up this call. But I maybe saw Jake kill a man. One of the possibilities. Out in Nebraska, trying to get to Denver. We'd been hitching rides all the way from Omaha. This driver made a move on Jake, a pass. I was stretched out in the back seat trying to sleep. Would have been a while after midnight, not another car on the road. A chilly clear night, no moon, a million stars. Jake and the driver fought in the front seat until the car ran off the road. Then they got out and fought some more in front of the headlights until the driver pulled out a little pistol, and Jake took it away from him. All Jake had to do was get in the car with that pistol and drive away, leave the man stranded, standing by the side of the road watching taillights disappear. We could have gone west awhile and dumped the car outside North Platte and walked into town and caught a train. Which is exactly what we did, except first Jake shot the man. Guy was standing there with his hands held out to the side, totally conceded the point. Three times, man. It was a small-caliber pistol, but still, three times. Maybe he lived. I didn't see where he got hit.

—Shit. This is truth? I said.

—Truth's the first thing smart people deny. I'm breaking my rule here. I've been trying to warn you since he was up here knocking me around, but you won't listen to me. Past two or three years, when he comes around, I try to keep him calm and keep him moving along. He got scary and still is. So yes, you two would be smart to move on down the line.

—All right, I said. We'll get out of here tomorrow. Probably y'all should keep an eye out too.

—For what?

—In case he loses track of us and comes back to Seattle looking for someone to blame, I said.

—Goddamn, he said.

I couldn't tell whether we were done or if he had any more truth to impart.

Finally Donal said, Hey, when this all blows over, you ought to swing by. Me and Fawn miss you.

—You keep asking, I might take you up on it, I said.

I HADN'T LOADED LONG'S LITTLE Browning semiautomatic since Florida, but I did after that call to Donal. I tried it under my jacket at the small of my back, tucked half under my belt. But pulling it out was awkward and slow. I felt sure Faro and the cowboys would've had a laugh watching me practice in the bathroom mirror.

Eve paced between the window and the bathroom door.

I said, The calculus has changed entirely.

—Did you just notice?

—I'm saying he's watching us and he's getting madder by the day, I said.

—I know. Let's pack our bags and hit the road first thing, come back in a couple of weeks to see how Horowitz did with the Renoir.

—Fine, I said. One thing at a time.

WE WOKE UP AT DAWN ready to roll, but Eve began to worry that if Jake was watching, changing our normal schedule too much would make him suspicious, so we planned to leave around lunchtime instead. Casual. Taking our time.

First thing, as usual, I left the hotel and took a walk, though I kept it shorter than most days and stayed closer to the hotel. Every step wary. Not long after noon, Eve got the car and cut a few blocks, watching for anything following. I waited with our two small bags around back of the hotel. She swung by, I tossed the bags in the back seat, and we hit the road.

SOUTH OUT OF SAN FRANCISCO along the coast, Highway 1—fleeing, in flight, scared. Eve said, We could keep going. The road never ends. At least that's what some of us used to say.

It hit me wrong.

I said, Yes, it does. It fucking absolutely does end. That's fake, crazy hobo wisdom or real estate salesman wisdom or politician bullshit. When people come all the way across the continent and see the Pacific, they usually know for sure the road has ended, maybe in a way they hadn't planned on, but that particular dream or fantasy of running away forever from your problems is done. You can't keep running west forever. Whatever they thought they were running toward or away from, all the way from the Tidewater or Plymouth Rock or the Lost Colony, they know that dream of freedom forever has ended when the road stops in front of them and there's nothing ahead but thousands of miles of water.

—Val, you're in a different conversation. Two-lane ribbons of pavement are not what we're talking about.

—Not what I was talking about either.

MOST OF THE WAY TO Half Moon Bay, fog swelled between the ocean and the highway like a bank of dark smoke from a vast forest fire. We gassed up and changed drivers, and once we were back on the road, Eve said, Keep looking back. It feels like we're being followed.

I tried to tease and said, Old hobo wisdom—*Don't look back.*

—Not funny, asshole. You don't get to joke about that.

—Yeah, I'm sorry, I said.

Eve didn't speak for miles. Then, very quietly, she said, I never did work artichokes, but I knew a lot of people who did. Somewhere down around here is where most of them come from.

We hit Santa Cruz and stopped for a late lunch at a fish house near the water. Eve insisted on a table where she could watch the street and the parking. In the distance, we could see the boardwalk with its tall white roller coaster, dizzying even from afar. Eve was jumpy, eating in fits and starts.

I nudged into her with my shoulder and said, You never know, we may have fooled him this morning. Could be he doesn't even realize we're gone.

—You can't know that. Maybe he's real good at following us. Not a good time for rosy optimism.

After lunch we drove down the road a ways, then pulled over and watched again. I started feeling a little cornered too. I thought maybe I'd seen a dove-colored coupe more than once since Santa Cruz, but didn't mention it to Eve yet.

—We should keep moving, she said.

ONCE WE'D GOTTEN DOWN BELOW Carmel, not far above the Bixby Bridge—another of the country's shiny new amazements scattered like diamonds among all the poverty and loss—Eve became more nervous.

She said, From the map, looks like if he's following us we'll be trapped on this crazy road for miles.

—See if there might be choices, another road if we get in a tight spot.

She flapped the map and said, That's what I'm doing. Farther south, this road's not even finished, but until that point it looks like it's going to be more of what we've been seeing—road right by the ocean, sometimes hanging over it. To the left mostly mountains. And to the right, a long drop to the rocks and water.

I said, Long's paying a lot for the view, so we should enjoy it.

—This is not funny, Val. I'm feeling like something's not right. And part of why I stayed alive out on the road is because I learned to pay attention to those feelings. It looks like the farther we go, the fewer choices we'd have if we were trying to get away from somebody following us.

She studied the map a while longer and then said, Hang on, looks like the old road is still there. Heading south too, but farther back from the water. A thin squiggly line. Turn left just before Bixby Bridge, and maybe we'll at least be able to see if anybody's coming behind.

I tried to watch in the rearview for the gray coupe when I turned, but there were several cars behind us, and the road was curvy enough that I couldn't be sure. The pale dirt road was wide enough for two cars to pass, and it bent immediately around a low hill, then began climbing away from the ocean. We drove up curves onto tan grassy ridges. At a pullout looking back the way we came, I stopped. The bridge looked impressive from above, seeing the whole span of it stretching in an elegant arch across the deep green gully of Bixby Creek. The sun hung low on the horizon, and the Pacific stretched hazy blue forever west. You didn't have to know a thing about world geography or maps to look out into that widening space and know in your core that this ocean was vastly more voluminous than the Atlantic. Maybe you could feel the mass of water and empty air, nothing mystic, just an effect of gravity. If it was a physical thing, I ought to be able to transfer it to canvas. Maybe.

Eve said, Let's sit here and watch. Anybody following us we can see if they pull onto this road.

—And anyone else making the turn for their own reasons.

—Sure, but I'm particularly looking for a gray car.

—So you've seen it too, I said.

—Three times since Santa Cruz, Eve said.

—What do we do if a car like that turns in?

—Drive like hell. And look for little side roads. The map shows a couple, but they don't go very far.

Only a few minutes later, the dove gray coupe turned onto the dirt road. It pulled to the side and stopped. We both froze.

Tiny in the distance, a figure, likely a man, got out, crouched down, stood straight, walked back and forth across the road three times, and then got back in the car. When he started driving forward on the old road, I cranked the engine and threw it into gear.

I said, How the hell did Jake get his hands on a car that nice?

—Hot-wired it. Not hard to do.

We drove over the ridge, and the dirt road drew down to one lane and sloped toward a creek, and then climbed up into dim coves of redwood. I was trying to find the speed between getting caught and sliding head-on into a tree or down a bank.

Eve said, Goddamn, go faster. Do you need to pull over and let me drive?

We were in a possibly tight spot, and I didn't think. I said, Sure, why not? I'm just along for the ride and to get the shit beat out of me by the whole goddamn Orson family. So now you might as well have a go at me too. You're the one who chose to link yourself to that bunch of criminals until death or convenience do you part.

Eve shifted sideways in the seat and hit me. Not a slap or a loose, half-hearted roundhouse, but a hard, tight fist straight to my right eye socket. She hit me like I was a boxcar rapist, one of the wolves about to tear her apart.

I slammed on the brakes and the car went almost sideways before finally skidding to a stop. I touched my eye and nose and lips and looked at my fingertips. I'd never checked myself for bleeding as much in my life as I had since I met Long and Eve and the damn Orsons.

Eve sat looking straight ahead, breathing hard. Then she yelled, Go, go, go.

The coupe stayed well back, three turns at least, so that you didn't know it was still there until the road opened up and you could see behind for a quarter mile. And then there, faintly, would be the gray coupe. If it had been another shade toward clay, it would have melted into the roadbed. It never came closer and never fell farther behind. It knew we knew it was back there.

We drove as fast as we could on the one-lane road, but not crazy fast. Eve kept her eye on the map and finally said, Half a mile. Should be a little road on the left. Looks like it goes up in the hills a few miles and has a couple of side turns. Nothing goes very far, but there should be places we could get out of sight.

I turned and drove on. The sun set and the woods dimmed. I figured we'd be better off hiding than driving around with our headlights blaring. We found a likely spot and pulled well off the road behind a crowd of trees and rocks, the car aimed forward so we could watch for headlights. We cranked the windows half down so we could hear if anyone approached. The air coming in was cool and damp.

Eve touched my face very carefully where she'd hit me. She said, I didn't mean that. Then she kissed me like she did mean it, and said, Sorry.

She leaned into me and ducked under my arm and tried to settle in. She felt like what she was, a ball of clenched muscle. Sometime after dark, she started talking about a friend, a boy named

Bobby, from her tramp days. A few sentences in, she relaxed. It was a sleepy story, her voice dreamy and slow. She and Bobby spent a stretch of time traveling together, who knows how long. She said Bobby never pushed himself on her. He didn't care for women in that way. Or men either, but maybe he just hadn't figured all the confusing angles out. She said, We could hug tight and sweet and warm all night on a freezing freight train heading west out of Denver in November, climbing up into even higher country, and neither of us worrying about the other digging and grappling to get under our clothes. Both of us smelling of the road, which was mostly bad, but not entirely—free and real. In a hobo jungle, though, Bobby could be tough as anybody. I saw him beat a big full-grown man into a curled-up ball after he'd tried to fool with a pale, white-haired boy about twelve years old and traveling alone. Bobby had a skinny body like it was made out of tight-wound wire, but that man next day in the light, his face looked cut up and swollen like he'd been run over by a truck on a gravel road. Then one night climbing the rungs getting to the top of a closed boxcar, Bobby fell between cars onto the tracks. The train rolled along at a good clip. This was somewhere out on the prairie. Western Nebraska or Kansas, eastern Wyoming or Colorado. He didn't make a sound when he fell, and nobody saw him again, so probably the wheels chopped him to pieces and the wolves and coyotes and birds scattered him. A lot of kids died that way all over the country, and there won't ever be any record of it. No marker, gone for good.

I remembered her telling a shorter version of this story back at Long Shot. No funeral for a kid killed falling off a train. I pulled her closer to me and listened to her and to the road, but there'd been no sign of another car since we stopped.

Eve said, I mostly try to remember Bobby from one particular time. We spent a February together camping in the dunes near the

Fountain of Youth in Florida. The weather was not nearly as warm as advertised. A con like most everything in Florida. Nights were freezing cold, and the Fountain of Youth wasn't a fountain, and all the water tasted like sulfur. But we ate well on little fish and shrimp we caught in backwater with a piece of seine net we found washed up on the beach. We cooked on driftwood fires that burned in unusual colors. The ocean hummed and boomed and hissed through the nights.

As Eve's story went on, the pauses between sentences stretched longer, like she was back singing at the club, extending a three-minute ballad to a dreamy fifteen. I slouched against the driver's door, Eve's head rested on my chest, my arm around her shoulder. We half dozed. We were in a car in the dark on a remote dirt road on the far edge of the continent.

Listening to her old beach memory, I began inventing my own. Evading Jake, hitting the road together, brand-new life. We could take our time crossing the country, on our way to my beach shack. I couldn't stop myself whispering it to Eve like a story, past tense like a shared memory. The names of towns we had stayed in, that herd of sheep in New Mexico that blocked the road for an hour, the thunderstorm near Amarillo when we couldn't get the top to go up, that little tourist cabin right beside the water on a big lake in Arkansas. Then how we lived on the beach like shipwreck survivors through a long stretch of impossibly good weather, the books we'd read, watching osprey hunt at sunset.

Eve said, Do you remember that lunar eclipse? The sky was so clear, and we sat in the dunes and watched it from start to finish.

At some point we both dozed off, tangled together.

OUT OF THE DARK, A MAN'S VOICE SAID, IF Y'ALL
have a pistol, don't get stupid and start shooting.

Instantly we were breathless awake. The first elements of dawn
were hours away. I couldn't see the face of my wristwatch but guessed
it must be about one or two. We froze quiet, waiting. But not another sound, not a light. Under the redwoods, with only a wisp of
moon showing through hazy air, we couldn't see even the shape of
a person.

Eve slowly reached the pistol from the dash.

—Be calm, children, the voice said.

Eve cranked her window the rest of the way down and said,
Faro?

Silence.

Eve said, If it's you, say so. Or else next sound I hear, I'm shooting at it.

There was a little laugh in the dark, and then Faro said, Damn,
Eve, gun me down. We need a little confabulation. Y'all get your-
selves collected or dressed or whatever you need to do. I'll set fire
to this pile of wood I've been working on. I thought I'd have woke
you up rattling around getting the makings together.

We got ourselves organized in the car, whispering, What the hell? Faro squatted and matched dry tinder and fed dead sticks to his tidy fire.

We walked up to the fire, and Eve said, So it was you following us all day?

—All day today and yesterday both. And maybe a little more. But to be accurate, some of the time two of us tracked you separately. And then at some point last night we kind of consolidated.

—You're with Jake now? What? He got in touch with John, and John sent you out here, and now you and Jake and John are working together against me?

I said, I don't see it playing that way, but I can't see what else *consolidated* could mean.

Faro made a damping motion toward me with his right palm. He said, Val, you and Eve sit down and listen a few minutes.

In the firelight, we could see that Faro had a bruise and a boxer's cut under one eye, and on his right forearm, sticking out from the sleeve of his jacket, a long wrap of gauze bandage. Rusty bloodstains soaked through in blotches that if I were taking an inkblot test I would've said looked like a parrot in profile.

Faro said, What happened was, John got a phone call from this other husband late at night. Said something like, Saw our wife in San Francisco singing in some shit bar. Her new boyfriend seems nice. But right now we got some stuff to settle, you and me and Eve. You want me out of your hair, that's going to take ten thousand dollars. What I hear, you've probably got that in your sock drawer. Then Jake just hangs up, soon as John starts talking. So John bangs on my cabin door and says to me, OK, I need you to go find out what's going on. I'll drive you to Denver tonight, then you'll fly out first thing. When you get to San Francisco, go buy a car. If you see a new Buick coupe, buy that.

I've been wanting one anyway. Don't let Eve and Val know what you're doing until you know what they're doing. And this grifter husband who wants things settled, well, the first thing he needs to learn is that we'll be the ones doing the settling. He doesn't decide anything.

Faro paused and said, So, I'm here. Flying was horrible. Won't do that again.

Eve shook her head and said, He had you buy a new car?

Faro said, Would've taken too long to drive out here, and turns out buying a car takes no time at all when you show up with a fat roll of hundred-dollar bills.

—And you've been trailing us how many days total? Eve said. Two?

—Rounded down.

—So three?

—OK, Faro said.

I said, How'd you find us on this road?

—Simple, Faro said. Back in San Francisco, I cut a notch in one of Eve's tire treads in case y'all might do exactly what you did—drive away, turn onto some little dirt road. Like tracking a horse, cut a notch in one hoof. Got out and looked for your tracks and sure enough, there they were. I've never tracked anyone this easy to catch.

Eve said, You could have come to me first. I thought we were friends.

—And if it was down to me, I'd have trusted your word, but John needed more. He wanted me to check things out. He's your husband after all, or at least he hopes he still is.

Faro paused and looked at me and then at Eve again. He said, And whatever y'all two have going on isn't my business. John's suspicious because of what Jake said on the phone, but I kept telling him all the way down to Denver that he needed to consider the source. Either way, John knows how I do when it comes to morals. I'm not going to take his word or anybody else's on when somebody's guilty and when they're not. The only time I was on jury duty, I ended up needing to take a pistol off the foreman. Had to break his nose doing it. He thought he could bully me into agreeing with the other eleven.

FOG HAD RISEN UP THE hills from the ocean. At first it filtered moonlight and starlight funny and strange, and then it blanked the sky entirely. In that dense wet air, the fire cast a dome of amber light over us.

I said, The fog's getting so thick it's gonna be hard to tell what's up or down.

Faro leaned over and picked up a rock the size of a chicken egg. He held it at arm's length and dropped it with no comment.

—Mystery solved, I said.

Faro tossed a few more forearm-sized limbs onto the fire. He said, I'm going to tell you a campfire story that illustrates how I do things when it comes to law or matters of right and wrong. All of this is to say, I'm trying to figure how to deal with Jake. I'm not seeing a clear right direction.

He said, This goes way back. I was about eighteen or twenty and got hired to uphold the law. I was the youngest deputy to a county sheriff in the hillbilly mountains of Arkansas. Not much in the way of mountains compared to Wyoming, though. I'd already learned you're swimming against the river if you're looking to force justice on a world where it's an unnatural idea. Sometimes you've got to invent things as you go along.

It was between New Christmas and Old Christmas, and I was

out looking for a man, a veteran of the early part of the Indian Wars. His brother had reported him missing. His farm was a day's ride west of the county seat, so I spent a night at a tavern on the way and rode up to the frame house shortly after dawn on a bitter cold morning hoping to find the missing man lounging at the kitchen table eating his breakfast. An enormous dog greeted me in the road, barking in spasms until it stood with its legs spraddled and its head down, breathing hard and wheezing wet. Its breed, if it had one, was unclear because it had been sheared—only its head and tail had hair.

A round and good-looking woman, speckled as a guinea egg with freckles across her cheeks and nose, and about my same age, came to the porch and stood with her arms folded under her breasts so that they rose up above her bodice in two smooth domes.

I called out, What's the matter with that dog?

—I was fixing a hole in a wall and needed hair to swell up the plaster, she said.

I told the woman my business concerned her missing husband, and she said, I've not seen him lately.

—Does he go off much?

—Some.

I sat my horse and thought.

To fill the silence, the woman offered the opinion that maybe her husband had left to buy whiskey to honor the anniversary of the Christ's birth and had perhaps fallen off a cliff or into a river.

—Yeah, gravity and all, I said.

In order to get inside the house to look around, I asked the woman if she might offer me a cup of coffee, and when she said yes, I got down and went inside and looked about the place without actually letting on I was searching. Nothing of interest presented itself except for the patch of new plaster in the parlor wall.

I stepped out the back door and onto the porch. What I discovered lying on the frosted ground, at about the distance one would pitch cracked corn for chickens, was a man's entire head. It rested neck-hole up and facing away. He'd been red-haired.

Of course your natural reaction to such a sight is to pull your pistol. Once I had it out, I was not sure what to do with it. Maybe march the woman out at the end of its muzzle and lock her in the smokehouse until I could figure out what had passed in that place.

The woman came onto the porch and saw the head.

All cheerful and friendly, she said, Shit fire, where's that thing been at?

I let down the hammer and put the pistol back in its holster.

The woman and I went inside and sat across the kitchen table and drank black coffee together. I learned that her husband, previous to fighting with the Indians, had been a sweet and loving man, but he came home from the plains completely changed and crazy. In particular, she held General Miles and General Sherman to blame.

—Those two were his gods, she said. But I've decided in that case, maybe there ain't really one at all.

For a whole year her husband had mostly lived farther up in the mountains, he said in a cave, but could have been he had another wife. He only came to stay at the farm for a few days at a time to get food and demand his rights on her and give her thrashings with a length of old plowline. He would hardly speak other than to threaten to kill her in her sleep and to curse her when he was on top of her. He kept his shotgun propped by the bed, and he'd point to it and say, See that standing there? I've got buckshot in one barrel and a slug in the other. Most of his time at home he spent piling brush into the road, trying to seal their cove from the rest of the world and from the spirits of the people he had helped kill on the plains, men and women and children. The ones who specially lodged in his head were the old people who couldn't even run from you, just shuffle. She told him over and over that no one looking to do him harm, especially ghosts, would be stopped by a mere brush pile. Still, at the least sound, he would put the bores of the shotgun to her head and threaten to shoot her if she yelled out to his enemies. She got to where, even when he was gone back into the mountains, she could sleep only in quick naps with a butcher knife in her hand.

One night, when she couldn't take it anymore, she knocked him in the head with a stick of stove wood as he stepped through the door. Once he was down, she put the knife in him right to the handle, dug the blade way up under the rib cage. That took the fight out of him, and after he died, she cleaved his head off with a mattock and dismembered him with a bow saw. She put the head down in a big bucket of gray water where she had been soaking a ham to draw out the salt, and she set it on the back porch. She tried to burn the other pieces up in the fireplace, but they were too wet to light. So she spent several days trying to hide the charred parts in the wall and under the floorboards of the house and in hollow gum trees and in shallow caves.

As for the head now sitting in her yard, the only way she could explain it was that on the night of the killing, the weather had turned bitter cold and the bucket on the porch froze solid. Being in a raving mood for a few days, she forgot about it. In her mind, all the parts had been accounted for. When she needed the bucket for another chore, she tapped out the gray ice block and threw it off into the yard. She would never have been discovered as the killer except that the night before I got there, deer must have been drawn to the salt in the water and licked at it until they had melted the ice.

—How much of him's behind that new plaster? I said.

—One of his hams is all.

I thought how things might play out. Tearing into the dog-hair plaster. Employing some neighbor's scent hound to locate the rest. Reaching up into hollow gum trees and pulling out arms in a disgusting handshake. Burnt feet buried under floor puncheons. Then returning to town with the man's rotting parts all jumbled in hemp sacks hanging paired across the rump of the horse the woman would ride. Her wrists bound to the saddle horn, her ankles tied with a rope under the horse's belly so that if she tried to jump off she would drag along the ground. Then a jackleg trial with only one possible verdict.

Some men find law work satisfying. They see themselves setting right the violated order of things. Mostly, I found it sad. After all, which order? It sounded to me like the man had it coming. If he tried to do me the way she described, I'd have been a lot less patient. But she would certainly be hanged anyhow.

I said to her, You swear not to do this sort of thing again?

It wasn't a fully thought-out position, but I'll stand by it.

—Lord God no, she said. Not never.

—As soon as the ground thaws, can you remember to bury that head good and deep way out in the woods?

—Oh my, yes.

—Take a shovel and the head and walk until you feel like you've walked a mile and then dig a hole two feet deep. Say it back.

—Mile, two feet.

—Then I will maintain the opinion even under oath that your husband's gone to Texas to take advantage of the unlimited personal freedom that's offered there.

—Many have gone there before him for that exact reason, she said.

—Look me in the eyes and say it back to me.

—Gone for Texas, the woman said.

EVE AND I BOTH SAT silent. Faro poked the fire with a stick. Orange sparks rose in sprays and quickly snuffed out in the wet air.

Faro said, I could have sheltered myself this past half century under the letter of the law to keep from feeling guilty for letting that woman hang. What I did seemed like approximately the right thing to do at the time, and it still does. I've never felt guilty one minute for letting that woman go free. My point is, Long knows I work that way. So he knows I won't do just anything he tells me to. If he pushes me toward something I think is wrong, I'll tell him to kiss my ass. And if he doesn't like that, he'll fire my ass, if I don't quit first. What that amounts to is kind of like we keep each other from getting things too wrong. He can fire me, or I can quit mad, which is not pretty.

Up above the redwood tops, chalky black light swelled. On the ground, green-tinged darkness.

Faro said, I need to show y'all something. It kind of happened, and I'm trying to figure what to do about it. Don't know which way to go. I need advice.

We walked with him to his car. The Buick was all curves, and the sloping trunk seemed like it took up half the car's length. Faro opened the door and folded down the front seatback. He leaned in and took out a bundle, gray wool. He unwound the Renoir, flicked his lighter for a second, and snapped it shut.

Eve and I looked at each other. Faro said, That doctor was happy to get this off his hands. Hardly cost anything to buy out his interest, the deposit he gave you and a little bit of gratuity. Paid him a visit an hour or so after you three made your deal, and he seemed relieved to make a profit and get shut of the whole matter.

Faro wound the painting back in the blanket and went around to the trunk and keyed the lock and raised the lid. The space was cavernous. A body didn't crowd it at all. It rested half covered in a coarse gray wool blanket identical to the one wrapping the painting.

Natural instinct, Eve and I both stepped back, but Faro motioned us forward. He thumbed the lighter again and held the flame so we could see that the body was Jake.

Eve whispered, God almighty, Faro. What have you done?

Faro moved the flame closer to Jake's face for a second. Jake groaned and rocked slightly side to side. His eyes stayed closed. Faro flipped the lighter cap shut and said brightly, He ain't dead yet. He'll resurrect by sunrise.

Jake began to heave from the pit of his stomach. Faro wrestled him out of the trunk and staggered him to the trees for a wrenching vomit before walking him over and settling him on a log by the fire. Jake breathed several big huffs and then leaned forward loose-necked, glaring at the flames. His hands were tied in front of him, and he wore dirty socks but not shoes. Faro draped the blanket over Jake's shoulders.

FOG TANGLED HEAVY IN THE first layer of trunks and limbs. Above that, perception dulled to nothing. Faro cooked coffee at the fire. He had a shiny new cheap percolator and tin cups. Jake sat at about a forty-five degree angle to gravity, and the blanket wrapped around his shoulders stayed exactly as Faro had arranged it. Even in yellow firelight, Jake's face was pale as lard except for eggplant-colored half-moons under and over his eyes. I felt like I was in a particularly vivid dream, but Eve and Faro acted like this was normal life.

—I'm going to need you to catch me up, Eve said.

Faro said, Last night got to be a goddamn mess all of a sudden. You two and your routine had been so easy. If I lost you, I'd soon find you at the hotel or the bar. So for a couple of hours at a time I went off following him, trying to figure out his patterns, his play. He was mainly living in a series of stolen cars, but that's neither here nor there. Didn't take long to realize I could follow you by following him. My mistake was, I believed he was too stupid to know I was watching him. So last night I was tracking him while he followed y'all on your little date. And then he came at you. I had my pistol in hand ready to rush out of the dark to save your asses, but pretty quick it got clear that he hadn't hurt you too bad. Everybody was still well enough to talk snotty to each other. So once he was gone and you two finished licking each other's wounds and drove off, I walked on down the street following Jake. He walked the same direction I'd parked the coupe. If I'd been thinking, that should have set me on alert, but I'd been distracted by being concerned with you two idiots. To make it short, he hid and then jumped me as I was unlocking the car. I haven't been that stupid since I was about twenty. He waved his knife around and asked why I was following him. Did John Long send me to kill him, or was I just one more con artist trying to edge in on Long's money? He had strong feelings about not sharing the pot. Not with y'all and definitely not with me. He was fairly jacked up, and I could tell he was looking for a reason to put that knife in me if I let him get close enough. Well, I convinced him to change his mind. Which I did hard. And now we're here.

Eve looked at Jake. His eyes were closed, and his head wobbled slowly. She said, How'd he get like this?

—Well, first, back in the old days, opium was a daily fact of life. Mostly you took care of yourself, so you got to know doses. He'll be fine, except he's a mean little shit, and the amount I gave him is only a temporary cure for that. I'm keeping him soothed way down for a while. Brought syringes from the barn. I can give muscle shots and vein shots both. Basic barn skills, but handy elsewhere too.

Eve walked over to Jake and squatted down a little more than arm's length away. His eyes were half open now, but he didn't seem to recognize her. She said, I wish you didn't have to be like this. Once upon a time, I thought you were better. Maybe you were different back then. Maybe both of us were, but maybe not. You should have gone off and lived your life.

Jake looked at her with an instant of recognition, and then he dazed off again.

I said, If that's you rehearsing how to talk to Long about all this, I'm not sure it's the angle to take.

Faro huffed one laugh. Eve looked at each of us in turn and said, Two-thirds of the idiots who thought I ran off to be with some long lost love are sitting right here, and so is the one y'all thought I ran to.

She tossed her hands in the air and said, Goddamn. I can't believe the mess that I've got to clean up. Sitting here looking at the three of you, I'm thinking I might've been better off if I'd sold the picture fast and kept the money for myself and moved on.

—The picture part is settled, Faro said. It's going back to John. The rest of the money he sent me with is still in the air. I've got a fair pile to get things done with and free rein to decide my methods. Point being, there's ways to clean this up without you having to be the one doing it, Eve.

She didn't say anything. My neck itched, and I scratched it without thinking. My fingernails scraped over the thin scab, and immediately a drop of blood tickled at my collar line. Faro reached for the coffeepot, and a thin trail of blood ran from under his bandage. Eve looked at both of us and touched her earlobe and came away with a drop of blood domed on her fingertip.

Jake's head flopped back as if he was looking up at the sky to a brilliant full moon, but there was nothing to see except fog. Slowly and with great effort, he lifted his head and leaned forward toward the fire, staring at Eve. She stared right back at him. It was hard to tell how lucid Jake might be. He sat quiet awhile, groggy. Then, fairly clearly, working hard to enunciate word by word, he said, I will kill you someday, bitch.

Faro stood up and said, Enough.

He pulled Jake to his feet by his shirtfront. With his free hand, Faro reached into his jacket pocket and slipped out a fat metal-and-glass syringe.

He held the barrel of the syringe to Jake's eyes and said, See how full that is? If I emptied it in you, you'd never threaten anybody again. He put the syringe back in his pocket and helped Jake lurch toward the car.

I looked at Eve, her profile beautiful and grievous in the firelight. I said, I'm sorry.

We heard feet shuffling, then the trunk lid closing.

Eve said, Great. You're sorry, but you don't even know what to be sorry about.

FARO WALKED INTO THE LIGHT. He looked at Eve and then looked at the ground.

She said, You two want to know what you were missing? All the ways you were wrong? Tracking the wrong trail? Investigating the wrong case?

277

Faro topped off everybody's coffee and sat.

He said, You know I wouldn't work against you intentionally. Not ever.

—Maybe, Eve said. I didn't think you would.

First signs of early dawn in the trees. First faint light in the fog. A good bed of coals inhaling and exhaling with every shift in air, checkered logs, piney incense rising.

Eve said, I'll tell a campfire tale too, but no ghosts or big bears that need to be killed. Or pretty women with big tits that need help from handsome young deputy sheriffs. My story is messy. John pretended to be shocked when I told him I didn't want to have a baby, that I wasn't ready now. He'd waited this long, so why rush when we'd gotten married quickly and hadn't been married very long? Settle in, the two of us, and be sure before adding a third. But his hurry was obvious. He'd never much cared whether he reproduced in general or whether he and I specifically had children until he got so serious about a position, a seat. Being a US senator, alongside his war medals, would be achievements he could dangle over his sorry family and outshine every member of his generation of freeloaders and also the one before. Plus, I suspect he got a taste of the kind of fortune to be made from that land deal with the government, and he figured he might do even better working both sides. He wants that real bad, and he sees parenthood as a great benefit to his image. Having a younger wife, either knocked up or else sporting a brand-new baby, could be very useful. Imagine the photos in the paper. If the governor and the state legislature—who'd have to say OK to his appointment—and the newspapers and the ordinary people have any reservations about him, he evidently thinks I can take care of that.

I don't know what folks in Dawes and Cheyenne all thought about John before I came along, she said. Confirmed bachelor, playboy, loser who couldn't get a woman. But I know people gossiped about his never being married, no kids, until all of a sudden I showed up fairly perfect for the role. Not snobby and East Coast, which a lot of people would have expected. Rougher-edged, but not bad-looking, with some show business glitter trailing behind. Much better for that particular audience than a beautiful snooty rich girl. The fact that lots of them had been to my shows or heard me on the radio before I ever met John was another selling point.

Bottom line, folks thought I was real and he was not. In Cheyenne, when some politician's wife got drunk enough at a late-night party at the governor's house to ask John about being a childless bachelor so long, he'd say, You're right, I have no kids . . . not that I know of. That wink-wink man thing—the stupid pause meant to be comic and sophisticated. Then sometimes, to cap it off, he'd look at me and say, But we're working on it all the time. And then wait for the laugh. I hate it when amateurs try show business, and John is particularly not suited for it. He has a hard time being crude. But at least he usually apologized to me later for sinking to the level of the room. Back when I was in Ronnie's Rangers, I had a little onstage back-and-forth double entendre comedy thing with the bandleader, Ronnie himself. I didn't mind it so much because it was part of the act and everybody was in on it. That felt a lot cleaner than playing along with John and the politicians.

She said, Truth is, I don't really know why John waited so long to get married. Maybe he was having too much fun being a bachelor in the wide-open twenties.

—Or was waiting for the right person? I said, not entirely serious.

—Sure, that must be it. Moping around waiting for me to show up and make his life complete. She paused and then said, Drag a hundred-dollar bill all the way along Route 66 from Chicago to LA, and you'd catch thousands and thousands of me.

—You know that's not true without me having to tell you, I said.

Faro shook his head and said, Val, good Lord, you don't interrupt a campfire story.

—Thank you, Faro, Eve said. My point is, as soon as I suspected I was pregnant—the very first moment—I knew I wasn't interested in being the vessel or vehicle or pickup truck or wheelbarrow to carry John's ambition forward. Not right now, maybe not ever. Flirting with the current governor or shabby state legislators for a few minutes was cheap-feeling enough, but having a baby I didn't want just so John could prove to voters what a big potent man he is, well, that's a whole other thing. I knew too many women who gave up dreams, or gave up their actual lives—meaning they died—because they got pregnant at a bad time. And others who wanted a baby but couldn't feed the ones they already had. Being on the road broke was hard. Being on the road broke with a baby was horrible, and it could kill you. A fatal condition.

Confused, I stupidly said, But when you found out, you weren't on the road. At least not until you left Dawes.

Faro pointed at me and said, Shut the hell up and listen.

—I knew John would use the baby for politics, Eve said. And I didn't want any part of that. It made me wonder things I didn't want to, like was that why he married me to begin with? Breeding stock? I felt like maybe I was nothing but a necessary step in a plan. Like some olden-days queen, kept around only as long as she's producing heirs for the king. Or all those Italian and German and Soviet women who are right now being told it's their patriotic duty to make more sons, to fulfill a quota. Read that in a magazine a couple weeks ago.

We sat a moment, Eve looking off into the trees like she was collecting a thought. Then she continued.

—When it's the two of us, John doesn't like to talk about my time in the bands. He talks about it plenty in Cheyenne, though. Sees it as an advantage that a lot of those politicians who've seen me perform seem like they also remember the thoughts they had watching me. Which is neither here nor there. When you throw yourself under the lights, you have to quit worrying what thoughts churn in other people's heads about you. If you can't do that, it eats you up. But it was the lights that pulled John in too, no matter how much he wanted to think otherwise. He wanted what he saw up onstage, but once he got it, he wanted to pretend those couple of years in my life never happened. It was the first thing I did after I left home in Tennessee that felt right and felt like mine, standing up there singing to a crowd, whether that was a couple of thousand at a big dance or thirty-five drunks scattered around in a cowboy beer bar. Every other part of life had felt like waiting, killing time. I even learned to love the long bus rides because they were taking me where I wanted to be—making my own living doing something I loved. And John wants me to pretend all that never happened or at least never will again. The exception being when it helps get him what he wants. I had some talent. I don't know how much, but some. Maybe I still do, though some days what there is of it feels like a waning moon. The gig in San Francisco felt good, but not as good as it used to. Something was different.

—I sat for two hours and listened to you in that nightclub, I said.

—Bar.

—My point is, I wanted to keep watching and listening. If I'd walked in off the street and didn't know you, I'd have felt the same way.

—Intermission, Faro said.

He stood up and stretched. Joints cracked, the friction of bone and cartilage. He walked off to the edge of the trees. After he came back and fussed around with the coffee a minute, he said, OK, you're pregnant, but you don't want to be. Not the first time I've encountered that situation, by the way. So what do we do now?

Eve shook her head and looked at me and said, You remember that office you went to in Seattle? The Acceptance Company?

—Of course, I said.

—Its full name is Pacific Medical Acceptance Company, but they don't put *Medical* on the business cards or the sign in the lobby. What you saw was the first part. Weeding out. If they hadn't weeded you before you got more than just your nose in the door, and if you weren't a man, you'd have whispered with the receptionist about having a medical condition that interferes with your monthly cycle. Then you'd talk money—need a loan or paying cash? If you had cash, you'd sign a form and a nurse would examine you and assure you that your normal cycle could be restored with a simple procedure. Doctors and women all over the country use that same wording. The only difference with the Pacific Medical Acceptance Company is that they have a chain of offices all the way from San Diego to Seattle.

When what Eve was telling us sank in I asked, Are you OK?

—Better than I was when I left Dawes.

—We've been so far off the mark, I said.

—No shit, Eve said. Big of you to admit it. You asked last week about why I was so upset after the dinner with the gas producer guys. That was the first time John asked me to be on display, to perform, in our own home. Knowing what I knew, that dinner sealed it, and I decided to take Donal up on his offer to help. Well, Fawn's offer. She's the one who knew where that office was, how to talk to the grumpy lady at the door so she'd let you in, how to answer the nurse's questions in the exam room. Fawn's helped a lot of girls and women get to that office, and now Donal's helping her too. And I can tell you two are struggling right about now, maybe wondering why I'm not all broken up and sad. But let me tell you what's sad. Some imaginary kid growing up unwanted, whole life a thing for the parents to argue about. I didn't want to bring that kind of resentment into the world. Being pushed out of the house as a teenager was a different situation than this, but it gave me a taste of what it feels like to be a burden to your family, more trouble than they think you're worth. So I see the decision I made as a kindness, to the imaginary child and to me. And now I'm done explaining myself to y'all. If you've got questions or opinions, too bad. We're moving on. New topic.

I nodded. Didn't dare say a word, but looked over at Faro. I saw his face change, that cold look, the minuscule tilt of his head I'd seen on the ranch a couple of times. Primordial and a little scary.

He cleared his throat with one sharp cough and said, Way I see it, Eve, nobody but you ought to be making the calls here. All I have to do for John is settle with Jake some way. He was kind of vague on method. Just make him go away. I think I know what John's preference might be. As for me, back when I was about twenty, we'd have shot somebody like him and ridden away without worrying about it. He came at me in San Francisco intending to kill me. He thought it was easy to cut up an old man and walk away untouched. Yet, what do you know, he's not at all untouched. I don't owe him jack shit. Should have killed him on the street when I had self-defense on my side. But this is a different time, or so I keep being told.

He poked the fire and said, Eve, I owe it to you to go however you say.

He looked at me but didn't ask anything of me.

I said, Same for me, Eve. Your call and we'll stand by you.

Eve said, And it's none of John's business what we do here or what I've told you?

Faro and I both nodded. Faro said, And not anybody else's either.

—Good, Eve said. Be that young deputy looking the other way.

AN HOUR LATER, LIGHT FELL through the trees the color of an oyster. Faro and I held either side and staggered Jake far out into the redwoods. Looking up into the columns of trunks and vaulted limbs was like entering a cathedral. Jake was awake enough to know us and cuss at us a little, but he wasn't able to resist. We sat him down by an enormous tree trunk, and Faro took out a fat syringe and topped Jake up with a touch more opium.

—Noon at the soonest, Faro said. Then he'll have a moment of reckoning. He'll have to figure out where the hell he is and why.

Jake's spraddled legs and splayed socked feet, dirty at the pads of his soles, made a *V* in front of him.

Faro pulled a little drawstring canvas bank sack from his jacket pocket. It wasn't all bulged and heavy with treasure like a pirate hoard of gold and silver. Ten thousand in paper money is light as air in comparison. He placed it between Jake's legs and took out a little notepad and pencil and jotted a message and then showed it to me—*Don't come back for more. Not ever. This is it. Next time, no way out of the woods.*

Faro didn't ask for revisions, and I didn't suggest any.

We walked away, back toward the campfire. Halfway there, the fire winking tiny and yellow through the trees, Faro patted his pockets and said, Oh, shit. I forgot something. You go on and make sure Eve's all right, and I'll be back before you know it.

When I got back to the fire, Eve looked up and the light caught her face, and I knew I'd never have the talent or skill to paint it and get it right. The hundred questions in her eyes.

When Faro joined us, we drank coffee and ate yesterday's stale doughnuts from a box in the Buick until all of us were jangling with sugar and caffeine.

Very quietly Eve said, I think from here, Faro and I need to head back to Dawes. And Val, maybe you need to have something real important to do here for a couple of weeks. Give things time to settle down before you come out. Let everybody get a better sense of what's real.

I looked at Eve and she looked down and then looked up at me. It was a moment, a hinge of time. I didn't say anything. There wasn't anything to say. The questions were all gone.

Faro said, Yes, I think Eve's right.

After a long silence all around Eve said, Send a telegram to John saying I'm ready to come home. Tell him Faro caught up with us, that he and I are on the way back. Maybe say you're tying up loose ends and will follow soon with my car. OK?

—OK.

—The following-soon part?

—Yes, I said.

Mid-morning, the sun a bright, hazy disk in the pearl sky, Faro and Eve got in the Buick and headed for Wyoming.

I wanted to walk back into the redwoods and look at Jake. But if someday I needed to testify, I wanted to tell the truth. Last time I saw him he was alive.

I SPENT A PERIOD OF time that felt like months but was actually a couple of weeks wandering the strip of coast between Big Sur and Half Moon Bay. If you have to wander around feeling dead, you couldn't ask for more beautiful country to do it in. Just enough artifacts of man—cars and roads and late-night diners—to offer welcome relief from all that ocean and wilderness, the empty light and space and dimension, all the shapes and colors and distances.

The first three days I penciled my guesses where Eve and Faro were along their thousand-mile drive onto a gas station map of the Western states. Somewhere in that first week I stayed at a place called Tassajara Hot Springs Hotel. Everybody working there kept telling me that the name came from the original people who'd inhabited the land and that it meant *place where meat is hung to dry*. Which felt like exactly where I needed to be for as long as I could afford it, which was two nights. Hung to dry.

In Carmel I bought paper and watercolors and drove back into the hills on oiled dirt roads and sat in the car with the top down and watched the light on the Pacific or the shadows in the redwoods for hours. I painted smears of pointless color. In Half Moon Bay I stayed in a big frame boardinghouse, a third-floor room up under the eaves, and in Monterey I stayed in a place too shabby and tiny to be called a bungalow and not charming enough to call a cabin. It was a shack, a walled shed with running water in the kitchen but only an outhouse toilet. I attempted sketches from memory for portraits of Eve and Faro and Long. Jake would have to wait. I painted small watercolor landscapes of bright open hills and dark redwood coves, flowing two-tone abstracts based on the shapes of car fenders and geometric locomotive cow-catchers and smooth curves of rifle stocks and pistol grips. Nothing I painted worked. I needed time to edit memory.

Eve rode my thoughts. And Long too. And questions like, why had Eve decided to go back? How would she account for her time away—especially the past couple of weeks—when Long asked?

I went on night walks in the Tassajara redwoods and the cannery streets of Monterey and the ocean emptiness of Half Moon Bay. I looked at the sky, the stars and waxing moon, big bright Jupiter and Mars nearby. But nothing looked right. Patterns of constellations seemed deformed, as if some force vast as precession had accelerated and shifted even the stars in the sky.

v

—

INDELIBLE
BLACK

WANT TO TALK AWKWARD MOMENTS? WALKING
into the lobby of Long Shot was high tide for me. I didn't know
anything. Not where Eve and Long stood after two weeks and not
what Faro might have told Long. Not how Eve and Faro had accounted for my lapse of communication and especially not how
they had explained the most damning contents of Jake's concise
telephone call. No way to know before I arrived all the ways our
lies might fail to overlap. Faro didn't have a phone in his cabin,
of course. And calling Eve in the big house was impossible. Who
knew who would pick up and talk to the long-distance operator and
get curious why I was calling. All I could do was send a telegram
from Salt Lake saying that I'd get to Dawes Thursday or Friday.

So, Friday—coming on sunset, dragging it out as long as I
could—I drove through the ponderosa entrance into blankness. I
knocked on the big door to no effect, and then let myself in. The
lobby was the same, nothing out of place, including the Renoir and
the .30-06 sniper rifle I'd fired. I counted fingers to number the
weeks since the prairie dog massacre and was surprised I'd hardly
been gone a month.

I called out, trying to sound cheerful and innocent, Hey, anybody home?

Long came from his office smiling. He gave me a hearty politician handshake as if I were a constituent, and said, Welcome back. What long journeys you've made to bring my wife home. Eve and I both owe you a debt of gratitude. I want to hear all about California, but there's plenty of time for that tomorrow. I've made plans for a picnic. The last warm days of the year need to be celebrated. Right about now, in the next couple of weeks, the weather usually changes drastically. We'll ride out. Things will be set up for us, and I think Faro will be coming too.

—Surely Faro and Eve told you some of our trials in California?

—After a fashion. Don't worry about that.

He paused and said, Anyway, you must be tired from the long drive. The blue-door cabin is ready for you, same as always, and Julia will have some supper shortly.

I said, The Renoir looks good back home.

Long looked at it as if slightly surprised and said, Yes. Thank you for that. Faro tells me you kept it from being sold in San Francisco.

I only nodded in acknowledgment.

I carried my bag around to the cabin. Wiltson was still shoveling shit in the round pen at sunset, so he must have pissed Faro off yet again. When Wiltson saw me he said, Look who's finally back. Faro kind of said you fucked up in California. Way he put it was, you did nearly as bad a job as I would have done.

I said, Faro has a vivid imagination, doesn't he?

—If that means sometimes he makes shit up in his head and wants us all to take it for truth, then yes. Same as everybody.

In the blue-door cabin, I unpacked and cleaned up and went

to the kitchen. A brown paper bag on the counter held my supper, but Julia looked at me and said, You look terrible. So skinny. What have you been eating? You need more than a sandwich tonight.

She sat me at the kitchen table, put the paper bag in the icebox, heated an iron skillet blazing hot, and seared a T-bone that must have weighed a pound. At the same time, in the same pan, she reheated a split baked potato with about a quarter cup of butter mashed into it. She tipped the food onto a plate and set it in front of me and said, That and about ten hours sleep will make you right.

Afterward I managed to stay awake maybe an hour rehearsing how to behave the next day and guessing what would help or hurt Eve based on what had happened or might have happened since the clearing in the Big Sur redwoods. I trusted that Faro would protect Eve, but that was all I trusted at Long Shot.

NEXT MORNING, NO SIGN OF Eve. While I was eating breakfast in the kitchen, Long ducked in and refilled his coffee mug in a rush and made a wiggly four-finger signal conveying *too busy to talk*.

Midday, Faro lunged a new gelding in the round pen. The weather didn't feel different, but the light did. It fell at an angle that carried a thin and brittle sadness, the sense of an ending. I stood at the fence until Faro got to a good stopping point and came over.

I said, I'm in the dark. What do I need to know?

Faro looked down at the footing of the pen, formulating his comment. He finally said, High tension, if you know what I mean. Loud for a couple of days and then silent. Not good.

A couple of cowboys came out of the barn and headed our way, and Faro said, Bad place to talk. This afternoon try to follow along.

I said, Thanks for giving me credit for saving the picture.

He shrugged and walked back to the horse.

EARLY AFTERNOON WE ALL RODE deeper into the ranch for an hour to a high hill with a sunset view toward the mountains. Eve barely spoke, only said she hoped my drive had been nice. No emotion, just mildly interested. A wife asking one of her husband's employees how their weekend had gone. I understood why, but her ease in playing the part hurt some.

Long had sent a couple of cowboys out earlier to stomp down a space in the tall grass the size of a tennis court. Tall grass meaning five feet, six feet, eight feet high. They'd dug a shallow fire pit and had a blaze going and a stack of firewood enough to last through the afternoon and into the night. Four campaign chairs with canvas slings striped soft red and blue and cream stood around the fire at the cardinal points. Each chair had a heavy Pendleton trade blanket folded at its foot. A table, white tablecloth, loaded with stacks of china plates and piles of silverware. A platter with a great deal of sliced rare roast beef and a basket of Julia's yeast rolls, several kinds of cheese, enough potato salad for a football team, various pickled vegetables and horseradish and relish in little white bowls, three pies with brown cinnamon-apple goo seeping through slits in the top crust. And a case of Gigondas with a corkscrew and eight stems. Half of the bottles were already open and breathing deep breaths of Rocky Mountain air.

—You're aiming for the four of us to eat and drink all that? Faro said.

—We don't have to, Long said. First rule of hosting, excess is always preferable to shortage.

Faro paused awhile after the words of wisdom and then said,

See that little brown bird over there sitting on a grass stem? It's a grasshopper sparrow. Spring, when she has a nest and chicks, she'll nab a grasshopper and shake it until the legs fall off before she feeds it to them. Flies not much better than a chicken. Mostly runs around on the ground. Usually you see them sitting on the lowest strand of fence wire.

Nobody had a response.

The view from the clearing looked westward toward the Winds. Almost all the snow had melted during summer and not yet replenished, so the blue-gray mountains barely differed from sky.

Faro fussed with the fire, revising the geometry of wood until it suited him, while the rest of us settled into the chairs. Long sat north, Eve east, me south, and Faro west. Long unfolded his blanket and draped it over his feet and lower legs, so the rest of us did too. We drank wine, and a silence swelled around us.

Eventually, to fill the tense air, Faro told a story he said was prompted by the time of year and the place. September high plains along the edge of the Rockies, specifically the Wind River Range and the Absarokas.

He started his tale by saying, This happened way back. I've wandered all over these mountains and high plains from Mexico to Canada. You get to know a place pretty close traveling that speed. It's a land of extremes. Always has been, still is. If it's not dust, it's mud, or else snow and ice, or it's sand, or hardpack ground like concrete. For a couple of months, when the skies are so blue and dry and cloudless, you ache from the beauty and the hardness of the sun on the land and trees and mountains. But come September, it can go from warm days to driving snow in about eighteen hours.

Picture way up in northwestern Montana, exactly this time of year, fourteen wagons scattered without pattern across two acres of scrub grass, hunkered down outside the last damn frontier fort, the final edge of what we pretended back then was part of the United States. A batch of earnest settlers bogged down on their way west. From that fort to the nearest evidence of our civilization, you either turned around and traveled many days backward to where you came from, or you forged on through hundreds of miles of high mountains aiming for some town toward the Pacific coast, which was where these people—probably from Illinois or that kind of place—were trying to get to with their wagons and children and their granny's rocking chair. Except they ran out of food in Montana at the end of summer, a bad time and place to do that. They believed that out in the wilderness somebody other than themselves would save them, meaning the army fort. Except the fort's running low too, having hunted out the surrounding territory and mismanaged their staples and their chickens and hogs. Suffice it to say, plenty of idiocy to go around. Hard fact, everybody in the fort and the wagon train is looking at starvation come February. You ever hear about the Donners? It's a long time from Christmas to Easter, and people get hungry.

Meanwhile, I'm all the way down in southeastern Wyoming, hired to take care of horses at Fort Laramie. Not a soldier, let me emphasize, just one of many such independent contractors. This young officer's name was Blevins. I don't recall his exact rank. He was about my age, and he was put in charge of a resupply mission to that outpost way up in Montana. The weather still felt like summer, so Blevins decided our little train of supplies could take our time getting up there. Scouts hunted and brought in fresh meat every day, and we had barbecues and sometimes camped a couple or three nights in the same place if it had good water and game.

Then, middle of the month, weather blew in. After a day of

rain that soaked everything, including the horses and the wagon canvas, wind picked up from the northwest and the temperature fell nearly fifty degrees in a few hours. Snow went sideways and the men driving the wagons couldn't see the horses in front of them, couldn't tell whether they were going straight or in circles. I felt like I was riding into a gray wall three foot from my horse's nose. We made camp the best we could, but the wind didn't allow fires. Mercury fell all night, and by next morning the horses had icicles hanging off them. Water freezing in the barrels.

Blevins didn't know where he was because he had lost the main compass and the spare compass during the night. Besides which, the location of the sun remained uncertain. And then, instead of sitting tight for a couple of days until the sky cleared and the situation revealed itself, Blevins suddenly got in a hurry and gave the order to move on. So we meandered in a roughly easterly direction—the exact wrong direction—until the men and the horses were exhausted. I kind of mentioned it to Blevins, but he told me to shut up.

After that I kept track of our headings best I could. I tried to feel when we bore toward one direction or another, when we climbed away from a creek or descended toward one, and when we crossed a creek, I noted which direction it ran. In other words, I paid attention, which is a big part of what people call having a good sense of direction. But it's also true that some people have a feel for the cardinal directions. North pulls at their blood like a compass needle.

So I let Blevins go on about his business, but every chance I got, I tried to nudge us back the way we needed to go—northwest. Blevins, left to his own devices, would have run around and around in a circle about five miles in diameter.

When the storm cleared and the sun reappeared, every direction you looked was flat white. For a couple of days, the temperature stayed cold, but then it warmed back up to cool days and cold nights. Snow melted quick, and after a couple more weeks, we finally made it to the fort. We lost three horses, but we delivered all the provisions for the starving idiots of Montana. Blevins lost a toe or two. If he's still alive, I guess he's been walking kind of funny all this time. Before I headed back down to Wyoming, he came up to me and said, You knew where we were all that time.

I said, I wasn't the boss. You kept reminding me of that. If you'd ordered something sure to kill us all, I'd have done something drastic about it.

And believe it or not, he didn't thank me. He called me an asshole.

Long laughed and, tongue in cheek, said, Where does this parable lead us Faro? What lesson did you learn from that experience? Maybe you became a cynic or learned the importance of faith?

Faro smiled and said, Lesson? You know me better than that. I didn't get a drop of wisdom out of that miserable trip. Except that maybe I should have cut out on my own as soon as I recognized Blevins for the fool he was. You can't put yourself under those kind of people and keep your self-respect. I should have stood up after morning coffee the second day out of Laramie and said, Gentlemen, I'll be going now. Good luck and farewell.

Long said, You can't have an army if everybody thinks like that.

—Exactly, Faro said. Got to convince people to take orders whether they come from a genius or an idiot. Right, boss?

Long laughed and said, The way you've constructed the question, if I say yes, I'll indict myself.

Faro turned his hands up and said, Who am I to say?

THE SUN HOVERED OVER THE jagged far peaks. Faro added wood until the flames stood waist high. We'd all eaten roast beef sandwiches and potato salad and pie, and we'd already made our way through the majority of the opened bottles of wine, Long drinking almost as much as the rest of us combined.

Long said, One thing I don't get is . . . Well, there are many things I don't get.

He lost the thread of his thought and paused. He finally said, I'm confused about the timeline. Val, you got to San Francisco and started looking for Eve, and it took how long to find her?

I tried not to glance at Eve. I said, A week, give or take.

—So somewhere between four days and upwards of two weeks?

I said, Not quite so much in either direction.

Long said, OK, so about a week.

—That's what I've been saying. The timeline was confusing to me too. When things started happening, they happened fast.

Long said, Not that damn fast.

He turned to Eve and said, You'd been singing in the dive for how long when he found you?

Eve said, I don't remember exactly. The rent where I was staying was due weekly, in advance. I think I paid four times, but I can't swear to it. John, we've been over this.

Long said, I was hoping maybe Val could help focus memory since you and Faro can't seem to recall much. I'm wondering, for example, in all this running away and searching, when did each of you have your first contact with Jake? Val, did you have any contact with him before you found Eve in San Francisco?

—Nope, I said. And I wish I'd never met any of the Orsons. They've been nothing but trouble, and he was the worst of them.

Long said, Eve, your turn.

—John, I'm done. I've answered questions for going on three weeks, and I'm finished. You think if you keep asking, I'll start giving new answers.

—Fuller answers, Eve. Because sometimes your stories lack detail and consistency. The timeline doesn't flow. It needs to flow.

Eve said, If you're talking about something I said at three in the morning after we'd been fighting for hours, then maybe I was inconsistent. I don't know what . . .

Faro cut in and said, I met him for the first time when he came up on me in the dark and made me take a knife away from him pretty hard. If he'd known more about how to fight, I'd have lost because he was stronger. By *lost*, I mean he probably would have killed me. It was that kind of fight. At the end I was bleeding and had to control myself not to finish him with his own knife. Might have been a mistake not to do it right there on the street and walk away. But I've told you that already.

Long sat and looked at the fire. He said, Maybe I need to let this go. That would be best. Except questions keep whirling around my mind. Such as, if this Jake was so ominous and scary and threatening, why didn't you two come straight home? I mean, we do have a ranch full of cowboys with guns. And why didn't you keep in touch with me about what was going on? And really, Eve, why did you marry that criminal in the first place?

Eve said, That's not the point. I'm not talking about that anymore. I thought your big question was, am I still legally married to him? Isn't that your main concern?

—*A* concern.

—I'm telling you this one more time. Maybe we were legally married, maybe not. In some little town, we asked where to get married. We went to an old guy's house and paid him a couple of dollars. His wife was the witness. I didn't check out his credentials.

I guess he was a preacher. I don't remember going to a courthouse. I don't know whether papers got filed properly. That was the least of my problems. It wasn't much of a ceremony. And as for the divorce, after that flood, I thought Jake was dead. No way to prove it, though. I'd have gone on thinking it if you hadn't gotten this all stirred up. When I took off, I didn't do it to find Jake. I panicked. I started thinking I'm not the right person to be a senator's wife. You could boil it down to this—I ran off because I didn't want to be the person to fuck up your dreams.

When she'd mentioned the flood, she had given me a quick glance, and I guessed she was wishing she hadn't told me the alternate story in San Francisco.

None of us spoke until Faro said, Sun's getting near the ridgeline. We riding back in the dark?

—I'm tired of this picnic anyway, Long said.

He got up and wandered over to his horse and mounted up slowly, drunk and awkward. We all followed and rode back in the gathering dark, none of us daring to speak.

THAT FIRST WEEK IN SEPTEMBER had been unquestionably summer. Then a front pushed in over the mountains from the northwest, but not nearly as dramatic as Faro's story. A couple of gray windy days with falling temperatures, and then the sky cleared to a hard brilliant blue, and it was immediately autumn, as if the aspens on the lower slopes of the mountains began turning yellow at one precise moment.

Most days I drove into town and worked, or pretended to. Days when I couldn't focus my thoughts on the mural, I spent long stretches sitting in the diner sipping coffee and thinking. Well, *thinking* may be too elevated a word. Really, I sat and felt sorry for myself and worried about Eve but didn't know what to do to help. Over the days, tensions around the ranch seemed to have cooled some, and one weekend morning, Long proposed another outing, a ride together, the three of us. Two or three hours in the afternoon, a ragged circle into the hills to the south and then meandering westward upstream with the river for a while, and then north. Back home in time to get cleaned up for dinner. Long had everything planned.

But when we met at the barn, Long had a problem. He said, The governor wants to talk in about thirty minutes. His secretary called and said it was important. He believes everything is important, but I'm still curious what he has to say. His calls are always short, but they're also always late. Sometimes pretty late.

He leaned and pecked Eve awkwardly on the cheek and said, Sorry. I don't want you to miss this beautiful afternoon. I've never taken you on this ride, but you can hardly get lost. Ride south on the farm road about half an hour until you hit Elk Creek and then follow it upstream, which is roughly west. Never lose sight of the creek. About an hour later—the sun will be lowering by then—turn right on another farm road, the one the cowboys call Rocky Road even though it isn't rocky. It heads north and brings you back here. If I haven't taken a shortcut and caught up with you somewhere along the creek, I'll be coming down Rocky Road to meet you. It's simple. Two rights and home. Now say it back.

We said the directions like first graders reciting the Pledge of Allegiance.

EVE RODE PÁLIDA, OF COURSE, and I rode Mopsy. The sky was blue and dry, uniform horizon to horizon unlike any Chesapeake sky ever in history. A perfect example of my ten-thousand-foot blue. We rode at a walk and talked.

Eve made it clear that she did not want to discuss California. Not now, not ever. The terms of our deal had been clear going in. It was my problem alone if I had let myself fall into something I imagined to be endless love.

She said, We were friends before the deal, and we're friends again now that we're back here. We needed each other, and in a way, we love each other. The good news is the worst of it will fade away.

I forced a quick laugh and said, Yeah, but I got shortchanged on time in California.

Eve smiled at me and said, That wasn't specified in the deal.

About halfway into the ride, the creek on our left and the lowering sun ahead, I shifted and asked how matters stood with Long. Eve took her time answering, but finally said, He behaves himself in front of you and Faro, but otherwise, he's not at all good. He's mad and sad in about equal measures. Sad about me leaving, and angry because he thinks you and I slept together.

—Thinks? I said.

—I've denied everything, she said. Told John that Jake was lying to upset him, which is true. What Jake told him wasn't based on any fact—far as I can tell, Jake made that phone call before we made our deal. But John's struggling to believe me. Which is why it's odd he sent us off alone.

A couple of hundred yards farther along I said, Does he know why you went to Seattle?

—That's personal. All I'll say is that he knows what my feelings are about having a baby right now. He's still trying to negotiate about it, though.

—Doing business about having a baby?

—Val, everything's *doing business*. Every waking minute is a deal. If you don't see that, you're a lost soul.

—Everything? I said.

—Dreams, maybe. Dreams aren't business. They're all yours with no butting in by the real world. They're free of charge. Everybody's head cranks them out every night. You don't even have a choice. That's the definition of worthless. So don't talk to me about dreams. I knew a lot of people, teenagers, who didn't live long enough to get to think much about dreams. They got separated from dreams early. I'd be saying *we* instead of *they* except I fell into luck, and suddenly I had some choices. Or at least I thought I did. Lately my choices feel narrower every day.

—Talent combined with work produces choices. Hutch said that to me.

—The great Hutch speaketh. And he's maybe right about that. But pulling a pistol and robbing a bank does it too. Go down to the town in Tennessee where I grew up and say this kind of stuff, talk about choices, and then look around and see who any of it applies to. Almost nobody except white men in big white houses. I married one of those men, and now it seems like the only choices I have are stay or leave. Security or freedom.

I tried to come up with a response, but anything I said would have seemed like mocking or like I was asking her to run off with me, and it didn't feel like the right moment for the latter. So I just said, I'm sorry. Then I felt a tug at the sleeve of my Barbour high on my right arm. After a beat, a distant sound like breaking a stick. Not even loud enough to spook the horses.

I looked down at my arm. Right there where the shoulder muscle fades into the upper arm, the fabric of my coat was torn. And then immediately, a pain like being burned, like changing a rear tire after a flat and brushing against the exhaust pipe.

I pulled up Mopsy and dismounted and took off my jacket and then my shirt.

Eve stopped Pálida and said, What?

On my arm a raw red stripe, more a scorch mark than a gash or a cut. It wept a little blood, tiny drops like condensation on a glass of iced tea.

Eve said, Have you been shot?

A question, not a statement. I said, I don't know.

The moment lacked enough information to assign cause and effect. How did the snapping sound and the cut in the jacket and the burn on my arm relate to each other, if at all? The pain began to ratchet up and I winced.

Eve dismounted, and we stood looking off into the empty distances and then back at my arm.

She said, Are you all right?

I thought about the question and tried to notice the sensations in my body. I said, I think so.

Eve handed me a handkerchief, and I pressed it into the wound and put my shirt and jacket back on over it. We mounted the horses and rode forward at a faster clip.

I said, Did you hear that sound right after?

—What sound?

—A snap. I don't know. A click. A sound like breaking a piece of wood, a dry branch across your knee. Off in the distance.

—No, I don't think so.

LONG MET US AT THE barn, all apologies about leaving us on our own to find the way home. When he realized something had happened, he seemed worried in excess of the nature of my injury. In the house, he made me sit at the kitchen table while he got the first aid kit. He finished cleaning the wound and said, Really, Val, we should go into town and see the doctor.

Trying to act tough, I said, It stings and burns is all. I got hurt worse crashing my bike into a lamp pole in Norfolk when I was ten.

Long swabbed Mercurochrome on my arm in great quantity until I had brownish smears seeping into the skin from my elbow to my shoulder.

I looked at Eve, and she shrugged almost undetectably.

Again Long said, We really should go into town and have this looked at.

I said, Come on, any number of Orsons have mangled me worse than this in the past couple of months. Including their dog.

At least that got a laugh out of Eve, but she quickly went quiet.

Long's jaw tensed. He finished with the bandaging and then said, Tomorrow morning after breakfast, we'll dress this again and decide how it looks. A wound like this, passing through clothing, carries a lot of grime with it. We have to be careful about infection. Back in the war, infection killed more than the projectiles themselves.

Long poured three short glasses of Irish whiskey. It was the first time we'd all sat together at the kitchen table. Eventually Long said, The past few years, we've had trouble with poachers. As long as they only shoot antelope, we leave them alone. Well, I mean we escort them off the ranch and warn them not to come back, but we don't call the sheriff or rough them up. If they ever went after cattle, we'd have to do something. Faro will tell you, we've spent a lot of time talking about all this. How hungry people will take chances. And we've thought a lot about how to deal with poachers in a way that acknowledges this is not the Wild West and that we're in the middle of a bad time in this country. Things haven't been perfect here, but we've been lucky.

Eve said, Nope, can't have hobos with high-powered rifles killing cows and building fires and having barbecues.

Point being, Long said, that may be the explanation here. Poachers. I'll have Faro and the boys ride around and check.

Eve cut her eyes at me and quickly looked away.

BACK IN THE CABIN, I thought about how Long hadn't spent any effort at all wondering what could have caused my wound other than a bullet. He either knew the answer or assumed it and went straight to gunshot while I was carefully avoiding that word.

I tried to sleep but couldn't. I replayed those few confusing seconds when the single sound, delayed by distance, arrived. Maybe it sounded like striking one piece of granite with another. Crack, pop, or click. A directionless sound. Except maybe not completely directionless. The brand on my arm was a horizontal stripe, so the shot must have been fired from in front or from behind. Either from the direction of the ranch house or away from it. If the shot had come from a .30-06, how far away would the hunter or the marksman need to be to make that sound?

Middle of the night, I walked through the kitchen door and on into the lobby. I pushed a chair very carefully and quietly against the shelves and stepped up to sniff the barrel of Long's sniper rifle, killer of so many during the Great War, which now seemed much longer ago than it really was. I didn't touch the rifle, afraid it would somehow come crashing down to the stone floor. I leaned my nose close to the black hole of the muzzle and breathed in deep. I smelled the strong odor of gun oil, but also burnt gunpowder in the background. I was no forensic firearm expert, so I couldn't have said whether the rifle had been cleaned that evening or the previous month, after the prairie dog massacre.

My mind spun. Maybe Long had ridden with the big rifle and its trumpet-shaped scope to a knoll far from the ranch. Coming up from behind when he had told us to expect him from the front. Set up the small bipod and waited for us to offer a good target. But no sniper was good enough to intentionally graze from such a distance. Maybe he hadn't hit his target. But then, which of us would he have been trying to shoot? Eve was only a few paces ahead of me. From the right angle and distance we could have been seen as overlapping. I decided it would be much simpler for all of us to assume some poacher was shooting at an antelope and missed and the bullet ruined my Barbour. End of story.

I also decided it would be better all around if I moved into town and finished my work and then got the hell out of Dawes.

EARLY THE NEXT MORNING, I packed my things in the woodie wagon. Over in the round pen, Faro worked a young horse and watched me. I closed the back of the wagon and turned to go speak to him, but then Eve rushed out the back door with a coffee mug in one hand. She paused between the house and the blue-door cabin, looking confused.

—You're leaving?

I touched my arm and said, Might have worn out my welcome. I'm moving into town to finish the last few days of work. Then I'll head home.

She took a few steps toward me like she might want to say something, but before she reached me, Faro shouted, Hey Eve, you mind grabbing some ointment from the barn for me? This one has a scrape on his ankle.

Eve looked at the ground and then back up at me. Turning to Faro she said, You got it, boss.

She faded into the shadowy barn. I nodded at Faro and got in the wagon. In the rearview I watched Eve walk to Faro, and then they both turned and watched me drive off.

Within an hour, I'd found a room over the drugstore on Main Street. At the PO, I told Don Ray the mural would be done and I'd be leaving in a week at most.

—Looked done to me some time ago, he said.

—The last few touches is all, then I'm out of your hair.

UP ON THE SCAFFOLD A FEW DAYS LATER, ADDING another layer of shadow to one rib of a covered wagon, my face inches from the wall, I heard a woman clear her throat and looked around to see Eve. She tilted her head, and I climbed down the ladder.

She said, After Coit Tower, I'm beginning to see what you mean about the shapes, the mass and weight. And about optimism. Who am I to say, but for me it stands up to all those murals.

—Thanks. I'm about medium happy with it.

She looked away and said, I'm headed out.

—Headed out?

—I can't go on here with him. Wasn't meant for it after all, so I'm gone. And don't you come looking for me.

I moved toward her, and she held one palm up, chest level, to stop me. A handful of people milled around nearby, checking mailboxes and chatting.

—We could have more privacy if you'd stop at my room later instead of here, I said.

—Exactly why I'm here now. No temptation.

—That's it, then? So long, Val, have a nice life? I don't imagine falling on my knees and saying, Baby, please, would change a
thing?

She said, Wasn't it always how this arrangement would end?
You'd finish your work and head back to Virginia. Only difference
is I'm not sticking around here either.

—Ride off into the sunset?

—Feels like I've done it a hundred times, she said. No different
really from what you're getting ready to do.

I shook my head.

—Remember in the car out in the woods, thinking Jake was
chasing us, I kind of dreamed of us taking off together? Shack on
the Chesapeake?

Eve said, I remember.

—The offer's still there. Lots of beautiful weather in September
and October. No promises or commitments. No phone and not even
a real address. A place to be and to think about what's next.

She looked like she was about to say no, so I held up my hand
for a pause. I went to the counter and laid down a penny for a
postcard and wrote directions from Norfolk—*Ocean View Ave to
Shore Drive. Left just before Lynnhaven Inlet. Less than half a mile, a
path between scrub pines into the dunes. General delivery, Chesapeake
Beach, Va.*

Eve looked down at the card and then put it in the pocket of
her jacket. Looking straight in my eyes she said, I'm glad I knew
you, Val.

She rested her hand on my arm for a moment, then turned and
walked out. At least she didn't peck me on the cheek.

I climbed the scaffold again and watched through the high
window as she drove away in the red convertible, top down.

Glad I knew you. Maybe worse than my fiancée pretending

unconvincingly that it tore her up to walk away right before our wedding day. Except in that case, I was happy she walked.

I sat on the scaffold facing my work, ass hanging half off the boards like Rivera in the fresco. I imagined a couple of years on, or ten, listening to the radio and hearing a voice sounding like Eve singing something slow and haunted.

IN MY ROOM AFTER WORK, two knocks, very restrained. I opened the door and let Long in. That handful of days since Eve's goodbye visit, I'd half expected him. He stood inside the door and surveyed the metal bed frame and sagging mattress along one wall, the beat-up piece of furniture squatting on the opposite wall that the land-lady had pointed to and called a chester drawer when she showed me the room. The drawers smelled like mustard inside.

Long examined the plaster walls as if trying to determine whether they were intentionally tan or just dirty. He walked over and looked out the single, painted-shut window and studied the view—twenty feet of flat tar roof and then a blank brick wall. He turned to the uncleanably stained porcelain sink hunkered in a cor-ner and said, Imagine how many thousand late-night pisses that's received. Then Long smiled and spread his arms and hands as if to claim the space or bless it or condemn it.

He'd been drinking. Quite a lot, it seemed. He wavered where he stood and said, This is your natural habitat, Val. But you and Eve imagined you might be king and queen at Long Shot someday. That somehow, natural or unnatural, I die. Then she gets every-thing, and you hang around enjoying it. No kids in the way to inherit. But there's a flaw in the plan. Eve doesn't know anything about my will and hasn't ever asked. But know this—it's written so that however I die, Eve won't really get jack shit except through the generosity of an heir. Except, to my amazement, there isn't one. The will is very tightly written. But because I'm not a pure asshole, it's written so she'll get just enough annually to remind her of me until she finds another man. Which won't take long even if she's being picky. She has a few more pretty years left, don't you think? Otherwise she can roam around in a bus with some cowboy band, singing in beer joints and fucking sad little dudes like you when she gets bored or depressed. And if she never gets married, she'll collect that very small annual stipend forever. Let's call it minuscule, Val. That's the verbiage for us to focus our thoughts on. Somewhere in that area between minuscule and zero. And right now, I wouldn't agree to a divorce. Let her deal with that.

I stood and watched his speech. In that moment, he seemed more like the sad little dude.

I said, How about drawing a deep breath and sitting down?

He didn't argue. He sat on the edge of the bed.

—One of us is going to die, he said. Isn't that the direction we're going, Val? I'm good with that. You?

I thought, I've stayed out here too long in this empty country.

I said, I've got about three more days to finish in the PO. I'll sign my name in the corner, and then you'll never see me around here again. Gone for good.

—You could have bothered at least to tell different stories. It's insulting.

—I don't know what you're saying.

—She's gone, and she said the same as you, gone for good, no coming back this time. What a coincidence. So then you go meet her somewhere, and you're off together?

I said, John, I don't know what Eve's plans are. But I do know she didn't run off to be with me. I'm certain of that.

Long sat hunched forward, propped with his forearms on his

knees. He said, I could take it if she'd talk to me and say, I'm going away for a week, a month, whatever, but I'll be back. I wouldn't ask questions. But all I get is a note written on the back of an envelope—*Can't go on here, won't be back. Sorry. My mistake*. Like she was sending me a telegram.

I waited. After a long pause he said, There's a way things fall out so that there are no winners. Everybody loses.

—I figure Eve probably doesn't feel like she's losing, I said.

—Someday off in the far future, I bet she'll start calculating what choosing freedom every time the choice came up has cost her, Long said. Then he leaned very slowly over onto the bed, his feet still on the floor, until his head rested on the pillow.

I stood and watched, somewhere in the range of puzzled and amazed.

He appeared to fall asleep, so I sat in the one straight chair and studied him. Through the wall, I heard a radio playing a song too faint and thin to recognize. Finally I got up and tapped him on the shoulder. He raised his head and looked at me as if I'd interrupted him.

I said, Let me drive you home.

—No, I'm fine.

—You're not fine, I said. You'll have that new coupe wrapped around a power pole in half a mile if you drive away from here.

He fumbled in a pocket and reached me his keys. I helped him downstairs and propped him in the passenger seat and drove one last time from Dawes to Long Shot.

LONG WAS ASLEEP WHEN WE arrived, so I went hunting for Faro and found him oiling a saddle in a late sunny spot past the exaggerated angles of the barn shadow.

—Didn't guess I'd ever see you here again, he said.

—Long's drunk. Came by my room in town asking about Eve. He made a few vague threats, and then he lay down in my bed awhile. I couldn't let him drive. Help me get him inside?

Faro shook his head slow and said, Of course. Let's get the son of a bitch to bed.

Once we'd gotten Long settled upstairs—a sort of awkward ceremony, the two of us helping him onto the bed and covering him with a blanket—Faro shook Long's shoulder hard enough to make him alert.

Faro said, Hey, piece of shit, I'd fucking like to beat you down for driving her off. And I'm still trying to decide about that.

Long said, You can't talk to me that way.

Faro said, I just did.

Long muttered something and struggled up with his back against the headboard to watch us walk out the door.

Down in the lobby, I asked Faro if one of the boys might be free to drive me back into town.

—I'll do it. I need to get the hell out of here and I kind of like driving that coupe, he said.

WE PULLED OUT OF LONG Shot and onto the main road. Faro drove poorly, clashed the gears and jerked the wheel. The day dimmed down. Gold sky behind the blue Winds faded to indigo straight overhead.

Faro said, How's that little wound doing?

—Almost healed.

—You have a theory on who did it?

—I have nothing but theories. I'll never know what happened.

A little farther on I said, There's something I've wondered about

since that morning in the woods in Big Sur. You said you forgot
something and went back to where we'd left Jake. What was that?

Real quick Faro said, Realized I still had the knife I'd taken
off him in San Francisco. Figured I ought to return it to him.

I paused and said, Generous to a fault.

—I've always been known for that.

I tried to remember details from that morning, asking myself
questions I didn't really want answered. Like, when Faro came
back to the fire, how did he act? Did he carry anything? I knew I
would wonder all my life about that knife and the syringe and the
money bag.

We rode on a bit in silence, and then Faro said, Part of me
wishes Eve hadn't run off again, and part just wishes she didn't
have to. She needed more than what Long was ever going to give.
You can either settle or you can't.

I said, She stopped at the PO to say goodbye and told me she
wasn't meant for it, staying here. Any idea what her plans were?
Whether she has money to live on for a while?

—Oh, I wouldn't know a thing about that, he said.

—Of course not.

—Don't you go looking for her again, he said.

—I'm under orders not to, straight from Eve. I wanted her to
say, Follow me. What she said was, Goodbye.

Faro gave one quick nod and said, Good. Best for both of you.
You know, that kind of bullshit people say to each other.

We rode the rest of the way in silence until, parked in town,
Faro said, I'm guessing you're smart enough to head out of here
soon and not get talkative about all the time you spent away from
that picture of yours.

—I am smart enough to do that, yes.

—Where to from here? Virginia?

—Probably. I'm not sure. I've got an invitation to stay in Seattle awhile. It might be a place to figure out what's next. Ride out the disappointment, pass the days reading ominous headlines with pretty good people and a cellar half full of very good wine.

If I were being honest with myself, I'd have admitted there was a better chance of bumping into Eve in Seattle than in Virginia.

Faro said, Hell, every choice doesn't have to be perfect, specially at your age. Month or two loafing in Seattle might do you some good. Either way, best of luck to you, Val.

—You too, I said.

I reached over to shake his hand, but Faro said, Shit fire, why do y'all young men need to hold hands all the time?

I gave him a two-finger eyebrow salute instead and closed the car door. He laughed and drove away.

AFTER MIDNIGHT, TAMBOUR DOWN AND the building empty, I sat on the floor studying the painting. In my mind, I had projected it large as Benton's Chicago murals, so large part of the brick wall of his studio had to be cut out to remove the sections. But my entire piece of PO wall might have fit the dining room of my parents' house in Norfolk.

I felt like a tire with a slow leak. Thinking back on the past three months—tracking Eve, and then Jake and Faro tracking us, and then the day Long might have done his own tracking—the calendar shattered into potsherds, puzzle pieces, broken mosaic tiles of days that I was unable to fit back together into shape. Even when I tried to reconstruct memory into its simplest form—a line, a grid, an order corresponding with days and weeks and months—it swelled against me like an oncoming wave.

Out the windows, stoplights flashed yellow. The woodie sat packed to go. Chesapeake or Seattle? Still hadn't decided.

Standing in front of the mural, I felt too distant from the earlier version of myself who'd dreamed up the image to be overly critical of it. In a way, it was like looking many years later at art you made in high school. You'd probably think, Maybe that's naive and earnest yet technically not bad. Like something Hutch said about a painter he didn't completely endorse—He can paint, but he doesn't have anything to paint about.

Looking now, I realized the missing element—and it was down in a deep crater—was the violence of the West. Not so much the physical geography, but the violence inherent in the concept of the West, the politically and culturally and religiously ordained rapacity smearing blood over all the fresh beauty. Hutch had made the limits of the job clear and strict, though. The work needed to express hope and pride, optimism and energy. No looking back in guilt and gloom. You can't paint a PO mural of the Sand Creek Massacre or of the murderous rudimentary capitalism of the Lincoln County War.

I took my fountain pen out of my shirt pocket, a cellulose Parker with an extra-thin gold nib that Long had given me. Almost like a note to self, in the bottom right corner of the mural—a space of brown and tan grassy plains—in indelible black ink I sketched a tiny gunfighter in a slight crouch, in the split second of drawing his pistol. The image so small you could cover it with your thumb. I paid attention to the angles of his knees and elbows. The pistol barely clear of the holster, still rising. Half a second from killing to get something he wants, even if that's simply not being killed himself, or to protect someone he loves. I figured if Faro ever came in and recognized my tiny representation and carried out his threat and tracked me down, then let him come. We'd have a drink together on the dunes at sunset.

I stepped to the other corner and scratched a lean man reclining facedown, legs apart, his body and rifle and bipod geometrical, a Y-shape on the ground. His face almost merging with a long trumpet-shaped scope. Maybe he's aiming at the gunfighter or maybe far into the distance across the vast landscape. For a moment, I wondered how many people Long and Faro had killed between them. What would the number be?

I sat on the floor twenty feet back and looked some more. From there, the figures were practically smudges. To see them clearly you'd have to run up close like Anna had done in those early days, before everything. Back when the making of a picture on a PO wall was all.

I stood and walked to the wall and signed, tiny as insect tracks, *Valentine Montgomery Welch / 1937.*

ACKNOWLEDGMENTS

I WOULD LIKE TO EXPRESS MY APPRECIATION, thanks, and love to my wife, Katherine Frazier, who has supported my work, put up with my writing schedule, read and commented on draft after draft, brainstormed character and plot, and managed the business side of things ever since I took the leap to write my first novel over thirty years ago.

I thank my daughter Annie Crandell and her husband, Kyle Crandell, for the many ways they've worked to preserve my time to write these past few years. In addition to innumerable careful readings, comments, critiques, and suggestions, Annie has also taken on everything from Covid haircuts to Greek translations.

Many thanks to my agent, Amanda Urban, for twenty years of thoughtful advice and support.

Much gratitude and appreciation goes to my editor, Sara Birmingham, for all her meticulous, smart, diligent work in helping make this book better. Thanks also to Sonya Cheuse, Miriam Parker, Allison Saltzman, and the whole Ecco team for their expertise, collegiality, and enthusiasm.

AUTHOR'S NOTE

FOR THOSE INTERESTED IN THE HISTORY BEHIND the fictional world of this novel, I would point first to the following sources of information:

Particularly helpful in constructing Val's cross-country journeys were volumes from *The American Guide Series* covering Washington State, Florida, and California. Those three guides alone add up to more than two thousand pages of detailed period travel information. The guides were published from 1937 to 1941 by the WPA (Works Progress Administration) through the Federal Writers' Project. Among many noted writers who worked for the FWP are Saul Bellow, Ralph Ellison, Zora Neale Hurston, and Studs Terkel. The WPA guides are widely available online in both digital and physical forms.

The Living New Deal (https://livingnewdeal.org) is a brilliant project that provides an indispensable treasure trove of information on New Deal projects nationwide, particularly artwork.

Thomas Minehan's *Boy and Girl Tramps of America* (New York: Grosset & Dunlap, 1934) is a remarkable account of Minehan's experiences traveling with homeless teenagers in the early 1930s. The book has been long out of print and hard to find, but at the time of this writing, a welcome new edition is scheduled to be published by University Press of Mississippi in 2023.

Also very helpful were Francis V. O'Connor's *The New Deal*

Art Projects: An Anthology of Memoirs (Washington, D.C.: Smithsonian Institution Press, 1972) and Leslie J. Reagan's *When Abortion Was a Crime: Women, Medicine, and Law in the United States, 1867–1973* (Berkeley: University of California Press, 1997).